Chasing Forever

1st in the Beachside Romance Series

Carrie Thorne

Published by Thorny Books

Carrie Thorne

https://carriethorne.com/

Standalones

The Christmas Bet: A Double Feature Christmas Standalone.

Enjoy free books, first looks,

review team access,

and occasional hellos from Carrie?

Let's do this: carriethorne.com/newsletter

1

3 Months Ago: Offshore Oil Platform, Gulf of Mexico

STATIC ECHOED IN HIS ears, barely discernable over the piercing, high-pitched ringing. He blinked repeatedly, trying to clear his hazy vision.

"Chase? Do you copy?" A frantic voice echoed, bringing him back to the present. Jose, his dive supervisor, called his name repeatedly in a broken transmission. Chase tried to shake away the fog that had encompassed his brain.

"Yeah, I'm here. Explosion knocked me out for a minute. I can't see much. Everyone ok?" He searched in the debris for the cause of the blast. Couldn't have been too big as the rig was still standing, but it was definitely close. "Hank?" He called for the other diver, searching around but knowing he wouldn't see much with such poor visibility.

"I'm sending down help. I know you're hurt, but we need to you stabilize the... loose in... "

The voice cut out again. *Loose* was never a term you wanted to hear that described anything that supported an oil rig. He'd been inspecting the structure with Hank when the nearby explosion struck. Chase put his hand on the blowout-preventer in front of him and felt an unusual vibration.

Shit. If that came loose, there could be a catastrophic rupture. At best a leak, at worst, a bigger explosion that could risk everyone on board the platform.

He kicked his legs rapidly, following the metal down until he found a weakness in the structure. Explosion must have knocked the stabilizing mechanism loose; normally the back-ups would have shut it down. Wasn't this the section Hank was inspecting? The voice crackled but was too broken up to understand.

His head throbbed. At least his mask hadn't cracked.

Finally, he reached the affected area of the blowout-preventor and pulled the emergency wet-welder out from his toolbelt. His shoulder was on fire as he pushed the loose BOP component back into place, trying to hold it steady so he could weld the weak zone together. The rattling clamp shook violently as he struggled to hold it in place.

Movement out of the corner of his eye. Ivy, his dive tender. He held steady despite the startle she had caused. Without words, she pulled out a hammer to knock the clamp back into place where it had slid.

Crack, the sound of the hammer hitting the metal reverberated through Chase's body, making his head pound even more and a wave of nausea passed over him. He slowly breathed in and out, suppressing the need to puke as his head throbbed. Vomiting would be more dangerous than if his mask had cracked in the blast.

The rattling stopped; the well-placed hit had worked. Chase didn't hesitate, knowing it wouldn't last. He quickly started the welder and sealed the weak zone. Despite the urgency, he took his time, ensuring the weld wouldn't come loose in the coming storm. His shoulder screamed under the strain of holding the heavy equipment steady against the strong current.

He held his position against the force of it. Even an emergency weld needed to be done right.

Repair complete, he gave a thumbs-up to his partner. He scanned the area, but it wasn't easy to see through the debris. The pair swam together through the critical zones, checking for any other areas that had weakened in the explosion. No more major weak zones, but they patched up a few spots that looked unstable.

Reassured they had dealt with any critical hazards, they searched for Hank. Visibility was poor, but even a dark shadow would be worth investigating.

Jose's voice crackled through again, "Chase, we pulled out Hank. Come on back up. Take it slow. You've been under a while; you'll need to decompress within 5 minutes of surfacing and stay in there a few hours." He and Ivy silently and slowly rose back to the surface. He was glad Ivy had been his dive tender this excursion; she was shockingly strong for her 5'5" height, and he'd yet to see a challenge she didn't face head on.

As they surfaced, a huge hand reached out and pulled him up the rest of the way. Sitting on the lift, he managed to pull off his mask and gasped in the fresh, albeit smelly air.

"Chase, you ok?" Ivy pulled off her mask as well.

He looked to the other diver. She looked as exhausted as he felt. Her spiky black hair was wild, her brown eyes at half-mast with exhaustion. They sat side-by-side on the dive lift, shoulders hunched forward, eyes half closed.

"Yeah, no worries. Glad you stopped by; my shoulder was about to give out. Must've hit it on something in the blast."

She weakly elbowed him in the side, a tired smile on her face. "Excuses, excuses."

As they neared their destination, they quickly stripped off their gear and climbed into the decompression chamber. A familiar face appeared in the window almost immediately. Through the speaker, a deep voice echoed, "You got lucky. Hank didn't make it. From the looks of things, that blast was an air pocket from his equipment. I figure, he'd gotten tangled in some debris and must have jerked something loose. His gear was all fucked up, and I think it was before the explosion. There'll be an investigation."

Chase looked up to see Jose looking down at him, face grim. They all knew it was a dangerous job. Hank had been in this business for over 20 years, twice as long as Chase. If you wanted to enjoy the hazard pay, you had to retire before your luck ran out. Hank had been invincible; pure muscle, pure stubborn, yet didn't even reach Chase's shoulder. He'd been planning to retire to Alaska, grow a full Grizzly Adams, and spend the rest of his days fishing on the Copper River.

Sitting quietly in the decompression chamber, listening to the rumbling of the contraption's aging but functional motor, Chase and Ivy shared a moment of silence for the lost diver and friend.

Unfortunately for his raging headache, the silence didn't last long. A shockingly chipper voice greeted them, causing screeching feedback from the aging speaker in the chamber. Chase winced, his concussion nagging at him. "Great work down there. We're back up and running." Ivy closed her eyes and tuned out the shrill voice. Stacy, the assistant operations manager pretended to ignore the snub. Jose was no help either; Chase could see him walking the other direction, disappearing from sight. Stacy pressed her face to the glass. "I'll put in a good word for you, Chase. With your quick thinking today, I'll be sure a raise is just around the corner for you."

Chase gave a polite, but empty smile. He couldn't motivate enough to come up with a decent response to her inanity. Having failed yet another of many attempts to be "one of the guys," she turned on her heel and stalked off. He could see her through the glass, strutting back to the office in her pristine blue jeans and very intentionally blue-collared shirt.

Finally done decompressing, Chase trudged to see the medic. Totally wiped out. At the metal door, he knocked his good shoulder into the door to get in. He was greeted with a gruff "Hello" as he parked himself on the exam table.

After a few minutes of poking and prodding, the medic gave him the good news. "Well, you didn't break anything. Pretty good contusion to your shoulder, maybe some rotator cuff involvement but should improve with time. And rest. Take it easy for a few days; 800 mg ibuprofen three times a day for seven to ten days. Maybe some physical therapy once you're ashore. The concussion's pretty nasty; you may have a headache for a few days. Total brain and body rest, got it? You're off duty until your head's back to normal." The burly medic gave him the serious-face. "I mean it Chase. You don't want another head injury while you're still recovering."

Chase nodded in ascent. "I hear you. I've got another 3 days left until I go ashore anyway. With that storm expected to roll in tonight, I think I'll be good." He grabbed his gear and headed for his bunk.

His tiny room was a mercifully quiet. The topside crew was working at full capacity, making up the time lost in the explosion and in preparation for the incoming tropical storm. Not quite to hurricane season yet, but nature didn't appear to care this year. Chase found that he had his cave to himself today, his bunkmate still on duty for the next 6 hours.

He stripped down to his briefs, too tired to wash up before hitting the sack. Over ten damn years of this. He'd run away from his hometown at the ripe age of 18 for diving school and hadn't been back since. Nearing 30, he knew it was time to get out.

He had no intention of ending up like Hank. He knew it was a good possibility, sooner or later. One didn't just work one of the world's most dangerous jobs if he didn't have a death wish, or at least a serious case of adrenaline addiction.

He'd never really had a death wish, nor an adrenaline issue. He'd had a contact at a commercial diving school and little else, so Chase had jumped at the opportunity for good money and an escape from his problems. Since finishing training, he'd picked up every damn job he could, appreciating that the intensity of the work had not allowed time to dwell on his past mistakes.

Chase crashed on the narrow bunk, not caring that the blankets were still in a wad at the foot of the bed after he'd kicked them off when he'd woken for his shift this morning. Twelve on and twelve off for 2 solid weeks; long damn days. His head still throbbed, but the nausea was fading. Just a few hours of rack-time and he'd be good as new. Until the sharp ring of the phone about pierced his skull.

No one on the rig would be calling, but who the hell would be calling from the mainland? He rubbed a hand through his hair as he leaned over to grab the phone. "Hello?" he didn't try to mask the confusion from his voice.

"Hey Chase, how goes the oil business? Staying safe?" Chase was surprised to hear from Frank but was always happy to hear from his best friend's father—and the closest thing he had to a decent father figure. Frank and his wife Laura checked in with him every month like clockwork. They normally timed their calls to catch him while he was ashore in his spartan studio apartment. Today's call while he was out on the rig was unexpected.

"Yeah, Frank, you know me, Mr. Safety," Chase dryly responded. He stood frozen with the phone to his ear, unsettled. "Good to hear your voice. What's up?

"Chase," Frank held for a long pause, "I guess I'll just get right to it, as I'm sure you're wondering why I'm calling you when you're working. I... well..." Frank stuttered, searching for the right words. "Your dad died. His liver finally gave out; you know he'd been dealing with the cirrhosis for a while."

The foul air felt suddenly heavier and thicker. He rubbed a hand over his face, trying to clear his already muddled brain. As angry as he'd been with his father for giving up and drinking his life away, it was tough to think of the old man dying alone. The heat was sweltering for mid-March, but the news made him break out in a cold sweat.

"You still there? Talk to me Chase." Frank's concern was almost palpable. Chase pictured Frank on the other end. How much had Frank's beard grayed in the past decade? Did he still have that lean fisherman's build and seasoned temperament, or had his years in management softened him?

"Yeah, I'm here. Just processing." Chase looked out the portal window. As anticipated, dark, ominous clouds were rolling in. At the moment, he'd rather be caught in the turbulent waves than resting in his bunk, his already sour stomach was now roiling with guilt... and relief.

Frank continued, "I've been doing some thinking. Now may not be the best time to bring this up. But... I'm hoping to give you something positive to consider. I want you to come and work for me, hopefully takeover McAllister Fisheries when I'm ready to retire. I know you Chase. You were a great son and provided your dad with the best chance to turn his life around. Even though that was never your responsibility. But, Chase, it's time you let it go and come home where you belong. You know none of my children have any interest in fisheries; who knows what I did wrong there.

"Laura's retiring in 3 months. I don't want her to have all the fun without me, so I'm hoping to start cutting back on my hours until I'm ready to retire. I'm a tired old fisherman set in my ways. We need some new blood around here to turn things around and diversify the business. Build a stronger future for this town."

"Frank, are you sure I'm the right guy? What about Steve? Or one of the other guys?"

"You know Steve. I tried to convince him to join me the office a few years ago. I told him he'd become a crusty old sea captain. He outright cussed at me and stormed out. He hardly spoke to me for a week. That man would be a fish out of water, bossing from shore." The two chuckled over the phone together at the image. Steve's permanently crinkled eyes, set deeply in his leathered face, his scruffy white beard; he may as well invest in a wooden leg and an official captain's hat.

"Think it over, Chase. Don't decide now. Why don't you get yourself back home, get back on the boat for a few days to get back in the rhythm. Try out the office for a few months while you make up your mind. Let's test out that business degree you finally finished." On his breaks from the rig, Chase had been restless, but refused to get trashed and waste his hard-earned cash like so many of the other divers. It had taken years, but he earned his MBA through a distance learning program.

"Frank, that sounds amazing. I'm not sure of the reception I'll get around town, but I sure miss you guys. I have a few things to wrap up around here and can be there in July." Chase stared back out the portal as they disconnected. Lightning lit up the small scrap of sky.

Yeah, Chase was ready to go home. If he stayed much longer, he had no doubt he'd end up lost at sea, another statistic, like Hank.

He paced back and forth, taking the four steps it took to cross the long-end of the room, restless. Knowing he needed the rest with his concussion, he forced himself to lie down and relax. He crossed his feet and put his hands behind his head.

Staring up at the ceiling, a nervous laugh escaped. He'd left town in a big hurry. Hopefully he wouldn't be returning to any open warrants but was sure Laura would have let him know.

He closed his eyes, allowing the approaching thunder to lull him to sleep. The rain was now rhythmically ticking against the exterior wall. He'd have to make sure the town was willing to accept him back before he took on anything as big as McAllister Fisheries. If that didn't work out, he'd built enough of a nest egg. He'd land on his feet.

2

"Stop! Put down the bag, remove your mask and put your hands in the air," Maddy demanded, posed to mobilize if the perp tried to run. Hand at her side, she was ready to grab her sidearm; which she didn't carry anyway.

Not in Seaview. Her most strenuous duties typically included breaking up barfights between fishermen or confiscating weed from underage tourists; no weapons required. Not like her time as a detective in Seattle working vice. Drug busts had been her favorite, but she still felt shaky with domestic violence.

In this case, however, she'd likely have no need to run and absolutely no reason to draw a weapon. This would probably be the biggest arrest of her week... if she actually arrested him. Not likely.

Grayson Reeves, 12 years old and desperate to be larger than life, had made off with Mrs. Daniels' purse in a classic caper. She pasted a grim look on her face to mask her internal giggle fit as she assessed his uniquely clever disguise, which comprised of black sweatpants, black t-shirt, face covered by a black ski mask with rough-cut holes for his eyes and mouth. In broad daylight. On Beachside Avenue. Maybe she'd talk with him later about the superiority of subtlety when committing a crime.

Not today. She would not provide any encouragement for this budding criminal.

Why on earth did he think he could get away with stealing his grandmother's friend's purse? In this town? Well, he wasn't thinking this through. Hence, the exciting 20-meter foot-chase.

Knowing he'd been caught red-handed and was outmatched in speed, Grayson finally came to a stop and his shoulders slumped. He slowly turned back towards Maddy, voice cracking with either puberty or sadness... or both. "I'm so sorry, Officer McAllister. I want to buy Call of Duty. Everyone's going to be playing it all summer, but my mom said it's too expensive. And, she says it's too violent anyway. I know Mrs. Daniels keeps a hundred-dollar bill stashed in her purse for emergencies, and this is an emergency. If I don't play online with my friends, I will become the social outcast for the summer. Come September, I'll have no friends left." He kicked an imaginary clump of dirt. He was so young.

Younger than she'd felt at that age. At least his rebellion came in the form of videogames, rather than sneaking out for a beach campout. The sneaking was the best part, although she later discovered her parents were onto Aiden and her schemes.

Maddy took pity on the poor kid. He looked almost comical with his dark hair now standing on end, wearing the most dramatic frown she had ever seen. She gently took the purse from him and placed a comforting hand on his shoulder. "Grayson, I'm sorry about the videogame. I understand wanting something so badly it hurts. Let's put this in perspective: attorney fees are a lot more than $100, trust me, I'm sure my brother charges a lot more than that. Look at his fancy new office."

She gestured to Aiden's office, located in a prime location one block up from Beachside Avenue. Aiden McAllister, Attorney at Law. Their mother clearly had made a strong impact on the decor. Coastal gray cedar shingles, crisp white trim, topped off with an anchor-shaped knocker on the front door.

She looked back to Grayson. His lower lip trembled. Tears flooded his eyes. He was just barely holding on.

She hadn't joined the force to arrest young kids, rather to guide them away from a dire path. She'd rather help them to *not* become criminals. As her mother had done for many potential juvenile delinquents.

"On the other hand, Mrs. Daniels could use some help weeding her front yard after her knee surgery. Let's return her purse to her, and you can apologize for stealing it. While we're there, I'll mention your excellent gardening skills. Hard work is much more likely to convince your mom that you're ready for Call of Duty. And, we'll consider this community service your sentence."

Maddy was tempted to smooth that mussed hair, wipe away those tears and tell him life wouldn't always be so confusing. But she knew that wasn't true. Life would be a hell of a lot more confusing as he grew up.

Grayson managed a weak smile and looked up at Maddy. He handed her the mask that he'd been clutching in his hands. She smiled back, took him by the shoulders and aimed his body towards Mrs. Daniels' house up the hill. "Go on now," she shooed him along, "I'll call Mrs. Daniels in an hour to check on your progress. If anything is missing from that purse, I'll know, and I'll come knocking."

"Thanks, Maddy. I'm sure glad I ran into you, and not Ian," Grayson hollered as he ran up the hill. Ian, Maddy's somewhat partner, had a reputation for being more of the bad cop of the pair. Maddy found the comparison laughable. Although Ian was at least a head taller than her own 5'7" and could manage a frightening glare, he was far more of a sucker for a sad story than she was.

Ian was a few years younger than Maddy. He'd volunteered with the department while still in high school and had proven himself to be worth the lack of experience. Andrea, the chief of police, had initially hesitated when she hired him last summer, but he'd caught on quickly. It was shortly after Maddy was hired after she had come home to Seaview, leaving a detective position at the Seattle Police Department.

Andrea had quickly appreciated the decision when she saw how smoothly Ian had stopped a vicious drunken brawl among some of the fishermen. He had made use of his young age, stepping in the middle of the fight and acting drunk and confused, until a punch had flown over his head and he blocked the fist from ending up in the other fisherman's face. Andrea had partnered them together while they both learned the Seaview police-ropes, hoping Maddy's more tempered approach would soften his jump-right-in approach.

Maddy smiled, shaking her head at how fast Grayson had run up the hill. Her enjoyment was abruptly disturbed. From behind her, a familiar, and painfully unwelcome voice, interjected, "Just letting the kid off the hook? You may as well earmark a cell for this future felon."

Chills ran down her spine. The previously pleasant salty breeze took on a noxious odor. Her tongue suddenly was made of sawdust. Swallowing the knot in her throat, she turned to find Dylan, her dreaded ex, smirking. Smirking like he owned the place.

There wasn't a day that went by that she didn't kick herself for failing to see past his handsome face and charismatic façade in the beginning. With his nearly-white blond hair, lanky build, and dashing smile, he'd been irresistible to her teenage self. The smile that now set her teeth on edge.

"Dylan, I didn't know you were in town. Thanks for your opinion, but it's not welcome. I've got work to do." She started to cross Beachside Avenue to head the two blocks up the hill to the station. Town was bustling with tourists as the summer was warming up. Maddy hardly noticed the crowded streets, the noisy laughter of folks meeting up for a weekend getaway.

Dylan stalked alongside her. He swept a rare stray curl out of his face and scowled. He smoothed the lapels of his perfectly tailored navy suit with coordinating starched shirt and metallic tie. Maybe she'd flustered him right back?

Doubtful. The asshole always took everything in stride. Particularly her attitude.

"I just got back. Thought I'd bring this fishing village into the twenty-first century. I'm negotiating a contract with a major cruise ship owner right now. Seaview will be a major stop for a new North Atlantic route." He looked down Beachside, greed dripping from him like a hungry rottweiler.

She followed his gaze. Where he no doubt saw the potential for money and power, she saw a charming fishing village and artsy tourist hub. The boats at the north end of the row were just docking for the day. Young families, college students, and retirees carrying bags overloaded with tourist-shop booty. Beachside Avenue and its tributaries were made up of an eclectic, coastal-inspired collection of tourist shops, restaurants and pubs, an old-fashioned-yet-modernized movie theatre, day-trip adventure tours, and a wooden boat builder. The town was in no way hurting.

Sure, it still heavily relied on fishing, but its tourism trade was bustling. Maddy had always appreciated the artsy vibe around town. Perched with a perfectly gentle-sloped hill in a dreamily arced coastline, framed neatly by a large spit that made for calm beaches, the town pulled in tourists from all over the region.

She couldn't stand the idea of the obstructing the incredible view with a huge ocean liner, the peaceful streets trampled by folks invading for a two-hour shopping spree and lunch break. She'd seen how small-town shops were run out of business by cruise-owned gift shops. She'd hate to see Seaview's charm crushed. Its locals wouldn't survive it.

She knew Dylan well enough to know, without even seeing the object of his gaze, that he was looking to the end of the street at her father's fish processing plant and docks. Half of the town worked out of those docks. For the past two centuries, fisheries had driven the local economy financially and culturally. The building and docks needed updating, but they operated efficiently and safely. Removal would mean most of the locals would be forced to re-locate to find work. Her father was working on a plan to re-vamp the entire business, to make sure it supported the town for another two centuries.

Dylan had worked for her dad the summer after their senior year of high school. Dylan loved to sail and assumed that meant he would make a good fisherman. After a rough two weeks, he announced that he was meant for a bigger future than that of a mere fisherman. Maddy had tried to pretend that was true at the time, defending her boyfriend, but she'd always known it was because he couldn't handle the hard labor. Not that he wasn't strong; she knew too well his physical capabilities. But, he was more of a thinker than a doer.

Disgusted, Maddy refused to acknowledge him further. Her lips pressed tightly together, she turned her back on him and walked swiftly toward the station. What an ass. She still regretted that she had dated him for so long. That she had dated him at all.

Before she'd started dating Dylan, Aiden and Chase were skipping school more than attending, avoiding her to "keep her out of trouble," and she knew it was time to take her future seriously anyway. The three of them had been inseparable since the seventh grade. Her brother and his best friend were a year ahead and had always found themselves in trouble. Maddy had always skipped the rabble-rousing anyway.

She'd always had big plans. Rather than dwelling in the self-pity of loneliness at the loss of her friends, and a broken heart from the crush she'd always held for Chase, she'd started socializing more with her twin brother, Ronan, and his crowd. All in advanced classes and clean lifestyles, she figured that would suit her better anyway. Dylan had proved eager to help her get back at Chase and had swiftly helped her lose her virginity. Everyone thought they'd be married and established as a power couple by now.

What a fool she'd been. She was shaking with fury. She refused to let him see how he could make her cry, even after all these years.

His hateful eyes followed her the entire walk back to the station. A chill ran down her spine. She feared his motives for returning were not simply financial. The way he'd looked at her. Looked down his nose at her decisions. Finishing her stack of paperwork at the office suddenly sounded incredibly appealing. It took a concerted effort to not sprint up the crowded sidewalk.

3

THE MISTY MORNING WAS making her wide turn, heading back to port with the day's catch. Within minutes of reaching the fishing grounds that morning, Chase's sea legs had quickly remembered the rhythmic oscillations as he trolled his line. Adorned with white and marine blue paint, she was a beautiful boat. Kept in pristine condition by her captain.

Hands gooey with fish scales, Chase shook off the slime and laughed, surprised at how much he was enjoying the disgusting mess. He lifted his tattered ballcap to wipe the salty sweat from his brow. Not that cod put up much of a fight. A lot easier hauling in a cod than welding oil-machinery underwater in ocean currents. Not to mention a hell of a lot more satisfying.

Damn, it felt great to be back out on the boat. Most of the other McAllister boats were out catching lobster and trawling groundfish. But, Chase had chosen to go out on his favorite boat. Focused on rod-and-reel fishing, a small team went out to catch fish the old-fashioned way. More sustainably, albeit more expensively, catching fresh seafood like cod and haddock to sell to local restaurants for tonight's dinners. The local restaurants made a fortune marketing today's fresh, sustainable white fish. Known for its fresh catch, the marketing ploy also helped out the Seaview tourism industry and gained support for local fisheries.

Adding the heavy cod to the holding tank, he took a quick break to clean up a bit. He silently enjoyed the comments from the crew about his huge catch. Ha. A few crude crotch grabs as he passed, guys comparing their mighty cods caught by their powerful rods. Shaking his head with a laugh, he scrubbed his hands in the utility sink, the icy water and orange-scented gritty soap stirring more memories than he was ready to dwell on.

Shaking the frigid water off of his hands, he dashed up the ladder to the flybridge to join Steve at the helm. Deep in thought himself, Steve didn't respond as Chase stood at his side, legs braced wide to keep steady as the boat cut through the waves at a good clip.

Chase inhaled the salty air mixed with diesel from the rumbling engine. He basked in the crisp breeze, a refreshing contrast to the warm summer sun. His gaze was drawn to the view of town as they moved slowly back toward shore. Seaview, his hometown, was now dominating the horizon as they approached.

The long stretch of ocean-front shops and restaurants would be quite busy at this time of day. On the far north end of the beach he could see their docks and processing plant. The building had seen better days, but it was clean and functional. His eyes were drawn past the row of the tourist-nirvana shops along Beachside to the south end of the avenue, where a clustered neighborhood of old beach cabins dominated the coastline. Some of the houses were small, weathered cedar cabins that had been in families for generations.

Behind those and further to the south, were bolder, and notably less charming, larger houses built in the 1960's when the town had experienced in influx of residents as tourists started to invest in beach-front getaways of their own, rather than vacationing at large resorts. Further inland, the rest of town covered most of the hillside, densely clustered around Beachside, but increasingly sparse as it sprawled over the hillside as the population grew.

"Hey, Chase, get your head out of your ass. We're docking soon." Chase glanced up, momentarily blinded by the sun just coming overhead behind the man hollering at him. Steve, his favorite captain and an old friend brought him back to the present.

Like the creaky old boat, Steve was crusty but sturdy. The old man had been fishing longer than Chase had been alive and had no intention of retiring. Ever. Always said his wife would hang him if she had to put up with him every day; early to bed and early to rise and couldn't sit still for anything.

Chase gave him a rough pat on the back. "Hell of a day to be on the water."

"Yeah, it was a good day. Made a good haul, and in good weather. Just wait until we get another damn 'polar vortex' like last winter. Damn boat was too frozen to even leave the dock," the old man gestured with air quotes as he described the weather phenomenon. The two shook their heads in unison, equally astonished at such inconceivable weather. "Course, you likely didn't run into anything like that the past decade. You prob'ly laid out and sun-bathed out on that oil rig. Where were at, Texas?"

"Something like that. Gulf of Mexico for the last few years, but I spent some time up in the North Sea. Now that's a damn polar vortex year-round. Can't stay in a heated dive suit all day. I gotta say though, hurricanes... a little bit of snow is nothing like securing an offshore rig in a hurricane, especially if you have to do an emergency dive in the middle of it to make repairs."

"You always did like to look death in the eye and laugh," the older man shook his head with a warm chuckle. "It is good to have you back Chase. Frank's counting on you to find a way to keep us running until my grandbabies retire." Chase looked through the salt-crusted windshield to the docks they were now rapidly approaching. He hoped he didn't mess this up.

Town certainly was hopping as the boat docked and the crew packed up for the day. Each one fatigued from the early morning and long day of physically demanding work. None complained though, as this was routine. Every muscle in Chase's body ached, having used muscles he forgot existed... and he was in damn good shape. Different set of muscles, he supposed. Different hours. Guys hollered to their drinking buddies, promising to meet them at Winter's Tavern later tonight, others off for a quiet evening with families.

"Chase, you in? We made a hell of a catch today. Think we'll go rub it in at Winter's. We owe a few bruises to Parker's crew after last week." Chase appreciated the invitation from Sean, a now-seasoned fisherman who had been a few years ahead of him in school. Sean had been one of those guys everyone got along with. Short, muscled, always sober but always with a jovial attitude, and downright kind. Chase was glad to see he hadn't changed.

There were several new faces as well. Most were curious about Chase. He'd only worked on the boats for about two years as a teenager, and now had returned a decade later, rumored to be taking over when Frank decided to retire. Chase would be irked at that thought too, seeing an inexperienced outsider set to be the new boss. He'd have to work hard to earn their respect.

Braden, a new face and a few years younger than Chase, responded before he could, "Hell no. Chase is gonna be the new boss-man, needs to keep his pretty nose clean. He can't be caught drinkin' with we lowly grunt fishermen." Braden sneered hatefully at Chase.

Braden was huge. He must have a good 3 or 4 inches over Chase's own six-foot-one and had at least 100 pounds on him. His shoulders were twice as wide as his own broad shoulders. Some of his bulk appeared to be due to a rock-hard beer belly, but most looked to be muscle. Steve seemed to like him, so he must not be a complete asshole. Chase wished he hadn't already had plans tonight; he might enjoy showing Braden a thing or two. Guys got real restless living on a drilling rig.

Chase looked at the larger man and smirked playfully, "Another time, guys. I have plans tonight." Tossing his pack of gear over his shoulder, Chase picked up the pace to catch up to Steve. The pair stepped off the dock together and walked across the processing plant to the parking lot. "You coming to Laura's party tonight, or did you con your way out of it?"

"As if Frank would let me off the hook. Frank's about as comfortable in that company as you or me." Steve, Frank's long-time partner and head captain, gestured toward the other fishermen, "Don't let 'em get to ya. You oughtta have a few beers with them at Winter's next time and let 'em know who's boss." He grinned at Chase, his crinkled eyes somehow crinkling further. Chase was surprised the leathery skin didn't crack under the strain.

Chase had always been fond of Steve. Like Frank, Steve had put him right to work and hadn't taken any shit from the smart-ass teenager. He may have been a smart ass, but even back then, in the heart of his rebellious days, he knew how to work hard. Maybe too hard; he didn't have much self-control in those days. For better or worse.

Chase knew that was a big part of why he had always found an ally in Steve. He had always brought an extra sandwich. Knowing Chase wouldn't accept the charity, Steve had always blamed his wife for packing him too much food. Chase had been too hungry to argue.

He casually saluted his friend as he hopped into his gleaming new black truck, relieved he'd have a few friends at the party. His first purchase after finishing his last rotation on the oil rig had been a shiny truck with all the bells and whistles. He'd packed his few favorite belongings, donating the rest of it, and drove the long trek across the country. Home.

It had been a dumb idea, giving him way too much time to think about his return. If the fishermen and the town would accept him. Ideas for McAllister Fisheries. If he could live up to Frank's expectations. What Seaview would feel like without his father around. What he'd need to build a home, a life, pretty much starting from scratch. If Maddy still made his heart stammer when she smiled mischievously at him.

Chase was already enjoying getting back out with the fisherman. The oil rig crew was great, especially his fellow divers. He supposed there weren't too many differences. Both were full of roughnecks, but tight knit. The divers were a bit different, especially when he'd go on the month-long saturated dives. Those guys had to have an amazingly calm temperament, mixed with top-notch brains, work ethic, and a fuck-load of stamina. The McAllister fishermen always had a camaraderie he enjoyed, even when they were throwing punches at each other.

Chase was ready to move forward and put his education to work. He'd already started brainstorming some ideas to modernize the company. As much as he loved being out on the water, he did not picture himself a crusty sea captain like Steve. He relaxed into the buttery soft black leather seats, taking in the new car smell that hadn't disappeared yet. He turned the key in the ignition, enjoying the deep purr of the powerful engine.

There was a bite of Spring still in the air. Not caring how un-manly it may be, Chase turned on the seat-heater to soothe his aching muscles. He had no intention of squandering his nest egg on frivolity. But, he deserved some fun new toys after living as a hermit the past decade. His first order of business had been to buy the heavy-duty pick-up he'd always wanted. He also had plans to buy a big home overlooking the ocean, but he wanted to wait until just the right plot became available and design the house himself.

He drove through town rather than taking the less crowded back-roads on his way back to his rental house. The town was even busier than when he'd left. Tourism certainly was booming. Kids were playing in the waves while their parents relaxed on their beach chairs. Couples held hands and weaved in and out of the shops with classically weathered cedar-siding and brightly colored trim. He spotted a cluster of teenagers prowling the street, pushing each other and laughing, completely carefree. Had Chase ever been that carefree?

Leaving the hustle and bustle, Chase headed up the hill. As he pulled into the driveway of his rental, he caught Lynn Hanson giving him the evil eye from her poorly shaded windows next door. Most of the fishing crew had remembered him and welcomed him back with friendly pats on the back. Those who hadn't accepted yet would come around. His years of work on the oil rig had gained some respect from the fisherman that appreciated similar souls that didn't shy away from hard work.

Others in town, however, had not been so friendly. Like Miss Hanson. She'd been his seventh-grade teacher. He assumed she was retired by now, at least, he hoped she was, out of sympathy for the current generation of awkward pre-teens. She had to have been 60-plus when he suffered through her class. An old 60-something that had survived the Reagan-era. Short, wearing nothing but polyester pants and stiffly starched blouses day in and day out, topped with stiff, gray, curler-perfect hair.

She'd been watching him not-so-discreetly since he moved into the house next door. He suspected she was just waiting for him to screw up so she could tell everyone she-told-them-so. *That Chase Anderson, always getting into trouble.*

Chase hopped out of the truck, giving his new neighbor a friendly wave with as warm of a grin as he could muster. She would see the smile as threatening, no doubt, but he tried to soften his naturally intimidating demeanor.

Miss Hanson lived in a small, but classy old brick house like his and the rest of the neighborhood's. The yards were all pristinely managed. He didn't mind a little gardening, but the other residents were quite particular about the neighborhood's appearance. He'd have to learn some basic gardening and lawn maintenance to keep up. Fortunately, his landlord had left some basic supplies for him. Some of the houses were fairly grand, but most were cozy brick bungalows like his.

Chase tossed his gear into the entry closet, trying to keep the inside as neat as the out. He stripped down to his boxer briefs, tiptoeing across the cold wood floor, through the sparsely furnished living room, straight for the laundry room. He tossed his smelly clothes straight in the wash, stripping off the briefs and adding them before starting the wash cycle.

Coffee. He made for the kitchen to brew a steamy cup. He'd brought very few of his belongings from his tiny Houston apartment with him, as most of his household items had been cheap, convenient items. But not his coffee pot. He'd invested in an efficient, grinder-attached brewer that made a perfect cup of coffee, every time.

It had been a long day, but the hard part had yet to begin. Laura's retirement party started in under an hour. Coffee brewing, Chase walked back through the bright and airy living room to the master bedroom. He'd picked up the rich brown leather sofa yesterday, but his coffee table was still a cardboard box. He didn't watch much TV, so that hadn't been a priority.

Thankfully, he'd only had to crash on the floor the first night he'd arrived. He picked up a large king-sized, espresso-finish headboard to go with the plushest pillow-top mattress the store carried. After such an impressive cash purchase, he'd easily negotiated a nice discount on the rest of the matching bedroom set.

He made his way into the master bath. The owner had made some premium upgrades before her work had transferred her to Chicago on short notice. Chase wasn't normally one to soak in a tub, but the over-sized tub had appeal. Maybe if he got around to dating, he'd get some candles to soften up his man-cave a bit. It had been too long since he'd even been out on a date. For himself, he preferred the walk-in shower with its over-abundance of shower heads.

Chase stepped into the brick-tiled shower. *Eek, cold*! He leaped back, avoiding the initially cold flow from the three black-finish showerheads.

Did he just say *eek*? Good thing no one was around to hear that high-pitched squeak. He was comfortable with his own masculinity, but the guys on the rig, or even the fishermen, would tease him to no end if they heard a squeak like that. First the seat heater now eek; life outside the rig was quickly turning him into a softy.

As the water warmed, he stepped in and let the water flow over his sore muscles. He tried to empty his brain but couldn't help but worry over the upcoming party. Aiden had stopped by the night before last to welcome Chase home and helped him unpack his few boxes of belongings.

Laura had insisted he get home in time to make it to her retirement party. According to Aiden, they'd planned quite the shindig. As a former member of the city council and long-time local judge, Laura's friends, and therefore most of the guests, would be established pillars of the community.

Drying off with his also-new plush gray towel, he debated shaving off his new-growth beard. The early morning winds on the boat would be frigid and the beard would be necessary. In the end he decided to neatly trim the beard for the party.

Nervous about people's first re-impressions of him, Chase made an effort to dress for the occasion. He'd made sure to buy a spiffy new get-up for the party to impress Laura and her cohorts. He'd spent all damn day shopping yesterday.

First new furniture, then new kitchen and bath necessities... he had certainly helped the local stores to meet their sales for the quarter. After his first night of sleeping on the floor in a sleeping bag and air-drying after his shower, he realized he had to do some serious shop-ping. He never imagined how many damn "necessities" one needed in a home. Sheets–two sets, bulk pack of dish towels and rags, bath towels, hand towels, washcloths. Laundry soap, dish soap, hand soap. Exhausting.

He hadn't left out the clothing retailers. In addition to house neces-sities, he picked up some very needed wardrobe updates. He couldn't remember the last time he'd gone shopping. It's like he'd been waiting for something, like his time away from Seaview was purgatory. Paying his dues. Lucrative, however.

The entire ordeal had sealed it, he officially hated shopping. Not his scene. He'd managed to buy himself a few basics. Who knew there were so many styles and prices of jeans and t-shirts? Maybe he'd try one of those personal shoppers for the rest of his new wardrobe and avoid the mall indefinitely.

Although, the clerk at the store had been a little too helpful. Perky, with her very-low cut top, the clerk had sold him on an "athletic fit" black button-up. Chase still thought it was a bit snug, but she had insisted it accented his well-earned muscles and was very "on trend." Which she had told him while she leaned forward to straighten the cuff of the black slacks she'd tried to sell him, quite intentionally giving him a spectacular view of the too-small black lace bra she was bursting out of.

Enough ego-stroking and he was suckered into it. He was a guy. A guy suffering from a very long dry spell.

A few years ago, he might have gotten her number. Or even taken her right there in the dressing room. But in the past few years, he'd lost his taste for quick hook-ups. He'd avoided any relationships in general, having grown tired of meaningless one-nighters. Nor would he put a woman – or himself – through the limited time he spent ashore, then lack of contact while aboard the rig.

He'd agreed to pairing the "sexy" button-up with some black boat shoes and coordinating black belt but refused the "skinny fit" slacks she'd pushed. When did those become in style for men? He settled on some casual khaki chinos. The chinos at least had some cargo pockets.

Catching his reflection in the mirror, he felt he was dressed to impress. He wanted to fit in, but he refused to be someone else. No one would have dared question his confidence on the rig. His past hadn't mattered to them. They only cared about his ability to get the job done efficiently, effectively, and safely. If not, he would have kicked their ass.

Chase finally chugged the luke-warm coffee he'd forgotten about. Among other frightening figures, Mayor Joseph Wilson would be there. Before his Honor was elected mayor, Chase had had a quick kneetrembler with the man's oldest daughter in the football stadium bathroom during the homecoming game. Making the homecoming queen late for her coronation. He sure hoped Mayor Wilson didn't know about that little incident. He was, however, fairly certain that his Honor suspected that Chase and Aiden had been the ones to graffiti his Porsche later that year, as the lime green paint they'd chosen had splattered and hadn't washed off of their hands or hair very well.

There would be others with similar memories or suspicions. Chase shook his head at the ridiculous egotistical invincibility he'd built around himself back then. He hadn't heard yet how Aiden's return to town went, but Aiden had always maintained a good image despite his antics.

Aiden's parents had been an important part of the community, and Aiden had a bright future, despite his rebellious teenage behavior. Chase had hardly graduated. He had the brains; he just hadn't given a shit.

Rolling his eyes at his own insecurities, he made for the door. Might as well get it over with.

4

MADDY WAS GLAD TO be done with the day. She'd experienced some intense days on the force when she first became a cop in Seattle. Long nights of drug busts, bloody murder scenes; she'd loved every minute working vice, but it was intense. She was good at it, too. Top of her class. Had quickly made detective.

Somehow, today had been harder. Dylan's return was hanging over her head like a thunder cloud. Maddy unlocked her front door and let out a tired sigh as she entered the cheery oceanfront cabin. The house was just south of the Beachside Avenue hustle and bustle, surrounded by wind-blown trees and similar gray, seasoned cedar cabins.

The cozy, two-bedroom retreat had belonged to her grandparents. They purchased the cabin when Laura was in law school. Years ago, they had discovered Seaview on a summer vacation. While Maddy's grandparents had fallen in love with the seaside town, her mother had fallen in love with a handsome young fisherman with big dreams.

Her parents had married as soon as Laura finished law school, and she had opened a small practice in town right after. Maddy's grandparents had jumped on the excuse to visit often and had invested in the cabin. It had been a great place to entertain their grandchildren and give the parents a few weeks off every summer. Not long ago, her grandparents decided they were too old to manage the summer home anymore. It sat empty for two years until Maddy moved back into town and bought them out at a very reasonable price – the promise of great-grandchildren... eventually.

Maddy was in no rush to fulfill that promise, as she was generally avoiding even the concept of dating for now. She wanted kids someday, but she wasn't too keen on finding a partner to create said offspring. Or partake in the act to get there. Maybe a sperm donor someday?

She was sure sex could be enjoyable. She learned how to enjoy herself. Despite Dylan's frequent digs, she knew she was not frigid.

Maddy had been thrilled to land the cabin. It was gorgeous, but in need of some serious updating. Which she had jumped into with both feet. She painted the ceiling and walls a bright coastal white, leaving the exposed wooden beams dark and rustic in contrast. She'd had the wide plank wood floors refinished rich walnut and invested in plush wool carpet, with facing white slip-cover couches and leather armchairs, all surrounding the wood-burning fireplace.

Since she'd moved in, Maddy had learned a lot about home repair. Trial by fire and a lot of YouTube videos. She painted the sturdy but depressingly dark wooden cabinets a bright white, topped them with concrete countertops, added new nickel hardware. Gradually, she was replacing appliances and light fixtures.

She loved her cabin, how she'd made it her own. Walking to the large wall of glass doors and windows, the best part of the cabin, Maddy took in the expansive view of the ocean and took some calming breaths.

At present, a certain prodigal son had just returned. Maddy hadn't seen Chase in over ten years. But she'd thought about him more than a few times. Was he the boy she'd remembered? In the public eye, he had worked hard to be the outcast that didn't need anyone and had no respect for society's rules.

Maddy had always known it was an act. He was polite, gracious, thoughtful. He'd always made sure she was safe and happy.

She was ten when they first met, he was nearly twelve. Aiden had invited Chase over to play for the first time. Maddy was spying on the boys and fell out of the tree. Chase had run to her immediately, checked her for injuries. She'd repeatedly assured him she was fine; when he was finally convinced, he invited her to play with he and Aiden.

She tried not to dwell on her memories of Chase, but he kept invading her head-space. It had been so damn hard when he'd pushed her away in one of many ridiculous efforts to keep her safe.

She walked into the bedroom and peered into the closet. *Hmmm. What to wear?* She was too emotionally drained to focus and found her imagination creeping back to Chase, the emotional safe place she'd built for herself when times became too tough. With an inward smile, she remembered how he'd rescued her on her sixteenth birthday. Her friends had decided spin the bottle was a great idea.

She and Ronan had normally celebrated their birthday separately, determined to be their own unique selves, but this time they combined parties. They'd held the party in the basement of their parent's house. She and her friends had decorated to the nines with funky lights, too many balloons, and loud music. She'd lost the coin toss and had to spin first. As her luck would have it, the bottle pointed directly at Bryce, an awkward friend of Ronan's with cold sores and braces. She'd been mortified.

Too cool to join in, being the oldest kids in the house at a very mature seventeen, nearly eighteen, Chase and Aiden had been playing video games on the couch. Maddy was not a quitter. Stubborn to a fault. She had accepted her fate, moving slowly but surely into the center of the circle to face Bryce, in front of all her friends.

Before she reached him, Chase tossed down his controller and strutted into the center of the circle, moving his taller, trimmer body in front of Bryce's. Chase stood in front of Maddy, but turned his head toward Bryce, raising a defiant eyebrow. "Back off kid, the girl deserves a real kiss for her birthday," he'd said to Bryce. Maddy had nearly swooned.

His face was illuminated by the sparkling Christmas lights strewn around the room. He'd looked her right in the eye before he cupped his hand around the back of her neck pulled her close, pressing his warm lips against hers. She'd expected a quick peck, but instead he lingered, slowly encouraging her mouth open and sliding his tongue against hers. He'd drawn out the kiss until she'd thoroughly kissed him right back.

Maddy had dreamed about that for years after. She knew he was just trying to spare her, but she couldn't help but hope there had been more to it. He'd played it off later to Aiden, that he'd been trying to save Aiden's little sister from herpes and braces-induced lip lacerations.

Chase's return had nothing to do with Maddy choosing her incredibly snug, dark blue jersey-cotton dress for tonight, she tried telling herself. It was her confidence-booster dress as it hugged all the right places without looking slutty. Not too dressy, not too casual. She even moisturized with her favorite grapefruit-scented lotion to perk her energy a bit. Smoky eyeshadow and liner boosted her confidence a few more points. To cap it off, she slipped into her strappy heels; too tall for comfort, but who cared when you looked this good?

Maddy looked in the full-length mirror she'd fastened to the inside of her bedroom door and took in her appearance. Feeling silly as she posed for herself, she laughed out loud. She was thin, mostly due to genetics, but she tried to take good care of herself. It used to bother her that she lacked curves, but now she finally liked her narrow frame.

It had taken a lot of effort to gain back the self-esteem she'd lost in those years with Dylan. He'd slowly chipped away at her self-esteem, and she hated that she had let him. After moving across the country to escape him, she'd found a great therapist that helped her take control of her life. She took a few of the centering breaths she'd learned.

The party was rumored to be quite the event. Her mom had worked for over 20 years for the county judicial system and had been an active member of the community. She'd served on the city council for the last few years, and before that the school board. She'd been a damn good judge. She was honest and fair. Laura McAllister had made a name for herself as listening to all sides in order to make a thoughtful, balanced judgment.

Knowing the cool, evening air was on its way in, Maddy grabbed her denim jacket from the hook by the door and headed out. She hopped in her dark blue, two-door Jeep Wrangler and voice-dialed Aiden. On a normal sunny afternoon, she'd have the top down and let the wind mess up her long wavy hair. Today, she'd spent too much effort taming each unruly chestnut hair with the flat iron to risk the wind. She pulled onto the road towards her parent's home on the hill.

Hearing the rumbling of her engine as the call connected, Aiden dove right in with the nag, "Maddy? Are you driving? Are cops allowed to break the traffic laws?"

Clearly her big brother enjoyed riling her, yet still looked out for his baby sister. She'd missed him so much she didn't mind anymore... mostly. "I'm on Bluetooth Mr. Big-Shot Attorney, which is not illegal yet. I'm finally on my way. I had to convince Mrs. Daniels to hire Little Grayson Reeves as her new gardener to spare him from juvey and a life of crime. All going well at the party so far? Have mom and the city council started pontificating on how they can personally reverse global warming, bring universal healthcare to America, and feed the hungry, or is everyone still sober?"

"All good so far, they haven't solved too many of the world's problems yet. She's got some great friends. I can't believe the turnout, it's incredible. I am really glad they hired a cleaning crew for after, because I'm not cleaning all this up."

"That's a relief. I took tomorrow off anticipating I'd still be there doing dishes. Need me to pick anything up on the way?"

"We're good, see you soon. Drive safe." She grinned at her brother through the phone as she hung up.

Maddy admired the last view of the ocean as the jeep hugged the big curve up the hill. It was nice to have Aiden back home these past few months. He'd buried his head in the sand to get through law school and pass the bar, then get some time under his belt as a hot-shot associate. Maddy had made it her personal mission to get him out of his shell again.

The jeep started to bounce a bit on the potholes as she turned down the long gravel road to her parent's house. Before she even could see the house, she noted the long line of cars parked along the driveway. Knowing there would be no place further along to park, she pulled in behind a gleaming black truck so new it had temporary plates in the window. *Nice*, she admired.

Stepping out of the jeep and walking the rest of the way to the house, Maddy stubbornly locked her ankles to avoid the un-classy wobble in her tall heels on the rocky drive. Her poor ankles felt the strain when she finally reached the cobblestone circle drive as she approached the house, but she maintained a steady gait.

Maddy took in the stunningly landscaped, appealing entry that her parents had lovingly created and refreshed over the years. The circular drive, flanked with mature, native trees and colorful shrubs, led to the welcoming entry. Although a few miles from the ocean, she could still smell the soothing scent of the sea air, mingling with thriving lavender warmed by the sun. From the back patio, she knew she would see a view of the ocean in the distance.

The tall, heavy oak door sounded the familiar squeak of its aging hinges as she let herself in. She gratefully appreciated the empty foyer as she stepped into the house. Peaceful, but she knew not for long. She took a moment to steady herself with a few extra calming breaths before braving the crowd.

The soothing atmosphere of her childhood home helped to calm her nerves. To the right, the large antique dining room table was clean and polished, the opening to the kitchen just beyond. To the left, she noted the newly re-decorated living room with camel leather sofas around an intricate tree-stump-topped-with-glass coffee table sitting on the plush white carpet. The cozy couches offered plenty of seating, surrounding the grand fireplace. A large bouquet of fresh flowers added a friendly splash of color.

That lovely arrangement wouldn't have lasted long when there were 3 young kids terrorizing the place. She pictured next Christmas morning with the new furniture. The past few Christmas's, it was just the four of them. Ronan hadn't been home in years. Maddy knew her parents grieved his absence, and wished he'd call more than the twice-yearly check-in.

With a gentle gust of wind, the sound of laughter trailed in as the patio door blew open. Yes, the party was in full swing. Clearly very happy guests; her parents were well-loved and knew how to entertain. Maddy hung her purse on the overburdened coat rack, hoping hers would not be the straw to break the camel's back. She turned and squared her shoulders to join the others on the patio.

Movement coming from the kitchen stopped her in her tracks. She could sense him before she saw him, her spidey senses on alert. No one else made her heart thunder quite so rapidly.

Her heart leapt into her throat. Words... and, well, the ability to think entirely, flew right out of her brain as she saw him come around the corner. She hadn't seen Chase in over a decade, and here he was, walking right out of her parent's kitchen like he owned the place. Never lacked for confidence, that one.

He'd certainly filled out nicely. He'd always been pretty built for his age, but it was a more... mature build now. His black button-down shirt was modern and sleek without being ostentatious; it hugged his broad shoulders and allowed her a sense of some impressive abs. He looked sharp in the black shirt and cargo khakis. The rugged stubble of a beard, albeit nicely trimmed in acknowledgment of the more formal occasion, added an edge she was thrilled to see he hadn't lost. His deep blue eyes held that same edge. Less angry than they had been when last she saw him, but no softer. He'd attempted to tame his sandy blond hair, but it had already gone wild.

Chase walked out of the kitchen, carrying two handfuls of beers by the neck. So far, the party hadn't been so bad. He'd assigned himself to serving drinks and manning the BBQ with Aiden, thereby avoiding any deep conversation with anyone he may have pissed off before he left town.

Chase was caught completely off guard as he strolled out of the kitchen and saw Maddy. Frank and Laura had emailed pictures over the years, especially when Frank upgraded to a smart phone and sent him ten photos a day. The photos were nothing compared to Maddy in person.

Long chestnut hair a few inches past her shoulders, smoky liner accenting her ice-blue eyes. Damn... that body in the snug blue dress – it went down below her knees but hugged her in all the right places.

In the shock of seeing her, the beers he'd been carrying back to the party started to slip. He tried to maintain his grip–and his dignity–but one got loose and slipped out of his hands. Miraculously, he managed to slow it's tumble by rolling it down his leg, catching it with his foot, thus preventing a dramatic crash and shatter as it hit the tile floor.

With the reflexes of a tiger, Maddy stepped closer and bent to pick up the beer that was rolling under the sofa table. Although failing miserably, he tried not to stare. But her top was just low enough that his eyes were drawn in, catching a quick glimpse down her top.

Maddy had filled out nicely since he saw her last. She was no longer the tomboy he'd competed with in beach racing and tree climbing. Her tight blue dress accentuated her lithe body and highlighted her subtle curves and long limbs.

He quickly averted his eyes as she stood back up. She calmly set the beer on the sofa table and turned back toward him. His heartbeat took on an unpredictable rhythm when their eyes met. Her icy blue eyes were a bit more knowing than they had been. Sharper and full of secrets. What had she been up to the past decade?

She was a cop now, and he'd heard she was great at it. Despite a rough freshmen year, she'd managed to graduate from college early. She'd made detective in record time in Seattle, but had come back home last year, as she had always planned. She'd always been independent and too mature for her age, but the hint of wariness was new since he saw her last.

His expression softened, as he realized how much he had missed her. How much he hoped she'd missed him too. Not that they'd ever really been romantic. As his best friend's baby sister, she'd been off limits.

...Probably still was.

Maybe...

Except for her sixteenth birthday. He'd been trying to ignore she and her friends playing spin the bottle; he was way too cool for such nonsense, of course. But when he'd seen she was set to kiss with that herpes-infected, braces-wearing moron that had been staring at her boobs in the strappy tank top all night, he couldn't help it.

He'd about thrown the Xbox controller to get to her before that dumbshit had the chance. He told himself he'd been playing hero. He knew better now. He had wanted to be her first kiss, had wanted to know her taste, even if only once.

He had no idea what to say to her now. Managing to not stare with his mouth gaping open, he managed, "Maddy... wow... it's good to see you."

She warmly smiled back, "Chase, hey. You look amazing. I can't believe you're back." She paused, looking him over. His imagination went nuts, but his thoughts were quickly doused. "I know Dad's thrilled to have a partner. Aiden has been driving me nuts. It's been a challenge to get him to leave the house since he's been back. Maybe if we both gang up on him, he'll come back to the world of the living." She was friendly and casual.

She must not feel the same sense of disequilibrium that he did. Like he'd surfaced too quickly and hadn't been watching his regulator. Like he'd succumb to nitrogen narcosis.

Her eyes swept downward, "I think I'll avoid the shaken one. Are those spoken for, or can I snag one?"

His cock twitched in his new, now feeling too-tight khaki pants as her gaze lingered in the area. His breath caught in his throat, his imagination running on overdrive as he imagined Maddy slowly lowering his zipper, hiking up that tight dress and begging him to take her against the back of the couch.

Trying to shake off the fantasy, he tried picturing her as his best friend's sweet little sister, which didn't work.

She'd played a major role in his fantasies over the years. Her fierce attitude and incredible body had gotten him through some rough times. Live and in living color, standing in front of him, it suddenly became way more difficult to *not* imagine her naked.

He closed his eyes for a brief moment to clear his head. Breathe in, hold, breathe out. She may be all grown up and sexy as hell, but still wasn't for him. He hadn't been good enough to even be her friend ten years ago, and he was certainly not good enough to be more than that now. He'd found peace after a decade of facing death on a daily basis, but still hadn't proven himself as worthy of Maddy McAllister.

Maddy cleared her throat. Was she smirking? More likely than not, she'd read his predictably male brain. "Beer? It's been a long day."

He quickly remembered where he was, feeling stupid for forgetting they were in the middle of her parent's foyer at a very crowded party.

Clearing his throat, he managed to respond, "I heard a few requests for refills, so I just grabbed a bunch."

He set the bottles on the sofa table and grabbed the opener he'd stashed in his cargo pocket. He popped off the top and handed her the cold brew. Her fingers brushed his as she took the bottle. They both stilled. He couldn't ignore the glimmer of hope that she felt the same fire at that light touch. Was she avoiding eye contact?

She took a long, deep swig.

"Long day?" he raised his eyebrows, hoping she'd stay and talk longer.

"Yep. I nearly arrested a gang of kids on break from college: drunk by noon and set on jaywalking through rush hour traffic. They sobered up pretty quickly when I asked for their parent's contact information. I later saved a young ne'er-do-well from a future life of crime. Survived a treacherous run-in with a hyena. And, nearly lost my arm handwriting reports when the computers went down this afternoon."

He pictured her intimidating the college kids. She had a hell of a death glare when she was angry. Poor kids didn't stand a chance. Wait... "Hyena?"

He knew she'd intended it as a joke, but winced at his stupidity for prying as she glanced away uncomfortably. Her brows scrunched together, voice pressured, "Dylan Maybrook has moved back to town and plans to rip off the tourists, buy out my father, destroy the local economy, and make my life hell."

He was relieved to see she thought as poorly of Dylan as he did but hated to see her so upset. He'd heard their break-up was rough, but he wondered how much more there was to the story. Her parents hadn't told him much. He'd been on a long rotation at the time. Incommunicado. Aiden refused to speak so much as the guy's name.

He should have guessed there was much more to the story than a bad break-up.

"That does sound like a rough day." As much as he wanted to spend more time alone with her, he felt a pang of guilt as he wondered if he may have prevented that heartache if he had held her close rather than driving her away her all those years ago. Not that she would have fared better, maybe behind bars rather than making the arrests herself.

During his last year in Seaview, he thought he had been performing an act of honor, to save her from the fallout from his mission of self-destruction. Maybe not. "Come on, your mom has been asking after you about every 30 seconds. She's getting a bit misty-eyed and could use a dose of your resilience."

5

Her anger with Dylan, or at herself for being so upset at his return, quickly faded as she admired Chase's very fine ass as he led the way to the back patio. She tried to not actually do a little dance as she followed him through the French doors, but she did a little dance in her brain and couldn't hold back the stupid grin. Resilience? She liked the sound of that, as she didn't always feel it.

She hadn't meant to mention her encounter with Dylan, let alone allow her emotions to take over, but she had little self-control when Chase was around. She didn't see herself as resilient when it came to Dylan, he was more of her own personal, emotional black hole.

As they stepped out onto the large flagstone patio, Chase distributed the remaining beers, and then beelined for the BBQ to join Aiden. Maddy was pleased to see her brother smiling and interacting with others. She felt a sense of peace as she looked across the patio. Maybe it was the beer and the smell of cheeseburgers emanating in a smoky cloud from the BBQ. It sure put Maddy in a good mood. And made her stomach rumble, realizing she hadn't eaten lunch today.

Her parents had built a beautiful patio. Much more elegant than the gravel patch when she'd been younger. A few years back, they had hired a contractor that had laid the gorgeous flagstone. The install had included a built-in firepit, with concrete benches and old whiskey barrel flowerpots scattered around the periphery of the patio. They had added plush patio furniture around the central firepit. The whole scene looked like something out of a magazine.

"Maddy!! You're finally here!" Her mom spryly hopped up from her spot on the bench next to Maddy's dad. Laura deftly stepped over the legs of her lounging guests as she made her way across the patio to her daughter. Maddy would guess she'd had about two glasses of wine. Not drunk, just a bit... sentimental. And still looked neat as a pin in her navy ankle length pants and pink floral sleeveless blouse. Her mother was certainly not a lush, so it was funny to see her get tipsy in a rare moment of total relaxation.

She was so proud of her mother's accomplishments; if the light-weight decided to drink five glasses tonight, Maddy would hold her hair back later tonight as she puked it all up. Fortunately for them both, that was not likely to be an issue. Despite the fun evening, she couldn't picture the judge giving up that much control, even to welcome in her retirement.

Neatly dodging a guest with their plate overloaded with spinach salad, Laura finally reached her daughter and pulled her into a warm embrace. Maddy squeezed her right back. "Mom, congratulations. Did you get all your cases wrapped up? Are you officially a retiree?"

They linked elbows and made their way across the crowded patio together. Laura whispered to her daughter, "Thank goodness you're here. You know I hate being the center of attention. Aiden has taken over the BBQ, and Chase volunteered to be a runner for drinks and supplies. I think they both are avoiding socializing. Your dad is on a roll; you know how he enjoys a good debate. He keeps trying to rope me in. I need an ally, and that's you, my dear." Her dad slid down the bench to make room for Maddy to squish in between her parents. Despite the cramped – albeit nicely cushioned – bench, Maddy was pleased to find shelter between her parents.

The crowd returned to their lively debate about the latest plans to increase tourism. The large patio was designed to entertain. The turnout was great. There were well over 50 guests scattered around the patio on various benches, with others seated on folding chairs scattered throughout. Some played games on the expansive green lawn, like croquet and horseshoes. Beyond the lawn, the hill gradually sloped down, and the forest filtered the view of the distant ocean.

Her gaze finally landed on Chase and Aiden surrounded by the smoke of the BBQ. She wasn't sure if it was Chase or the scent of juicy cheeseburgers making her mouth water. He threw his head back in laughter at something Aiden said. The smile stuck for a few moments. He shook his head while still smiling about whatever odd topic they were discussing and took a sip of his beer.

She couldn't help but remember the one time she'd felt those lips on hers. They'd both grown up since then. What would the feel like now? Would he taste the same?

Politely disengaging from Mayor Watson's gregarious jokes, Laura turned to her daughter, "I have a few days to put my feet up and enjoy retirement, then your dad has surprised me with a trip to Italy. For a month. You know how I've always wanted to go. You must help me pack. We'll need to go shopping. Or should I wait until I get there to buy some new retiree-and-now-international-traveler outfits? Maybe I should bring you back some Italian leather boots. I can't wait to do some fun shopping."

Her mother's exuberance was contagious, and a welcome distraction from her less-than-pure thoughts. Maddy visited with her mother about the upcoming trip. Yes, she should definitely bring her some Italian boots, and maybe a coordinating bag.

For the first time in her life, Maddy felt an odd pang of envy when considering her parents relationship. They'd been married and settled with their first child by Maddy's age. In her lifetime, Maddy had survived only two short-lived and not-so-satisfying relationships. She wasn't even sure it was worth pursuing, as her few failed attempts had been so awful.

Her eyes strayed to Chase, thinking about the fantasies she had allowed herself over the years. Now that Chase had returned, she felt unsettled, as if she were waiting for something. The sensation was entirely new.

He certainly had changed. He was dressed for the occasion, in what she suspected were brand new chinos with a pressed black button down and stylish black and white boat shoes. The pants were a bit more cargo than chino, his shirtsleeves rolled up, exposing muscled forearms with a hint of a tattoo peeking out, and I'm-not-shaving-for-anyone-but-me facial hair.

Like so many foolish women before her, she was a sucker for a bad boy. Well, one like Chase who acted like a bad boy but was a good guy deep down. A nice duality. Or maybe it was the ripped body. Or maybe that edgy look that said he wasn't looking for a fight but was prepared for it anyway.

Her father's shout over her head to his old friend, Steve, brought her back to the moment. She glanced at her mother and realized she was being watched. She failed at her attempt to not blush, but her cheeks burned red despite her best efforts. Dang her pale skin.

Her dad's voice resonated across the crowded patio, "Chase made it back in the nick of time to celebrate with us today. I hear he reeled in more cod than the rest of the crew today," her father shouted across the patio to his second in command.

His conversation across the patio was a poorly concealed effort to sow the seeds for Chase's acceptance in the community and as the future of McAllister Fisheries. "Chase, you'll have worked with several of the team before, but there are quite a few newcomers. Steve, you'll re-acquaint Chase with the ropes while I'm showing those Italian's how to properly catch whitefish? I know you hate the office, but let's get that kid using his brain for business matters. He's got that fancy business degree."

Frank gestured across the patio to his oldest friend. They bantered back and forth about fishing and travel, roping a few of the others into their conversation. Chase quietly listened while neatly avoiding joining the conversation himself. Maddy knew he was not comfortable with praise.

Maddy smiled inwardly as she watched Steve and her father promoting Chase. She had always enjoyed her dad's crew; the town cherished local businesses, and her father's was one of the major economic staples and charitable donors in Seaview. Steve had worked with him since before Maddy was born. He'd always been his right-hand-man. Frank had offered him partnership years prior, but Steve had refused, insisting he only wanted to catch fish without strings attached. They'd compromised on Steve managing groundfish operations. When they'd added the rod-and-reel route to sell to the local restaurants and seafood stores, Steve had called dibs on captaining that route himself; a fisherman's dream job.

After a few more lively conversations about how the local justice system would never be the same again and the must-see sites of Italy, the party finally started to wind down. Maddy let out a long sigh as she leaned against the door after having escorted out the last of the guests. She grabbed her jacket and made her way to sit outside and enjoy the last of the evening with her family. She saw Chase coming out of the kitchen, again with drinks. Coffee this time.

"I thought you were here as a guest, but here you are serving drinks again. You're in the wrong line of work."

The corner of his mouth turned up, "You know your parents love putting me to work. 'A helpful, busy body doesn't have time to find trouble.'" He quoted her mother with sarcasm, but it was impossible to miss the admiration in his voice.

She knew her mother had helped him out of more than a few scrapes, and not just when Aiden was involved. Not that he ever outrightly accepted help. Nor did he ever remain idle. The labor now, as it has always been, was likely more of his own choosing. Chase never was one to sit still, or one to let anyone wait on him.

She took the two mugs from his hands. Their fingers brushed again, and again she was overwhelmed by the zing. That was new. Their eyes locked.

She'd always been ridiculously attracted to him, and maybe had fantasized about his return more than a few times over the past decade but had never imagined this new sensation. Maybe because she had never felt anything like it before. Had read about it, but thought it was a bunch of romantic fantasy bullshit.

Chase quickly disappeared back into the kitchen and returned with the remaining three steaming mugs. Again, she followed him outside. Earlier, she had simply wanted to avoid the crowd. Now, she wanted to savor the moment. And the view. As he nudged the door open with his foot, he looked back and caught her checking out his ass.

He raised one eyebrow in challenge, "Enjoying the view?" The corner of his mouth turned up in satisfied smirk.

And here came the blush. Dang, she hated being such an easy mark. "Yes, I am. I've had an embarrassingly long dry spell. Now shut up and keep walking," she fired back with a flirty laugh. They were chuckling together as they stepped onto the patio.

She could swear she heard him mutter, "Me too," as she followed him outside.

Something in his brain shifted as she openly flirted with him. As always, she could dish out more than she took, but the flirting was new. He wanted to continue their easy banter, seeing where else she might take this. He was suffering from a ridiculously long dry spell too. He was sorely out of practice with any sort of flirtation, maybe even plain talking to an attractive woman. He hoped he could keep up.

He took his time and may have swaggered back out to the patio, knowing it would make her laugh more. That laugh was incredible, so unrestrained. So much passion in those few giggles. Giggles wasn't the right word; way too womanly and sexy for giggles, but whatever you might call it, she had a fucking sexy laugh.

As they walked toward her parents and Aiden, a rush of wind ruffled his freshly cut hair. Despite the unseasonably hot day, the ocean managed to bring in a cool breeze. Laura and Frank snuggled up in a blanket on a loveseat in front of the firepit. Aiden had pulled a chaise lounge up close to the fire, eyelids at half-mast, cozied up under an over-sized wool blanket. That left the one remaining loveseat close to the fire with a knit blanket strewn across the back.

Chase passed out the three coffees to Laura, Frank, and set Aiden's next to him on the side table. He turned back around to see Maddy handing him the extra coffee she had carried. Her hair, pin-straight when she had arrived, was now in a bit wildly in disarray.

When stressed, overwhelmed, or even while joking around, she ran her hands through her hair. He doubted she realized she was doing it. He wasn't about to say anything, as it was ridiculously sexy disheveled like it was. He briefly allowed the fantasy of her bringing him coffee and crawling back into bed with him in the morning, her hair tousled like it was now, but instead due to a wild night in bed with him.

Chase almost jerked when he realized where he had been allowing his brain to wander in front of Maddy's parents and very protective big brother. He blamed his long day. Waking up well before dawn, spending the first 10 hours of his day in the fresh sea air, on his feet on the rocking ship, then the last few hours at a big social gathering; he was practically falling asleep where he stood.

Observing his brief, standing nap, Maddy, already seated on the loveseat herself, gestured for him to join her. Not much space; they'd be pretty snuggly on the undersized loveseat. Shit. He finally settled at the opposite end of the small loveseat, squished against the arm of the chair to avoid touching her in any way. A few centimeters separated their hips. The cool night air was suddenly a hot, suffocating August day in Texas.

Chase tried to calm his thoughts. He looked around at his friends. His family, really. He no longer had his own father, and really hadn't had him in years. Who the hell knew where his mother was... he certainly didn't want to know at this point. Chase had berated himself enough over the years, struggling to save his own father from self-destruction after his mother had ditched them. Somewhere in the last decade he had accepted defeat, if not peace or acceptance.

The McAllisters and Chase slowly sipped their coffees in silence. The fire crackled between the five of them, their gazes all lost in the flames, eyes glazed from a hectic day. Each lost in thought and enjoying the silence. A great party; Laura had grinned all evening. He was glad he'd been here to see her so happy.

Maddy slipped off her heels. She rotated her body and tucked her ice-cold feet under Chase's leg. So much for keeping his distance. He gave up and pulled the blanket across them both, letting himself savor the closeness, but trying not to make anything of it. Keeping his imagination tamed.

After their coffees had gone cold and eventually drained, Laura's soft voice interrupted the silence. "That was a fantastic party. Thanks, guys, for making sure everything flowed so well and letting me relax and enjoy my party."

Without lifting his head from his pillow, Aiden rolled towards his mother and drolly replied, "Mom, this was a great party. A very crowded party. You've made an incredible impact on this community. Thank goodness you are retiring. Leave some room for we mortals." With a soft chuckle, he rolled back over, pulling the blanket tightly around him.

Laura's laugh warmed the night more than their coffee or warm blankets could hope to. "Oh boy. On that note, my dear sarcastic son, I'm heading for bed." Laura slowly stood, took a few steps towards Aiden and draped her blanket over him. Frank rose to his feet as well, his arthritic knees creaking as they straightened. He gently placed his free hand behind his wife's back and followed behind her. They gave sleepy farewells.

Aiden sat up just enough to fully recline his cushioned chaise lounge, then plopped back down against the makeshift bed. "Well, it's been quite a day. I'm crashing right where I am. 'Night." From all appearances, Aiden was asleep by the time his head laid back on the pillow. Chase and Maddy both stood on sleepy jell-o'd legs. Maddy carried their blanket and wordlessly spread it neatly across Aiden's sleeping form.

Chase followed Maddy back into the house as they walked through to the front door. The sky was dark, and the driveway was only visible thanks to the solar powered garden lights. Chase paused with his hand on his truck door, parked in front of Maddy's Jeep. He looked back to Maddy as she did the same, holding her gaze for longer than was appropriate. Each offered a soft, lingering smile, hesitating before climbing into their vehicles.

Chase waited on Maddy to turn her Jeep around first and head down the hill. He followed Maddy down the road back to town at a respectful distance. He had no idea what he was going to do. It was already clear that life with Aiden, Frank, and Laura would settle in a companionable routine. He was incredibly grateful they had accepted him back into the fold so completely.

Which he would completely destroy if he allowed his libido to take over and fulfill his very active, very naked fantasies of wild, incredible sex with Maddy. What a way to quickly lose their trust. Not exactly something they could really keep secret. That sort of thing was hard to keep quiet in a town like this.

6

THE NIGHT'S BREEZE HAD brought in some rainclouds that hung around the coast for the next week. Disturbing the pleasant serenity that had settled over the quaint town, the sun made another showing the following Friday morning, inviting a massive influx of tourists. The day could be considered unseasonably warm, but the gentle sea breeze kept the temperature perfect for a day at the beach.

Maddy finished up her daily patrol with a final check along the beach. Really, you never knew what trouble could be brewing along the beach on such a beautiful day. She'd ensured all was well in the busy areas of town before finishing the day at her favorite spot. The day had been amazingly peaceful. Not too many calls or disturbances, despite the crowds.

Maddy took advantage and stopped into Flotsam Antiques as she strolled back towards the station. The bells jingled to herald her arrival as she entered the store. Maddy inhaled deeply, loving the scent of old leather and wood furniture, with a fresh citrus, almost minty scent. Not a hint of must. The owner was quite particular about that.

The store was filled with antiques of all shapes and sizes, irresistible treasures for anyone who may stop in.

Payson Roberts: owner, proprietor, manager, accountant, and number one sales agent, and also Maddy's best friend, was finalizing a sale with a happy young family. Maddy paused to watch her friend crouching down to a chipper young girl in a sunny yellow dress, "I can't wait to hear what you decide to store in your new dresser. This dresser was once owned by a young girl just like you, nearly 100 years ago, and I'm sure she filled it with pretty dresses just like the one you're wearing."

The little girl beamed at the attention and smoothed the front of her dress. The family thanked Payson and said their goodbyes. Payson was dressed in her own soft blue cotton sundress and had clearly bonded with the young girl right off. Payson was a natural with people, old and young alike. Maddy envied Payson's extroversion.

As she walked across the shop to greet her friend, Maddy was distracted as she ran a hand along the dresser, admiring its fine craftmanship. "I've had my eye on this for weeks. If I can't have it, I'm glad that sweet little girl will get to have it. It is a bit too dainty and wouldn't have fit in with the rest of my furniture anyway."

Payson grinned at her friend, flipping her pin-straight auburn hair from her face. "I told you, you don't have room for another dresser anyway. Natalie will help me deliver it to their place tomorrow, so you won't have to pine over it much longer." Payson had a tough time sharing responsibility with anyone, so hiring Natalie part time as a delivery-driver-slash-emergency-sales-helper had been a big move. It had been helpful for Maddy as well, as she had often found herself as the involuntary volunteer delivery assistant otherwise.

"Town is hopping. Are you making good sales?"

"It's been great. I've met my sales goals for the entire month in the past 48 hours." Payson beamed, looking around at the inventory gaps that had begun to show, as her stock depleted with all the sales.

"Maybe you'll bring in enough this weekend to go on a real vacation, or at least take an occasional day off. Natalie is great, have you considered hiring her on full time?"

"I really want to ask her, but I doubt she would want to work in a shop full time. She's always game to come in and help when I'm overwhelmed; I don't want to push her too far." Natalie had moved to the area a few months ago and had stayed pretty quiet. She had seen the Help Wanted sign Payson had hung in the window and signed on to help Payson a few hours per week. The rest of the time, Natalie sequestered herself in her large studio apartment when she wasn't driving all over the coast. She was a spectacular photographer and sold a lot of her work at the local gallery.

Rumor had it, she and a few other local artists were doing so well, the gallery was planning to renovate the old chapel in a major expansion project. Natalie's latest project was a photographic journal of lighthouses down the coast. She mostly kept to herself but did agree to come out with Maddy and Payson for an occasional girl's night. At first, Maddy had thought she was pretentious, but she realized later she was just incredibly shy.

Maddy looked around at the shop her friend had lovingly filled with a collection of small and large antiques. As the name implied, she had a unique section filled with shipwreck finds near the front window. When Payson moved in two years ago, shortly before Maddy had moved back to town, locals had doubted that an antique store would succeed in the small tourist town.

But Payson had known what she was doing and had built a thriving business. She'd come with some impressive connections she had developed from her previous job in Boston, so her stock was always filled with new and interesting pieces. No stranger to the modern antique trade, she also rocked a great website and contracted with several online retailers. Even in the cold, blustery winter months, she stayed busy. Antique trinkets were a hit with the tourists looking for fun souvenirs, but she also carried high-end antique furniture, art, and jewelry.

Payson leaned across the old-style buffet that she had converted into a checkout counter. Her long hair slipped down her shoulders and rested next to her elbows on the counter. Waggling her eyebrows at Maddy, Payson changed the subject, "I saw your old friend, Chase Anderson, is back in town. Says he's renting a place in that beautiful old brick-house neighborhood on the hill. He bought that sturdy farmhouse table you'd been coveting. That is one sexy man. A killer body and those deep, stormy-blue eyes. And, obviously, great taste in furniture."

Maddy felt a rare wave of jealousy. What was that all about? Payson was beyond ready for a serious relationship, unlike Maddy. Despite going through some bad relationships as well, Payson was still convinced that true love was just waiting for her to find it. Not that she'd had any luck in the past few years, but she was out there and trying.

Maddy tucked away her feelings and would be supportive if her friend was interested. She deserved some happiness with a good guy. And Maddy wasn't interested anyway, not in anyone. "What did you think? Did you turn on some of that Payson flirty-charm?"

Payson flipped her straight hair dramatically and put on her sauciest face. "That man looked desperate for a good lay, so I closed up shop and showed him a good time. I was finally able to fulfill my fantasy of being taken behind the counter." Payson gestured with her arms spread wide and firmly gripping the counter, then paused just long enough to gauge her friend's reaction.

She reached across the counter and smacked her friend playfully on the arm, "Maddy, you dope! First off, yes, he's damn sexy, but the chemistry just wasn't there. He clearly felt the same way, sending no signals my way. Secondly, and more importantly, I know you've had your eyes on him since before you even hit puberty. So, tell me, did *you* turn on that Maddy flirty-charm?"

And Maddy's cheeks were officially burning red. Dang pale skin gave her away every time. "Fine, I may continue to try to lie to myself, but apparently I can't hide anything from you. No, I did not turn on the Maddy flirty charm," she vehemently denied. Then she remembered getting caught ogling. "Well, maybe I did. Just a little."

"Do tell!" Payson leaned across the counter and raised her eyebrows.

And, the blush spread down her neck. "Chase was at my mom's retirement party, but I haven't seen him since. I may have complemented his ass. But that's it. Mostly. Besides, I can't pursue Chase. He's my brother's best friend and my dad's protégé. I'm not good at this stuff anyway. Two very failed attempts at relationships. I'm officially done. Maybe I'll try sex again... maybe... but I just don't want to put myself out there again."

"You're so damn stubborn – which usually I love about you. But, in this case, you're only hurting yourself. Other men aren't like Dylan. The other guy, what was his name? Kent? Your rebound attempt. He doesn't even count. You went straight for an incredibly boring dud – that I suspect you weren't even attracted to – to compensate for your awful experience with Dylan. How long did you spend with him?" Payson ranted, still not letting Maddy answer, her finger raised to motion that she wasn't finished, "You spent like three months going on a very rare date before you even let him touch you. And, as I don't think you were the least bit attracted, of course you didn't enjoy yourself. And, I'm not sure he knew what a clitoris even is..."

"Hey, I'll have you know that he was very sweet, and I wasn't not attracted, just not... well... yeah, he was a total dud. I should never have told you about him anyway." Maddy paced, restless.

"You know and trust Chase. You know your family loves him and would love for the two of you to be happy together. And, most importantly, you're undeniably attracted to him." Payson was fired up on her friend's behalf.

"He's hurt me before, pushing me away when he and Aiden started skipping classes, staying out all night, trying to buy a ticket straight to jail." Maddy fired back, becoming defensive.

"Maddy, you both went through some awful stuff back then. I know you're scared; you have PTSD. Some serious relationship PTSD, thanks to Dylan. Both you and Chase ran far away to escape your demons. Now, you're both back. Come on Buffy, kill that demon by moving on. Don't let Dylan continue to hold that power over you." Payson's eyes softened as her fire fizzled, bringing it down a notch for Maddy's sake.

She'd never had a friendship with another woman her age like she had with Payson. It was a little scary having someone know her so well. Maddy's eyes welled as her friend came around and pulled her into a hug. "I can't go through another bad relationship. I just don't know that I can open myself up for that again. It sucked."

She'd distanced herself from Dylan as far as she could, emotionally and geographically. She'd run away to Seattle, changed her major and her goals in life. She had tried to move on—once, but that was a serious disappointment and didn't merit another attempt. Almost a confirmation that she wasn't any good at relationships. Or at sex.

Payson was right, she'd selected a dud that she'd felt was very... benign, i.e., not likely to hurt her. Well, he didn't hurt her, exactly. Only her self-confidence that was already at rock bottom.

Knowing her friend needed a reprieve, but maybe needed a push even more, Payson pulled back and looked at her weepy friend, "Maddy, I know you won't do relationships, and I know why. But maybe give him a one-night trial? Maybe see how it goes with someone you trust, and that you're actually attracted to?"

Maddy wiped her teary eyes and enjoyed a good laugh with her friend. "I think I'll hide in my bubble a bit longer. It's safer in here."

Finally granting her friend the reprieve, Payson changed the subject, "I'm closing up shop for the night. Want to grab a bite after work? Sit somewhere outside overlooking the beach and play tourist bad-lip reading?"

Before she could accept, her radio interrupted. "Maddy, could you call over? We have a bit of a situation we need you to check out."

Maddy checked her watch and responded back, "I'm off duty as of 5 minutes ago, can't Mike take it?" Maddy was always ready to lend a hand, but she really needed a girl's night.

"It's about Chase Anderson. His neighbor, Lynn Hanson, is calling saying she hears a fight going on in his garage. As I suspect it's nothing, I wanted to offer it to you first."

Maddy sighed. Great. Back in the day, Chase was frequently in trouble and was often the guilty party. Nearly as frequently, however, he was accused of something he didn't do. Lynn Hanson has always been a busybody. Her stereotypical spinsterhood might just be motivation enough for Maddy to change her own spinster tendencies. Scary prospect, ending up like Miss Hanson.

"Thanks Quinn, I'll head right over." Turning back to Payson, she asked, "Can I meet you at Antonio's in an hour or so? I need to go check this out and then go home and change. If you beat me there, get us a spot out on the deck and order me a big glass of wine."

"Sure thing. Let me know if you find yourself... *delayed*," Payson winked dramatically, grinning at her friend.

Rolling her eyes, Maddy headed out. She walked the two blocks west from Beachside Avenue to the station. She hopped in her official black Seaview Police Explorer and drove the two miles to Chase's rental house.

It wasn't a big house, a classic old brick with white trim, surrounded by well-manicured mature trees and shrubs. It appeared to be meticulously kept, not a weed in sight. Chase's shiny new black truck was parked in the driveway. Maddy parked on the street between Chase and Miss Hanson's driveways.

Miss Hanson wore her typical attire: hair in curlers, polyester pants hiked up above her belly button, with coordinating billowing floral blouse. Ouch. Yep, very motivating to *not* continue the spinster lifestyle.

She tiptoed toward Maddy, with surprising speed, as Maddy stepped out of the SUV. Whispering loudly to Maddy, Miss Hanson sputtered out, "Do you hear that? They're still going at it. I don't know what they were thinking, renting out that beautiful home to a known criminal."

Maddy didn't hear anything at first. Miss Hanson had amazing sensory powers, like an owl or something. Maddy shuddered, remembering the struggle to stay under the radar through seventh grade in Miss Hanson's class. Moving closer, she pressed her ear against Chase's garage door, finally hearing a muted cacophony of loud music, some bashing sounds, and an occasional grunt.

Maintaining her professional composure, as always, Maddy politely responded, "Miss Hanson, would you mind stepping back into your house while I investigate the situation? I would hate for you to put yourself in any danger." Miss Hanson's arms flew in the air as she abruptly turned and ran on her tiptoes back into her house. A moment later her face was pressed to the front window like one of those old stuffed Garfield toys that Miss Hanson still had stuck onto the rear window of her car.

Maddy knocked on Chase's garage door. No answer. She knocked more vigorously to compete with the rhythmic base.

In response, the music suddenly went quiet and the garage door slowly rose, dramatically revealing the scene. No wonder he parked in the driveway, the garage was filled with home gym equipment: punching bag, weight set and bench, treadmill, rowing machine. Holy crap, how much weight had he been benching? Although she appreciated the nice set-up, her eyes were locked onto Chase, standing casually in the middle of the garage.

Muscled arms across his chest, he raised one eyebrow as Maddy came into view. He wore a sleeveless old black t-shirt with gray cut-off sweats hung low over his hips. The corner of his mouth was raised in an expression somewhere between a question and a satisfied grin. He tilted his head, "Is there a problem, officer?"

Maddy was a bit breathless, but the humor of the situation helped her to hide her reaction to Chase's magnificently muscled body, glistening with sweat from and intense work-out session. Putting on her professional face, she responded, "Good afternoon, Mr. Anderson. I was notified of sounds of a disturbance at your residence. I will go notify your very helpful neighbor that all is well. Enjoy your work-out." She nodded politely.

They shared a humorous smile. Warmth traveled from her core clear to her extremities, yet she shivered.

She turned to walk down the driveway when Chase caught up to her, rotating her gently back toward him. "Hang on. You doing anything tonight? Aiden and I were going to grab a burger and a beer at Winter's Tavern. Want to join us? 6 o'clock?" His expression... was that nervousness?

Tingles rushing through her body, Maddy was torn between disappointment that he was not asking her out on a date, and relief that her brother would be there as a buffer. She hadn't been to Winter's in a while – outside of a professional capacity – but always enjoyed the old-school fishermen's tavern. "Sounds great. I have plans tonight with Payson, but I'm sure she won't mind the change in venue. Mind picking us up on the way?"

"Happy to. See you tonight." Chase jogged back into the garage and hit the button to close the large, noisy door behind him as he stepped into the house. Maddy tried to hide her smile as she went to notify Miss Hanson of the mistake.

7

At 5:45 sharp, Chase pulled in to Maddy's driveway. He had self-ishly decided to pick her up first, so they could have a few moments alone. No doubt, he was a glutton for punishment.

He admired the house as he hopped out of the truck. The location was perfect, right on the beach, just past the chaos of Beachside Avenue. He'd been over many times when her grandparents had owned the place; they'd had a lot of beach adventures in front of the house or used it as a meeting spot before walking down to join the crowds on Beachside.

She'd done a lot with the place. The cedar had aged to a silvery gray over the years, and she'd clearly recently painted the trim a crisp, fresh white with a contrasting bold blue front door. Brightly colored flowers flanked the walkway, clearly well-tended.

Chase rang the doorbell, feeling suddenly very much like he was picking up his date. He tried to keep a calm appearance as he anxiously waited for her to answer. He remembered the time he had been hanging out at Aiden's place and had answered the door for her date;

not uncommon for him to have opened the door, as he spent so much time there.

This time, however, Dylan was waiting on the other side to take Maddy to junior prom. Their first big date. It had taken all Chase's willpower not to knock his teeth out, that stupid smirk as the asshole watched Maddy come to the door in her pale pink dress – seemingly conservative in the front, but the low back made it damn sexy.

It had been of his own making, he knew that. Instead of going to the dance that night, he and Aiden had instead stolen some whiskey from his dad and knocked over mailboxes. A nice farewell to town, as he left a few weeks later.

The door finally swung open. Maddy stood in the threshold, wearing a short denim skirt that showed off her incredible, long legs. She topped off the look with simple, but incredibly sexy, slim white button-up top. Chase forgot how to speak for a moment.

"Hey Chase, let me grab my jacket." She quickly disappeared behind the door and re-appeared carrying a motorcycle jacket swung over her arm. She locked the front door, and he followed her out to the truck. Unable to shake the feeling he was taking her out on a date, he gallantly leaped in front to open the passenger door for her. He tried to calm his over-eager and ridiculously overzealous libido as he crossed over to his door. *Not for you*, he reminded himself.

They picked up Payson next from her apartment above Flotsam Antiques. She had been waiting outside when they arrived and hopped in the backseat. Chase suspected Payson was terminally feminine, dressed tonight in a long blue sundress with a leather purse swung over her shoulder. Her denim jacket at least was a nod to the fact that they were going to a rundown locals-only sort of tavern for dinner. "Thanks for the lift, Chase. How are you liking the table?"

"You were right, it's perfect for the space. I even bought that blue-glass candle centerpiece from the shop next to yours that you'd recommended. Now I have to start actually inviting people over for dinner or it'll get dusty." Chase didn't entertain much, so the table had been more than he needed, but the empty room had been far more depressing than a dusty dining room table would be. "You keeping an eye out for a coffee table for me?"

"Sure thing. I'd like to see the couch and chairs you picked out before I can recommend anything. Bring me some pics. Or, you can invite us all over for dinner one night so Maddy can visit her second favorite dining table. Lucky you bought it, or she'd have found a way to convert her spare bedroom just to make room for it."

Payson clearly loved her job and had a knack for it. She was more than just an antique shop owner. She'd told him about her studies in interior design and antiquities, her last job at an international antiquities dealer in Boston before moving to Seaview. He wondered why the move to such a slower paced life, but he didn't want to pry.

They drove the few more blocks to Aiden's. Aiden's house had belonged to a local accountant for years. The accountant retired a few months before Aiden moved back to town; Aiden had jumped at the opportunity and, like Payson, lived upstairs and ran his business downstairs.

Chase glanced in the backseat as Aiden walked out the door and was locking up. Shit, his new TV was taking up most of the backseat, leaving room only for Payson. Aiden opened the back-passenger door, "Uh, Chase, nice TV. But, where am I sitting?"

"Sorry, I forgot that was in here. I picked it up on my way home from work yesterday. I forgot how exhausting it is to be out on the boat all day. Normally I'm under the water, not on it. Plus, I feel like I'm working double-speed to show them who's boss, literally. I sort of crashed when I got home and forgot about it. Climb up front next to Maddy."

Chase pulled up the armrest and motioned Maddy to the middle seat while Aiden made his way around the back of the truck. On cue, Maddy slid across the bench seat. Her bare legs straddled the gear shifter, her left leg plastered to his right, almost as if he'd planned it.

His eyes went straight to her thighs, thinking her skirt wouldn't have to hike much higher for him to see her panties. Thong or bikini? Lace or cotton? His poor imagination was going a mile a minute, gaze stuck, hoping for a glimpse of heaven.

As the door opened and Aiden hopped in, Maddy tugged down her skirt, bringing him back in the moment. He quickly adjusted his own pants, that had grown a bit uncomfortable in the past moment.

There was little hope for improvement as he shifted into reverse, hand grazing her inner thigh. He was smiling inwardly, congratulating himself on his brilliant investment in the manual transmission and bench seat, but the knowledge that her brother was sitting on her other side was a harsh awakening, like jumping into the North Sea in winter.

He drove north through the backroads, neatly avoiding the dinner-hour traffic of Beachside Avenue. He would never admit out loud that his decision to take the path with the most stop signs, allowing for as many gear changes as possible, may perhaps have been intentional. He was a glutton for punishment. After passing the McAllister Fisheries' complex, they rounded the last bend past the tourist hullabaloo and drove a few final turns before pulling into Winter's.

Winter's was hopping tonight; filled with locals. It was mostly a fishermen's joint but was also beloved by many locals wanting to get away from the highly trafficked Beachside Avenue restaurants in summer. Well into his 60's, Winter had kept the place in good condition.

It looked to have been recently painted a deep blue color with bright white trim. Neon signs advertised beer of all varieties, blocking the view into any of the few windows.

Chase had actually never spent more than a few minutes inside, as Winter had always kicked he and Aiden right back out. Damn small town; fake IDs didn't work when everyone knew who you were. Chase didn't bother circling the crowded parking lot for a closer spot on the crowded night, instead he parked on the side of the building.

They all piled out of the crowded truck, heading together to the front door. Before even rounding the corner, the sounds of a scuffle were obvious. Chase knew Maddy could obviously handle herself, she did this sort of thing for a living. But, he found himself pushing her behind him as the fight came into view.

He saw a few of his own folks, Braden's massive form right in front. He saw Braden's fist connect with a guy he hadn't seen before, but clearly a fisherman and somehow even wider than Braden himself. The guy was built like a tank.

Neither he nor his friends looked familiar, must not be one of McAllisters'. Dammit. They didn't need anyone spending the night in jail or too badly hurt right now. They were a bit short-staffed as it was.

After Chase's hand grazed her legs during the drive over with every gear-change, at the many stop signs they had approached, capping off the drive with several attempts to reverse perfectly into the parking spot, Maddy still hadn't found her land legs yet. Sure, she could have adjusted so he had a bit more space to shift gears, but she rather enjoyed herself. That was a pleasant surprise.

As they headed for the front door, she was irked that Chase had pushed her behind him at the sound of the fight, but she found herself equally touched by his protective gesture. She noted Chase balling his fists at his sides, ready for a fight.

Shit. She may be off duty but would be forced to intervene or call for back-up if things got ugly. They were all used to the occasional fishermen's brawls and didn't get too worked up if it was just a few punches, or they'd have to permanently place a patrol outside the tavern and the poor fishing industry would struggle. But, if things got ugly, everyone involved got to spend the night in jail to cool down.

Chase turned toward her with a sly grin and asked she, Payson, and Aiden to hang on a sec. She watched Chase walk casually over to the small crowd, as if he hadn't even noticed a fight was in progress. Chase interrupted with a smile, "Braden, how the hell are ya? Heard you guys pulled in a huge load of lobster today."

The fighting pair turned back to him, surprised to have been interrupted so cheerfully. The man who had punched Braden turned to Chase, his expression wild and confused. "You must be McAllister's shiny new toy. Kiss my ass." The tank's fist flew out of nowhere, straight for Chase; a surprisingly quick move for someone so bulky. Maddy nearly shrieked but managed to keep silent, giving him a chance to cool things down before intervening.

Chase swiftly ducked to avoid the massive fist. As he bobbed out of the way, he caught the tank in a solid right hook. Chase quickly brought his other fist into the tank's abdomen as he recoiled from Chase's well-placed blow to his jaw.

The tank tried to straighten up and go for Chase again, but Chase was faster, knocking the tank onto the ground with his knee, as the huge man crashed limply to the ground. He laid on the ground for a minute, moaning and groaning.

Without a glance at the fallen tank of a man, nor even a glint of sweat on his brow, completely unharmed, Chase calmly looked to the tank's friends, "I don't think we've been introduced. I'm Chase Anderson. I'm sure Braden and my good friends here wouldn't have had any issues flattening you themselves, but it's been too long since I had a decent fight. Anyone else want a quick warm up?"

"Go to hell, Anderson," one responded. The others helped the tank up and stalked out to their own trucks, tails between their legs.

Braden stepped up, placed a friendly smack on Chase's bad shoulder, still painful from his injury on the rig, and laughed out loud, "Chase, I oughtta kick your ass myself. I've wanted a piece of those guys for so damn long. But I guess I'll let it slide this time, you being my new boss and all. Nice moves. Those pansy-ass oilers show you a few things?" The pair shook hands. "Buy you a beer?"

"Thanks Braden, but let me buy you one. That felt great. Oilers have nothing on fishermen when it comes to a fight," Chase said with a wink. "See you in there." Chase nodded to his crew as they headed into the tavern.

Aiden walked past and patted him on the back, "Couldn't have done it better myself. Frank'll be proud, but don't say anything to Mom; she'd have all of our hides." Payson followed Aiden into the tavern.

Maddy stopped in front of Chase and grinned, "You know I should probably give you a warning or something. We don't tolerate that sort of violence at the Seaview PD."

Chase held his arms out in surrender, "I'm all yours. Bring your handcuffs?" He waggled his eyebrows at her.

Maddy couldn't resist. She stood on her tippy toes and leaned in, whispering in his ear, "Anytime, sailor." She hoped she'd had an effect but didn't stop to see his reaction. It would really ruin that effect if he saw her blushing at her own rare, daring flirt.

She walked straight into the tavern, her heart about to beat out of its chest. She hadn't flirted in years, and found she was thoroughly enjoying it. Maybe she would consider sex with Chase. She had certainly enjoyed his hand *innocently* grazing her inner thighs on the drive over. She could only assume she would enjoy his not-so-innocent touch going a whole lot further.

Loud music blared from the large speakers hung from the ceiling. Classic rock, Winter's choice. There was no jukebox, no DJ, and no requests. It was Winter's place and he decided what music played. Usually classic rock, but he was occasionally in the mood for old-time blues, heavy metal, or even classical.

The bar itself was cut out of a huge old growth tree that must have been cut down a hundred years back, with a thick varnish that accented the natural woodgrain while protecting from slivers. The walls were a warm, dark green paint trimmed with dark-stained wood which gave the tavern a cozy feel. Pub-height booths lined the walls. Expansive plank wood flooring was nearly black from years of use. There was plenty of entertainment, with several pool tables, shuffleboard, arcades. Occasionally the tables were pushed to the side for dancing, but not tonight.

Maddy spotted Winter behind the bar and gave him a wave. She enjoyed stopping by for drinks now and again with her parents, as Frank was a regular of the joint. More often, however, she was here in a more official capacity. Winter ran a tight ship; like Maddy, he wasn't bothered by an occasional friendly scuffle, but anything more and he called in the law.

Winter waved back, ignoring the folks at the bar trying to order. "Maddy, my favorite cop. What can I get for you on this fine evening?"

Maddy strolled up to the bar. She squeezed into the middle of the crush, giving her friend a grin, "How about an IPA?"

"Coming right up." He slid the beer to her, not spilling a drop. "That one's on the house, thanks for the quick response the other night."

"Anytime for you, Winter," she warmly responded. "What's good for dinner tonight?"

"Sheila's trying out a new broccoli cheddar soup recipe; it's pretty amazing."

Maddy nearly drooled just thinking about it. "Sounds great. See you around." She headed for the high-top booth that Payson had nabbed for them.

Maddy slid in the booth across from Payson on the cracked leather bench. Payson rolled her eyes at her friend and smiled, "So, not sitting by me. Who are you hoping will squeeze in next to you? Maybe hoping for a little more thigh grazing from our hero with the flying fists?"

Maddy gently kicked her friend under the table. She opened her mouth to respond, but closed it again and shut up when Aiden slid in next to Payson. Maddy thought they looked great together, and had already hinted to each that they'd be a nice couple. Payson with her perfect skin, great figure, long auburn hair, combined with her clever wit, deep sense of kindness, and spunky attitude. Aiden was no slouch; he was tall, muscular without being bulky, a successful attorney, thoughtful.

Both had scoffed at the idea. Payson had laughed and insisted there was absolutely no chemistry. Aiden had looked confused at the prospect. Maddy had pushed and they finally agreed to try a date with each other, but it had ended with a polite handshake.

Funny how two attractive people with plenty in common could have zero romantic chemistry. Fortunately, neither had blamed her for trying. They had enjoyed their dinner out and were now good friends. Payson had furnished Aiden's office, and Aiden hadn't argued. Maddy thought that was a sign of a healthy friendship.

She looked across the crowded bar to Chase. As promised, he delivered a pitcher of beer and some frosty mugs to Braden and his crew from outside. She hoped Aiden didn't catch her staring. Chase had on a fitted black t-shirt and faded jeans that hugged his rear end nicely. He and Aiden were well matched in height, but Chase had few extra inches of muscle he must have earned after those years of demanding physical work.

He visited with the guys for a few minutes, then politely excused himself, taking his half-consumed pint with him. Chase slid in next to Maddy. The booth was barely big enough for the four of them, the twosomes sitting hip to hip, but the place was packed, so they were lucky to have gotten a table at all.

Maddy was on fire, her right side pressed completely against Chase. She tried to make conversation, but the connection had completely wiped her brain.

Sheila rescued her by popping up to their table to take their orders. An old friend of Winter's, but not romantically as both had repeatedly insisted, she had worked at the bar for the last year or so. She dabbled in the kitchen but spent most of her evening keeping the crowd happy with food and drinks.

From the look of her, she'd had a rough life prior to settling in Seaview, with white-gray hair and an almost bony build, balanced with her standard attire of navy-blue t-shirt with *Winter's Tavern* written across the front and classic blue jeans with combat boots. She almost looked frail, but Maddy had seen her carrying ridiculously heavy trays above her head all night without breaking a sweat. "What can I get for my favorite police officer and her friends this evening?"

Maddy beamed. "I'd love to try the soup, and maybe a caesar salad?" The rest of the group ordered. Sheila had the memory of an elephant. She never wrote down orders, and never got them wrong. She knew her regular customers and anticipated their needs before they did.

As Sheila walked away to fill their orders, Aiden prodded, "Maddy, no fries? Are you feeling ok?"

She laughed, "I don't need to order my own; I'll just eat yours."

"You can try," he teased and shook his head. "Do you work tomorrow?"

She focused on the conversation, distracting herself from the inferno, also known as Chase Anderson, pinned against her leg, "Sure do. Back to the rigmarole tomorrow. And it's the night shift, which I hate. But, it's my turn." Maddy loved how they rotated shifts, so no one-person was stuck with night shift, but hated when it was her turn.

Aiden nodded, then threw a curveball, silently gauging her for a response, "You see Dylan's back in town?"

Maddy glared at her brother, not pleased that he would bring that up when she was trying to relax with her friends. "Yes, why?" she responded through tight lips.

"I heard he's trying to buy out a big chunk of waterfront to bring in a cruise line stop. Wants to build a huge dock for it. I overheard him talking up his grand plans with some of his old friends yesterday. His docks would take out McAllister Fisheries and extend as far up the beach as Winter's. Fucking bullshit." Aiden shook his head, clearly as angry at the situation as she was. Aiden looked to Chase, "You'll let me know if he stops by? I already warned Winter."

Chase responded back, "Hell, yeah."

Payson interjected, "Wait a minute. Dylan is such a jerk; how would he accomplish something so major? How would he get the connections to represent a large cruise ship? With his criminal record and creepster vibe, what reputable company would hire that two-faced, evil, conniving, manipulative... grrr." She growled, running out of angry words.

Aiden teased her, "Grrr? You'd be fantastic in a courtroom."

She elbowed him in the side.

He dramatically feigned major injury to his ribs, which only earned him another jab. Calling for a truce, he continued, "He paid his fines and served his full sentence for what he did to Maddy. He's charming, charismatic. His dad is pretty high up in a successful mergers and acquisitions firm in DC; too big for our tiny town anymore, but he could easily help his son with connections."

Payson fired back again, agitated enough for the rest of them, "But, why would Dylan choose Seaview? We're doing just fine economically. There are a number of other tourist towns on the coast that would hand over enough property for such a good chance to boost their own economy."

They fell silent. Maddy took a long gulp of her beer, fearing the answer. Chase finally interrupted, "Because of Maddy." He looked over to Maddy.

She'd never told him what had happened, mostly as they hadn't talked while he was gone. She knew her parents and Aiden would not have told the whole story without her permission but would have told him the basics.

Chase looked deep into her eyes, expression pained, "Maddy, I don't know what all happened, but I gather it was unforgivable. I know he hurt you." Chase paused as if afraid to go on. Maddy nodded, silently giving him permission to continue. "Do you remember your sixteenth birthday party?"

Maddy and Chase's eyes connected. She was thrown by the reference to something she remembered so fondly in the middle of such a nasty conversation, but on seeing the glimmer in his expression and corner of his mouth turn up, she was quickly distracted. Neither had ever acknowledged the moment before now.

She tried to hide her blush, as Aiden would hopefully not remember the party the same way she did. "Yes... why?" she managed to ask.

"Remember when I knocked Bryce out of the way, so you didn't have your first kiss with him during spin the bottle?"

"Of course. I remain herpes-free thanks to you." She allowed herself to smile at the memory now. She wasn't quite sure how he knew that was her first kiss, but then again, she'd been a total tomboy for most of their growing up years and hadn't shown any interest in dating until around that time.

Payson's hand shot up, her finger raised between them, "Wait, what? Maddy, you didn't tell me Chase was your first kiss."

And now she was officially embarrassed.

Aiden fired back, and would have jumped out from his seat if Payson hadn't held him by the arm, "What? That was your first? Chase, what the hell? That's my little sister."

Chase shook his head at his friend and smiled innocently, "Which is why I saved her from herpes. Your sister. My friend. Thought you'd thank me for that." He smugly grinned as he took a swig of his own beer.

Aiden shrugged, "Maybe. It's just disturbing to think about. I really don't need a visual of you making out with my little sister."

Maddy rolled her eyes. "Aiden, I don't want a visual of you making out with anyone."

"Touché," he nodded in ascent.

Chase shook his head. "Back to my point. Do you remember Dylan's behavior at the party?"

Maddy shook her head in confusion; she had completely forgotten he was there. They didn't start dating until much later.

"He was starting to get up to take Bryce's place too, but I was faster. He was... not pleased. He came after me when you guys turned on the movie and were all absorbed in it. I had ducked outside for a smoke. I still remember the look in his eyes as he stalked onto the patio and went to slug me. I didn't even have to try to hit him back; he ended up knocking himself over a flowerpot and walked home crying."

Maddy's brow creased in concentration, "I don't even remember him being there."

Aiden jumped in, "I remember now. Why was Ronan even friends with him?"

Maddy knew this one. "Ronan wasn't very close with anyone, he was always in his own world. He probably didn't even care what a phony Dylan was. They were in academic clubs together, the same baseball team since little league; they were friends by default." Maddy looked back to Chase, "I still don't see how I'm the reason he's back. I haven't seen him in years and made it pretty clear I will flatten him if he comes near me again."

The tavern was briefly silent, as the music skipped to the next song. Metallica cried out, blasting from the enormous speakers, shaking the walls. Aiden spoke loudly, "Maddy, the guy had a thing for you for years. Good chance he feels that you ruined his future and wants a little revenge. However, he had a thing for you for years. He was... oddly attentive to you. Even before you started dating; you just didn't see it. Whatever his motive in coming back to Seaview, I suspect it involves you. His presence in town is not safe for you. Please, stay far away from him."

Now that, Maddy could easily agree with. Thankfully, their food arrived in a welcome interruption. If Sheila noticed the tension that had built at the table, she didn't comment, "Get you folks another round?" Aiden and Payson took her up on the offer, Chase declined as he was the designated driver. Maddy suddenly needed a clear head and declined as well.

8

AFTER HOURS OF READING through profit and loss statements, fish stock trends and regulations, inventory reports... Chase's brain had turned to mush. He'd had the weekend off to shift gears. From here on out, he was down to only a few days per month on the fishing boats, but the rest was dedicated to office time, as Frank would be leaving soon for Italy and wanted Chase to be in charge.

Thankfully, the rest of the office staff were well trained and supportive of Chase. They had converted the dusty old meeting room into a nice corner office for Chase, with a view of town and the ocean. Most meetings took place in the breakroom anyway, so no one missed the loss of space.

Laura had taken the liberty of decorating his office. She'd chosen an espresso-finished wooden desk with coordinating furniture, including a round table in the corner for smaller meetings. There was a large painting of an old school fishing boat in a storm hanging over the table. On the bookshelf, Laura had added a collection of framed photos.

She had been thoughtful in the photos she had framed for him. The largest was one of he and his dad in a rare happy moment when he was about 8 years old; he didn't reflect back on the good days often enough. Of course, she would have known how much that would mean to him. Henry had been a decent dad before Chase's mom had left. Hadn't been a stranger to liquor, but he hadn't started drinking away his worries.

There was another photo of he, Steve, and Frank smiling together with frozen beards on board an icy fishing boat the winter before he'd left. There was, of course, one of he and Aiden covered in mud with shit-eating grins, no more than 14 years old.

One of Maddy threw him off, a photo he hadn't seen before and wondered as to Laura's motives. It was a few days before he skipped town. Aiden's grandparents had thrown a graduation party for he and Aiden. The photo showed him grabbing Maddy from behind, his arms wrapped around her bare waist, lifting her and about to toss her into the coming wave. He remembered how she'd managed to twist around and dragged him into the wave with her. They tumbled into the ocean and had come up laughing hysterically, both soaking wet.

After the long day of research in his new office, Chase finally felt he'd gathered the overall feel of the past, present, and future of McAllister Fisheries. He rubbed his eyes to clear his head and looked up to see Frank watching him with bated breath. He was awfully sneaky coming into Chase's office, or Chase had been that involved in his research. "Frank, you've built an incredible business. You've managed to create a successful business with satisfied employees in a highly volatile market."

The older man nodded his head proudly. "Thanks, Chase. But, I don't know that it's going to survive the next century. Fish stocks are up and down – mostly down lately, and regulations are increasing.

Overfishing, global warming, ocean acidification, toxins. It's a lot to keep up with. This town counts on the fishing industry. I'm not leaving this business yet. For now, I need a partner to help me modernize this place, then I want you to take over, when I'm ready to leave and you're ready to boot me out. Let's see if we can build something the town can count on to provide for upcoming generations. Don't hesitate to let me know if you decide this isn't for you. Plenty of time and my feelings won't be hurt too much."

Chase admired Frank's dedication. Frank had started with a single fishing boat, following in his father's and grandfather's footsteps. When the processing plant had started to fall apart, more to due to poor management than lack of work, Frank saw the investment opportunity and bought out the processing plant. He moved into a new, clean structure at the end of Beachside Avenue. He'd upgraded the docks and expanded their fishing contracts over the years, diversifying to operate in every season and harvest every profitable species.

McAllister Fisheries was a successful business. Stable, but only if they continued to plan for the future. Chase could see Frank's concern. The fish stocks were declining and regulations understandably tightening. Chase was terrified of letting him down, and the town. He'd made a great income on the oil rig and had invested well, so he had some of his own money to invest into the business. He wanted to be a part of strengthening this community. It was a good chance to prove himself.

"Frank, I think we can do this. I've been doing some brainstorming. Have you ever thought about incorporating tourism into your business? I'd like to check out the potential for fishing charters and eco-tours. Seaview has been a growing tourist hub; I heard about that special on TV last summer. This town is a lot busier than it was when I left. We could tap into that, adding tourist fishing. Whale watching. Add a little historical tour with some of the old lighthouses and shipwrecks. Hell, we could even add a high-end seafood market storefront. Tourists could take home their own catch, or they could purchase and ship seafood straight from our storefront. We could do some marketing, for our options or even join up with other local businesses to advertise the town as a year-round destination."

"See why you're here? Let's get started on it. Adding the charter fishing line first makes the most sense. With some of the fish quotas going down, we could repurpose a smaller vessel as a charter fishing boat. May cost a bit to re-outfit it properly." Chase's chest figuratively puffed up with pride as Frank filled him with compliments.

"I made some good investments with my earnings and would like to start investing in the business to gradually buy my way in, if that works for you."

Frank leaned back and let out a boisterous laugh, his leathered fisherman's skintight in the big smile. "Chase, you've got a head for business. Glad to have you on board," they shook hands to seal the deal. "Write up some formal plans, and let's make it happen."

Frank stood from his chair across the desk and admired the homey touches his wife had contributed. She had even added a vase with fresh flowers on the small round meeting table to welcome Chase. Frank leaned forward to admire the photos. "I like this one of you, Steve, and me. We should blow that up and hang it in the storefront you're planning. Add a few neat pictures like that from the history of the business."

Frank's gaze landed on the photo of Chase and Maddy. The older man glanced over at Chase, an unreadable smile crossed over his face so quickly, Chase would have missed it if he hadn't been looking for a reaction. Frank chuckled and headed for the door. "See you Tuesday?"

Chase was puzzled. Today was Thursday. "Tuesday? What about Friday and Monday? I've never really worked this banker's hours nonsense, but I thought Monday through Friday included Monday and Friday."

Frank chuckled, as if Chase were a complete moron. "Chase, when one owns his own business, he sets his own hours. I put in a good day's work, usually here about 10 hours, so I made myself a 4-10's schedule. I refuse to work Mondays. As I am still your boss, I am assigning Friday as your day off. Friday morning is my Frank-time. I quite intentionally don't get much done, and you don't need to witness that."

Chase was still smiling as he left the office. It was a good day. Off work with plenty of daylight, perfect evening for a swim. He'd grab his gear and dive straight into the Atlantic, swim until his muscles ached.

His smile, however, wavered as he ran into a tall, lanky blond guy in a pressed khaki suit as soon as he stepped out the front door. It took him a minute to recognize him. Dylan.

Chase's hands immediately balled into fists at his sides and his lips pressed tightly together. "Mayberry. Excuse me." Chase went to push past him. Dylan stepped to the side to block his path.

"Anderson, I had heard you were back. So great to see you. I'm here to talk with Frank. I have a buy-out proposal for him. He's going to love it. I am negotiating a great deal to put Seaview on the map." Dylan smiled a bit like Wile E Coyote opening his box of ACME explosives. Chase had never imagined anyone could have the same ridiculous look; it was uncanny.

"Seaview is on the map. And Frank's not interested. Get lost." Shallow, he knew, but Chase clipped Dylan's shoulder with his own on the way by and kept walking. The collision angered his sore shoulder that still hadn't quite fully recovered from his injury on the rig, but it had been worth it. He would never know what Dylan's expression may have been, but Chase just kept walking, refusing to give the other man the satisfaction.

He thought again about Dylan's ridiculous appearance. Maybe too much cockiness for Wile E Coyote. Maybe that rooster character... or a peacock. Somewhere between Wile E Coyote and a peacock.

Damn he hated that bastard. He felt a sudden need to know exactly what had happened between Dylan and Maddy. Maddy was so gentle and funny and had a sexy rebellious streak. He'd never know what she saw in Dylan – but maybe that was the point. He was Chase's polar opposite. He thought back to that day on the beach. Maddy would never have laughed and played on the beach with Dylan that way.

"Son of a bitch." Chase berated himself aloud, hating himself more than a little at that moment. Needing that swim now more than ever, he hopped in the truck and tore out of the parking area.

9

Darkness had engulfed Seaview on the moonless night. Perfect. Dylan sat leaned forward against his steering wheel. His breathing was as slow and controlled as the speed of his car as he drove past her house. This had become his nightly routine, driving past Maddy's house to catch a quick glimpse before going to bed for the night.

Tonight, he could see that she was inside, her lights were on and he could see her moving back and forth inside. As usual, her curtains were closed. He tried to guess what she might be doing, as he could only see her lithe body's silhouette occasionally pass by the curtained window. He rarely parked, not wanting to get caught. His windows were darkly tinted, so he doubted she'd be able to see him even if she stood just outside his car.

One-night last week, she'd forgotten to close her curtains. Her reject of a brother had been visiting. Somehow, she always seemed to enjoy his company. Dylan had no idea why; Aiden wasn't as smart or clever as he was.

They'd been such an amazing couple. They had always been invited to the best functions. Both were on their way to successful careers, she one day a supreme court justice, he would dominate the finance world.

He realized he had been too understanding before, too soft when she'd begun making plans without him. If he'd cracked down on her secrets sooner, both of their futures wouldn't have been ruined. She wouldn't have tried to sneak out so clandestinely. He wouldn't have been so angry and wouldn't have struck her. He'd never hit her before that, he'd been able to control it, but she'd made him so furious he couldn't help it.

That night, she'd been too busy visiting and laughing to realize the sun had set and she was now in a fishbowl. And he was the cat, waiting to pounce. He'd fantasized about her leaning back in laughter like she had that night, but with pleasure as she rode him hard instead of laughing at a joke that ass had made.

He couldn't resist stopping again tonight. He pulled over and parked, allowing himself the rare treat. He closed his eyes and remembered their first night together. How she'd cried that she wasn't ready, that she wasn't sure it was right. She'd looked so hot in that red silk homecoming dress.

He'd brought her another shot of tequila and gotten her just drunk enough to be awake, but not so much she'd be sick and ruin his good time. He wasn't a monster; he wouldn't ever have raped her. She'd finally consented in a slurred "ok." He'd made her suck him before he drove into her. Told her that was how this sort of thing was done, how to properly pleasure a man.

Aroused at the memory, he loosened his belt and took his cock in his own hand. Despite the tequila, she'd cried out at the pain. He'd reassured her it was normal. Eventually, they'd found a rhythm in their relationship. He'd tried to be gentle and kind, but poor thing just wasn't capable of orgasm. She didn't believe him when he tried telling her that it was something wrong with her body, so he'd even provided her with articles to prove his point.

A loud knock on his car window broke the moment. He looked out to see a group of stoners giggling on the sidewalk. Grateful for the darkly tinted windows, he quickly tossed a sweatshirt over his erection. He relaxed his face and rolled down the window, ready to be polite like the rest of the idiots in this backwards town. He didn't want to raise any suspicion, especially outside of Maddy's house.

"Hey man, you from around here? We can't remember how to get to our hotel. I think it's the Seaview Inn."

Dylan answered in a gracious tone, "Two blocks north and three blocks inland." Morons. Once he had sealed the deal to take over the waterfront and bring in the cruise ship, eliminating that ridiculous antiquated fisheries business Maddy's dad ran, he'd help drive this sort of scum away.

He'd have to eliminate Chase first. The old fool was ready to retire and would jump at the opportunity to sell off his land. Chase was a problem. He always had been. At first opportunity, Dylan had stepped in to make Maddy his own.

He'd better move quickly this time. He'd already seen them together, pressed up against each other at the tavern. Like a pot boiling over, he felt himself becoming overwhelmed with anger and tried to calm himself.

He shouldn't worry so much. He'd eliminate Chase one way or another.

He glanced back across the street to Maddy's house. She'd turned off the lights and was clearly headed for bed. He'd have to finish reminiscing in the comfort of his motel room with the brilliant photo album he'd compiled. He turned the car around and drove back out of town.

10

MADDY AWOKE BRIGHT-EYED AND bushy-tailed on Friday morning. She dramatically swung open the bedroom curtains to welcome the day, causing the curtain rod to come crashing down, tangling her in the curtains. Perhaps she should have used those anchors the instructions recommended.

But even that couldn't spoil her mood. She inhaled a refreshing breath and took in her view of the morning sun shining over the smooth sand and calm ocean waves. Yes, it was going to be a great day.

Finally, at long last, her antiquated-in-a-bad-way ugly yellow dishwasher had finally kicked the bucket. She'd never been so happy to handwash dishes last night, she remarked to herself as she strolled into the airy kitchen.

A few months ago, she'd been thrilled to replace the matching behemoth of a refrigerator with a counter-depth side-by-side stainless refrigerator with ice dispenser. She was gradually upgrading her kitchen. The stainless appliances nicely complemented the concrete counters atop the cabinets she'd painted when she'd moved in.

Crap. A dishwasher was not going to fit in her jeep, and she wanted to pick it up today. Well, not without some serious creativity. She needed a truck. Maddy called her dad.

He answered on the first ring. "Good morning, Sunshine. What can I do for you?" Her dad was clearly as chipper this morning as she was.

"Hey dad, can I borrow your truck today? My hideous dishwasher finally kicked the bucket."

"No can-do. My truck has met an untimely death as well." She heard the phony grief through the line. Or was it through-the-air as no one had land lines anymore?

"You love that truck, why are you so perky?" She poured herself a steaming cup of coffee and leaned back against the countertop, staring at the broken yellow hideousness of an appliance.

"Sunshine, I've had that truck since you were in diapers. I was going to wait until after we got back from Italy to trade it in but looks like I'll be doing some shopping tomorrow. Borrowed your mom's car for today. I'm thinking I'll need something with GPS and heated seats for when the dementia and frailty of old age kick in."

Maddy rolled her eyes. "Dad, you just turned 60. But yes, maybe it is time for you to join the modern world. I can't believe you kept that thing running for so long. I think the rust was the only thing holding the tailgate on."

Maddy gently blew the steam over the top of her mug while she considered her options. "Why did Aiden have to get that ridiculous sports car? I've been keeping an eye on him so I can write him a juicy ticket while he's caught the eye of some girl as he's cruising with the top down."

She could hear her father taking a long sip of his own coffee as well. "Take it easy on the boy, he's just getting settled into town. Why don't you call Chase? He's got that beautiful new truck, and he's not working today. I've always worked a four-ten work week and told him to do the same. So, he took Fridays since I had Mondays already. Besides, he doesn't need to see my Friday morning routine." Frank chuckled on the other end.

Maddy could picture her father leaned back in his office, sipping his coffee and watching the boats out on the water. The man was a ridiculously hard worker, but Maddy knew he also savored his Friday mornings. Which was likely part of why he maintained such a good outlook on life.

"I'll give him a try. Mind texting me his number? Enjoy your coffee break." Maddy disconnected with a sigh she hadn't realized she'd been holding. Not an unhappy sigh, nor quite a nervous sigh, nor a contented sigh. Huh.

Her poor brain was racing to figure out how she was going to ask Chase. Since getting close at the tavern, and feeling his hand rubbing against her inner thigh while he shifted gears, she had reconsidered Payson's suggestion, to maybe give sex-only with Chase a try. She definitely did not do one-night stands normally. Nor did she do relationships. Hence, the serious lack of sex.

Maybe it was time to try? Her imagination had become ridiculously over-worked since Chase came back to town. He was all grown up and sexy and responsible but still had that appealing edge. She wasn't sure she could resist anyway.

Her phone buzzed with the text from her dad. She mustered up her courage and called Chase.

Maddy heard a "Dammit, hang on, dropped the phone." Some rustling sounds. A groggy voice finally came through clearly, "Hello?" Thankfully he didn't screen his calls.

"Good morning, Chase. It's Maddy."

Long pause. "Hey, Maddy. What's up?"

Maddy responded with a long pause right back. She cleared her throat, "Can I borrow your truck?"

He responded simply, "No."

Maddy tried to counter his refusal calmly, but found the words spewed out uncontrollably, "My kitchen needs your help. The hideous dishwasher finally croaked, and I need a stainless steel, low decibel, high efficiency dishwasher. The other appliances were embarrassed to share space with the ugly old thing. I picked out the one that I want, but it's in Portland. Don't get me wrong, I'd rather support our local hardware store, but Devaney's only carries two dishwashers and they're just not quite right. Can I please, please borrow your truck so my kitchen can be beautiful?"

Whew. That was embarrassing.

"Maddy, you cannot drive my truck. It's new and pretty and I don't share–"

Maddy cut him off, pacing back and forth with the phone to her ear, "Hey now, I'm a good driver. As an officer of the law, I am a very well trained, safe, and–"

Chase's laugh interrupted her diatribe, "Sure thing Rain-man. Despite my infinite respect for you as a human being and as a more-than capable driver, it's my new toy, and I'm not ready to share. However, I was planning to head down to Portland one of these days to pick up some herbs for my garden and would be happy to drive you."

"Apology accepted. Hang on. Herbs? Garden? When did you learn how to grow a garden, or even how to cook?" Maddy couldn't hold back the tone of surprise.

Chase feigned offense, "I've always been a good cook, I just never advertised it. It didn't agree with that bad-boy reputation I fought so hard to maintain. I've been in charge of cooking since I was ten. Somehow, I actually like to cook."

Maddy felt a pang of guilt. Of course, he'd had to learn to cook when he was so young, or chances were, he wouldn't have eaten at home at all. He was only at the McAllister house for dinner a few days a week. He would have had to put food on the table at their house the other days, knowing his dad wouldn't have tried. "Well, let's partner up then. You come pick me up, and we'll head to Portland. "

"Be on your front step with a big cup of coffee for me in 30 minutes. No cream or sugar. Black. A real coffee cup, none of that travel mug shit. I hate burning my tongue on that first sip."

"Yes, sir." Maddy saluted. She stared at the phone for a moment, collecting her thoughts. A whole day alone with Chase. She could handle it. She looked down at her yoga pants and dingy old white tank. 30 minutes. She quickly showered, dried and straightened her hair, slapped on some basic make-up.

Throwing open her closet doors, Maddy frowned. A trip to the hardware store said work-clothes, but she also was considering asking him to help end her dry spell. For one night. Maybe two; who knew how long the next dry spell might last. He was surely more experienced at this sort of thing than she was. What did one wear on a not-date to the hardware store?

Checking the time, Maddy realized she had stared long enough and was now down to 5 minutes left. Damn. She quickly settled on her favorite skinny jeans with her favorite no-bra-required pale blue strappy tank. She ran to the kitchen to quickly pour the coffee. She had two tall, not-travel-mugs, filled with black coffee. She dashed out the door to meet Chase, exactly on time.

Chase was just pulling up to the curb when he saw Maddy carefully balancing their coffees while shutting the front door. He hopped out and dashed to the sidewalk to lend a hand. He stopped in front of her at the passenger door, both stopping inches away from the other.

Chase gently took the coffee cup from her hand. "Thanks," he managed breathlessly. He flashed back to when he was seventeen, Maddy just a year younger, when he'd realized how much he wanted her. Hardly being able to speak in front of her. Wanting to ask her out, knowing he couldn't. Knowing he was leaving the day he turned eighteen and not wanting to leave her heartbroken. Or himself.

He realized now, he'd left them both hurting anyway.

He opened her door for her, and she brushed passed him, sliding into the passenger seat. As she got settled, he couldn't help but stare. Was she wearing a bra? He recognized the sway of unrestrained breasts under silk. He took his time walking around to his door. Shit, this was going to be a long day.

She deserved so much better than him. She grew up with a loving family. He hadn't even known healthy marriages existed until he'd met Frank and Laura. His mom had abandoned him, and his dad had emotionally pulled away little by little over the next decade. Eventually, Chase himself had abandoned everyone he knew and loved. Shaking off the regret, he focused his attention on the road as they drove out of town.

They sat in silence as they drove out of Seaview. Chase sipping the steaming cup of black coffee, the other hand on the wheel. Maddy broke the silence as they passed the *Seaview thanks you for visiting, come back soon!* sign heralding their exit from town. "So, what's your specialty?"

Chase glanced at Maddy, eyebrows drawn together in confusion.

"You cook. What do you cook? Steaks on the grill? Burgers?" She goaded him, the side of her mouth turned up in challenge.

Chase rolled his eyes playfully. She always did know how to both unsettle and soothe him at the same time. "I wouldn't say I have a specialty. Of course, I can grill a damn good steak or throw together an impressive burger, but generally, I just throw together what sounds good. What about you?"

Maddy considered a brief, feminist, 'why do you assume I can cook' retort, but she actually enjoyed cooking as well. "Same. I make good salads, pastas, veggies of any kind. I like to experiment with whatever is in the fridge."

"You said your kitchen would be complete once this amazing dishwasher is part of the family. Maybe you should make me a gourmet dinner as payment for driving you all this way for a fancy appliance." He turned his head to Maddy and gave her a quick look; she wished she could read the expression but was left in the dark. She'd play along, though.

"Or, maybe you could bring over some of the fancy herbs you buy and make me a gourmet dinner. And, I'll do the dishes with my new state-of-the-art dishwasher." Perfect. She could seduce him in the comfort of her own home.

Chase's face took on a pained expression. Was he regretting inviting himself to her place? She watched him from her seat, wondering what was on his mind.

They returned to a companionable silence for most of the drive, interrupted only by the occasional comment about the architecture or geography. Finally, they pulled into the hardware megastore. "We should have brought your old dishwasher with us to see if they'd dispose of it."

"I thought about it, but didn't want to miss my ride, as in, I didn't want to keep you waiting. Besides, I know the high school shop teacher. They love random crap to take apart and try to repair." Maddy slid out of the car and walked around to meet Chase at the front of the truck. "Ready to see the world's most high-tech but reasonably priced dishwasher?" She grinned and raised her eyebrows in a joking come-hither face.

Chase found himself laughing with her again. This was becoming a nasty habit. "After you." And he watched her walk confidently into the store.

Maddy was a determined woman-on-a-mission, going straight to appliances, until she stopped like a dog-after-a-squirrel in the lighting section. "Ooo, I love this chandelier. It looks like it belongs in an old castle. But I do love the one in my dining room. Hmm, maybe I need a chandelier in my bedroom..."

Chase took her hand and dragged her out of the lighting section. "Payson warned me about you."

Maddy paused. Maybe she was wrong about he and Payson. That stupid pang of jealousy returned. She looked back at Chase with questioning eyes.

"At the antique store. My new dining room table. Apparently, you'd been coveting it, despite you having a great dining room table. She knew we were friends and revealed your toddler-esque furniture-gimmes. I guess that extends to other home fixtures as well." Chase teased her.

An odd sense of relief overwhelmed her. This was not good. One night, maximum. Maybe two. "Maybe." She smiled back and allowed him to feel like he was dragging her past household decor to the appliance section. In reality, she wanted *him* much more than the chandelier.

Maddy was glad she'd done her research before arriving at the store. She despised wheeling and dealing. Several salespeople had attempted to sell her various protection plans and upgrades. Knowing exactly what she wanted, she brushed past them and pointed to the one she wanted. "I'll take this one and the hose kit. Can you ring me up here?" They promised to have the dishwasher waiting in the loading zone in thirty minutes. She turned to Chase, "Well, that was fun. Want to check out the plant section here for your herbs?"

"Let's head that direction." Chase grabbed her hand again to lead her to the plant section. Unnecessary, as she was walking with him anyway. More, she enjoyed the fire it stirred low in her belly.

Maddy enjoyed watching Chase pick out his herb collection. He'd studied and smelled each one with expertise, surprising Maddy. "I can't imagine how you would grow herbs when you spent most of your time away on the rig, nor can I imagine Henry giving you the cash for fancy ingredients or plants."

"No, you're right. I have absolutely no experience growing herbs." He picked up a full-bodied oregano in a 6-inch pot and added it to the cart, "But, I'm finding I like it already."

Maddy stood back to watch him perusing the herb section and putting the occasional plant into the cart. She never realized how sexy picking out herbs could be, but maybe it was the contrast of the delicate process of plant selection with his faded gray t-shirt with jeans riding low over his hips and wearing his signature day-be-yond-5-o'clock-shadow. The image would be permanently cemented in Maddy's mind. Which, inevitably, lead to a pleasant fantasy about how delicately he might touch her.

Soon, Chase finished picking out his new herb collection with a variety of ceramic pots and organic soil. They checked out and made their way to the truck. With Maddy's dishwasher loaded up, and Chase's finds secured into the back, they hopped in the truck. Chase turned on the engine and turned down the radio, "You hungry?"

"Starving. Want to grab some lunch?"

Chase found himself starving, but not for food. He looked across the cab at Maddy and tried not to stare at how her silky top caressed her skin. If only he could come up with reason for her to sit in the middle seat again; maybe he'd break the seatbelt when she wasn't looking. This was getting ridiculous. She was absolutely hands-off, and he found himself forgetting why he was trying to resist.

"I haven't been here in ages. Where do you want to go?"

Maddy closed her eyes and appeared to meditate for a moment. "*Hmmm.* What sounds good...?"

"Are you asking me or is this a rhetorical question?" Chase watched her and laughed.

"I'm imagining eating to determine what I'm in the mood for. It's a good strategy." With a satisfied sigh, she looked back to Chase. "How about Mexican? The quesadilla in my brain is delicious. There's a collection of food trucks at the beachside park that has amazing food." She grinned and looked back at him.

Shaking his head in amusement, Chase put the truck in gear. "Ok, you're the navigator."

They made pleasantly idle chit-chat as they drove across the city. Chase told Maddy some of the crazier stories about working on the oil rigs, some of the characters he'd worked with. Maddy shared a few stories about some of the more humorous arrests she'd made. He was not surprised to discover she had good instincts and a level head.

The sun was shining, weather a pleasant 80 degrees, the heat tempered by the gentle breeze. Perfect day to be at the park. As expected, the it was crowded. Chase eyed a family loading up their car right next to the beach. He neatly made his way over and backed into the spot as they pulled out.

Chase hopped out of the truck and dashed around to open Maddy's door, meeting her there just before she could open it herself. She eyed him suspiciously at first. Crap, that was a pretty date-like move, again.

"Thanks," Maddy smiled shyly as she slid out of the truck. He stood closely enough their bodies almost touched. Yep, it was a great date move. Chase couldn't help himself but took her hand in his as they walked to the food trucks.

Maddy ordered the quesadilla she'd conjured up with her mind earlier and had them top it with a mountain of avocado, tomatillo salsa, and sour cream. Chase ordered street tacos, as well as waters for them both. Maddy eyed the park. Not a picnic table or square of available grass in sight. "Looks like we're eating standing up today. This place is ridiculously crowded."

"Come on, I have a plan." She followed Chase across the crowded park back to the truck, dodging a stray frisbee, an out of control kite, and a large Labrador with its tongue lolling out the side of its mouth. Chase opened the tailgate and threw a blanket across for a makeshift picnic spot in the back of the truck. The fresh herbs, inches away, smelled amazing in the warm sun. They sat side by side, feet dangling off the tailgate as they devoured the food.

After they'd finished and watched the waves, Maddy broke the silence. "So, how are things going in the fisheries business? Life in the office agreeing with you so far?"

Chase ran a hand through his already naturally mussed hair. "Not bad actually. Frank lets me get out on various boats now and again. It's nice to get the fresh air, not to mention get to know the crews."

"Dad always did that too. He felt like it kept him connected."

"I agree. I think I'll actually enjoy the office work, though. I actually like the pace of the office. I just hope I can keep it so positive. There are so many fishing regulations that are constantly being updated to maintain the oceans, changing fish stocks. It's a lot." Chase was worried he wouldn't be able to sustain the business as Frank had. Tourism was probably the main industry these days, but fisheries was still the heart of the community.

"You'll make it work. Dad has complete faith in you, and he knows this business better than anyone." Maddy brought her leg under her and turned to face him. He was touched she seemed to genuinely believe in him. She had always been easy to talk to, and Chase found it even easier now.

"I'm thinking of adding some tour boat lines, like charter fishing, maybe a coastline tour at some point." He paused, looking out at the ocean. "As long as we're not edged out. Fucking Dylan. Wants to buy out our docks to move in the cruise line stop and take over the local tourist market with cruise-run shops."

Chase was seething and almost missed Maddy's reaction. He looked back to Maddy and realized she'd gone pale. She was looking down at her hands. She almost looked like her eyes were watering. "Hey, Maddy, you ok? I'm sorry. I shouldn't have brought it up. I'd like to hear what happened between you, so maybe I can understand better."

Maddy took a deep, steadying breath. She still was avoiding making eye contact but moved her gaze to a rowdy volleyball game on the beach. "It's ok. I usually do fine and don't even think about it, but since he moved back, it's brought back some memories I'd rather forget. His plan to tear Seaview apart makes his presence so much worse." Chase took her hand gently and sat silently, leaving her to talk more, if she was ready.

"Not many people know what happened. I want to tell you, but not today. Today's been too pleasant." Maddy shook off the sadness and forced a smile. "Thanks for the beautiful picnic and shopping day. Let's head home."

Dusk had settled over the neighborhood as Chase pulled in to Maddy's driveway. They'd been quiet since arriving in town. Chase was not surprised at the easy conversation they had shared all day. He and Aiden had been best friends since Chase moved into town in the third grade.

Most of the time Maddy had been there too. She had never been a third wheel; she was the soul of their little gang. Even on the occasions Aiden hadn't been around, Chase and Maddy had enjoyed hanging out together back then. It was almost comforting to see they shared that easy comradery now, maybe more than they ever had.

Chase put the truck into park. With tired eyes he looked across the truck at Maddy. "I'm beat. Mind if I head home and bring the dishwasher over tomorrow? I'll park in my garage tonight in case it rains. I can stick around when I deliver it tomorrow and lend a hand if you'd like."

Maddy turned to him and they locked eyes, her ice blue to his stormy. Seemingly realizing he expected her response, Maddy sighed as she finally managed to nod in the affirmative, "Ok."

Before he knew what had happened, Chase had pulled Maddy across and onto his lap, her legs straddling him. Without breaking eye contact he slid his hand behind her neck and gently pulled her toward him. He closed his eyes as their lips met, softly at first, tasting, teasing. Heat coursed through him. Her lips parted and she sighed.

Recognizing his moment, Chase kissed her more deeply, tongues met in a wild, hot tangle. He felt his control rapidly diminishing. She did taste familiar, thinking back to that spin the bottle kiss all those years ago. She wasn't hesitant now, she kissed him with equal veracity.

He'd completely forgotten his vow to keep his hands off of her and was quickly forgetting where they were.

Mouths still locked together, Chase's hands slid down her shoulders and he teased down her tank top straps. Chase pulled away so he could admire her very bare breasts. "I knew it," Chase savored that his all-day fantasy was correct, that her breasts were indeed without a bra, just waiting for his touch.

Chase forced himself to take it slow. His thumbs graced along her pink nubs in a light tease. Maddy's back arched as she subconsciously pushed her breasts further into his grasp. She was so damn hot; he couldn't hold back. He grasped her breasts in his hands, Maddy arched further, she cried out his name. Chase leaned and aggressively took her breast in his mouth, sucking hard. Completely caught up in her, he switched to the other breast and laved with his tongue, teasing the firm, pink bud, pulling it gently with his teeth.

Maddy about screamed in pleasure as Chase teased and devoured her breasts. Her hips rocked on his as she nearly orgasmed.

Abruptly, like a cold wave washing over her in surprise, Chase pulled away and looked up at her with a look of both shock and, she feared, regret. Before he could say anything, Maddy took his face in her hands and pulled him in for a deep kiss.

Slowly pulling away, she shook her head at him. She placed a finger over his mouth to silence him. She couldn't bear to think what he might say right now. Fearing rejection.

Maddy slid back to her seat and pulled her tank top straps back up. "Thanks for a great day. Really, I had fun. I'll see you in the morning with my dishwasher." He went to speak, and again, she silenced him.

"Please, please don't say anything. I don't regret a thing and couldn't bear to hear any regrets from you right now. We can start fresh tomorrow." Maddy eyed him seriously. She opened the truck door, pausing before getting out, "Chase, I want you. I don't do relationships; I think I'm just not built for that. But, maybe just once..." Maddy almost lost the nerve, but then remembered the feel of his mouth on her, "When you're ready, I want you."

Without looking back, she swiftly hopped out and shut the truck door, sashaying into the house. His complete silence, with mouth open in wordless astonishment, as if trying to figure out how to even respond, was quite reassuring that he would agree.

11

From across the street, Dylan sat in the dark, watching the disgusting scene unroll before him. He'd made it back out of the house in plenty of time, but he couldn't bear to leave until he knew she was home. She was gone all day... with *him*.

Dylan bit his cheek to keep from screaming out in anger. Years ago, Chase had driven her right into his open arms. She was his now, Chase had lost his chance.

Chase had proved useful this morning, however. Dylan couldn't believe his good fortune. He'd been driving by for his usual morning surveillance and watched her run out the door without locking it. After being away from her for the past nine years, he knew how to be patient and had bidden his time well.

After he was sure she wasn't coming right back, he made his move. Dylan casually walked down the sidewalk, and when no one was watching, he dashed into her house. Not wanting her to discover that he'd been inside, he was careful to not disturb anything.

Naturally, he explored her clothing, taking a few extra moments in her underwear drawer. He held up a miniscule black lace thong; she'd gotten adventurous since he knew her last. Just one little souvenir wouldn't hurt. Dylan allowed himself to peruse some of her photos, taking only a few for his collection. He made his time in her house count, taking full advantage.

12

MADDY AWOKE BRIGHT EYED and bushy tailed for the second morning in a row. Maybe she was a morning person after all. She took a quick shower. Well, not super quick. She did a brief touch-up leg shave. Just in case. And some lip gloss.

She drew the line at wearing a sundress. It would be downright slutty to install a dishwasher in a short skirt. She was working up her courage to make a move, but flashing him might be a bit too forward. Practicality won out. She settled on some ripped up old skinny jeans and a t-shirt.

When the bell rang at 7:45, Maddy nearly bounced her way to the front door. And... opened it to find Aiden standing there holding a brown paper bag. Chase stood right behind him, looking remarkably sheepish.

"Coffee, sis? If I'm getting up this early on a Saturday, there'd better be coffee." Why was Aiden irritated with her? It's not like she'd invited him. Aiden grouchily brushed past and headed for the kitchen.

Maddy stopped Chase in the doorway and quietly teased, "Call for reinforcements?"

He looked a bit ragged this morning. Clearly, he hadn't slept well last night. He had tried to shower off the fatigue, his hair still wet, hadn't shaved of course. His eyes couldn't hide the sleepless night, however.

Chase's face morphed into more of a sheepish grin as he stepped up close to her and whispered, "Guilty as charged. More of a chaperone, though. After last night..." He leaned closer, nearly pressing his cheek to hers and whispered softly in her ear, "I don't think we'd get much done if I tried to watch you wiggle your ass in front of me all morning while you install the dishwasher."

Chase grazed his hand along her hip as he moved past her. "Hey man, save me some coffee."

Aiden ripped open the brown paper bag he'd brought with him. He passed each of them a breakfast sandwich, tearing into his own, pausing only to sip his coffee. He glanced to Chase, "How was the trip to the hardware store? You talk her out of buying half the store?"

Before Chase could respond, Maddy interjected and elbowed her brother in the side, "Hey, I just drool, I rarely splurge." Aiden responded with a shit-eating grin back at his sister.

"Ok, break it up. Aiden, make yourself useful. Let's go grab the new dishwasher. Maddy, mind opening the garage so we can bring it in through the garage door?"

"Aye, sir." Maddy saluted and headed for the garage. She clicked the opener and daylight entered the garage. She returned to the house and grabbed some of her every-day tools from the kitchen drawer. She stared in the drawer for a moment. Where was her spare set of keys? That was the trouble of living alone, there was only one person to blame when things went missing.

Aiden and Chase shuffled into the room, cautious to not bump into any walls. Maddy had unhooked the old dishwasher last night when she realized sleep was not going to happen easily. She was glad to see Chase had experienced a sleepless night as well.

"Now you can move the old one out to the garage. It's nice having assistants," she added with a perky smile. Maddy was in full bossy mode and enjoyed it, knowing they'd tell her to shove off if they didn't actually want to help. "Hey, Aiden, do you have my spare keys? I couldn't remember if I gave them to you when you and dad came over to set up my porch swing."

"I'm not sure you can still call it a porch swing when it's on your back deck. And, no, I made a copy of your keys and gave the originals back to you. Why? Lose them?" Aiden wolfed down another few bites of breakfast sandwich before loading up the old dishwasher.

"I guess I did. And yes, of course it's still called a porch swing. What else would I call it? A deck swing? That would sound ridiculous." Maddy dove in to unwrap the new dishwasher while the guys carried out the old one.

The keys were quickly forgotten when Maddy got to admire her beautiful new dishwasher. Installation actually went fairly smoothly with the three of them. It likely would have gone better if she'd installed it without their "help," as they offered differing opinions at every step. Fortunately, they were able to laugh off their bossiness.

"Woohoo. Dishwasher installed. Who wants to do some dishes?" Maddy was not surprised there were no takers as the guys turned away, whistling and looking anywhere but at her. "Ha, you guys are very funny. I think I have to run it empty the first cycle anyway. Grab yourselves a beer and go sit out on the deck. I'll order pizza."

Chase did as instructed and headed out to the deck with his beer. Aiden hesitated before going out. "You doing ok sis? You seem distracted. Is it the keys?"

Maddy knew she had been distracted. The keys had bothered her, but she was sure she'd find them. She was more distracted by her response to Chase. She had felt disappointed when he had brought the chaperone, but it was probably a good thing.

After last night, she'd likely have jumped Chase as soon as he walked in the door, and the dishwasher would have gone uninstalled yet again. She should probably leave him time to consider her proposal first.

They'd had a good time installing the dishwasher anyway. They'd joked and laughed and worked well together, as they had when they were kids. She enjoyed the familiar and knew things would change for all of them if she changed the dynamics and slept with Chase. "No, I'll figure out the keys. I've been busy all week and probably misplaced them. It's just been a long week."

Aiden eyed his sister, knowing there was more. Thankfully, he didn't prod. Maddy watched him join Chase on the deck, both putting their feet up and apparently relaxing. Now, if only she could do the same.

13

Anxious to avoid Maddy, Chase neatly made himself quite busy at work over the next week. He researched other fishing towns to see how they stayed afloat in years where fishing was poor. Adding a storefront could increase the traffic to the end of Beachside Avenue so tourists could pick up some fresh local seafood straight from the docks.

Adding a charter fishing boat would be a perfect first step, and he already knew of few crew members that would jump on the opportunity, but they'd need to hire a few more. Folks with charisma and good instincts. Those who could entertain the guests, even if the fish weren't biting. He'd have to gather some legal expertise on taking the public out on the water. Chase felt excited at the idea of bringing something positive to the community.

He drew up a formal proposal including fisheries trends and financial projections for the next five years to present to Frank when he returned from Italy. He made some pertinent spreadsheets to analyze the numbers in detail. Just to show off, he made a brief PowerPoint presentation including photos from similar operations around the country including charts and figures showing their successes and failures. It would take a few years to pay itself off, but the eventual payoff would be significant. He'd have to inquire about advertising in tourist magazines.

A knock at the door interrupted Chase as he added some finishing touches to the presentation. It was Brent, the receptionist. "Hey Chase, there are some gentlemen from Briggs and Johnson Law Firm here to see you, says it's something about the docks and the processing plant."

"Any idea what they want?" Chase looked up from his screen. He had no idea who Briggs and Johnson were, nor why they would be making a surprise visit.

"They wouldn't say, said they wanted to talk directly to you. Said it was urgent, about the safety of our buildings." Brent shrugged, unsure how to even respond.

"Frank's in charge, if they have any official business, it would need to go through him." Chase shook his head. He knew Frank would support any decision he might make, but Frank was still in charge and should be present for any official meetings. "They need to schedule an appointment for when he's back in the office."

"I tried to tell them that, but they said it can't wait."

Chase recognized defeat. Slim chance he'd be able to hold these guys off until Frank returned, and what if there was something that couldn't wait? He debated calling Aiden but decided to feel them out first. Chase knew he could hold his own, but he wouldn't hesitate to call Aiden if anything felt off. "Fine, send them back." He stayed behind his desk as a power play. Let them know they were interrupting his day.

Brent came back with three men in very impressive suits holding leather briefcases. Dylan was among them. Chase was not one to be intimidated by suits, briefcases, or fancy titles. Had he known Dylan was among them, he would have refused the meeting entirely. He pretended to ignore Dylan, knowing Dylan would be expecting attention. "Gentleman. I am sure you have pressing business, or you would not have waited until a few days after Mr. McAllister left to pay us a visit."

The trio was a bit awkward. The front of the trio was a wiry, slick dressed attorney in a pressed navy suit with red power tie. He must be the silver tongue of the group. Dylan was similarly attired, but his smirk was downright obnoxious. The third of them looked to be more of a hired thug, hugely muscled, and looking more at his surroundings than at Chase.

The man in the front of the trio spoke first, introducing himself as Nielsen. "Mr. Anderson, we know your company is... troubled. Your equipment is outdated and you're barely passing inspections. We have a superb business opportunity that will ease your worries."

Chase stared unblinking at the man, refusing to acknowledge his insults.

The man cleared his throat and began again, "I'll get right to the point. This is an old, run-down processing plant with some boats that are even older. We can shut you down today if we want to. We'd rather do this fairly and offer you a buyout at a reasonable price." This guy surprisingly presented himself well.

But he vastly underestimated Chase if he thought his threats were going to help his case. If they'd done their homework, rather than listening to what was likely Dylan's delusional plan, they might have considered a different approach – or found a different location entirely.

Chase laughed humorously, "And what's your plan? Buy out our land and docks, for what, a cruise-line stop? Not interested. We're a solid company; your price is irrelevant, we're not for sale."

"Mr. Anderson, I don't think you're hearing us. We can have this place shut down before Frank McAllister gets back. I doubt he'll want to return to find his company in shambles, his people out of work." Dylan's smirk was so big, Chase was surprised he wasn't giggling maniacally. Chase held eye contact with Nielsen, still refusing to even look at Dylan. Just to piss him off.

Chase held a straight face. He was genuinely surprised at their boldness; these guys were little more than goons. He calmly responded, "I don't think you're understanding me. You won't shut us down. We pass all inspections and run a damn good business. Thanks so much for coming in today. If there becomes a reason to shut us down, I'll know exactly who to blame, and who to sue for damages and lost income."

Chase finally looked straight at Dylan and his comically giddy expression. Chase's expression was firm but sedate, his voice steady, "You're not welcome in this town anymore. You clearly have a personal reason for wanting to destroy people's livelihoods. I'm going to make sure you don't succeed," Chase paused, wanting to warn off Dylan to stay away from Maddy, but realized boldly threatening him in front of witnesses might not be the best thing for McAllister Fisheries, or for Maddy. He moved to his office door and pointed the way out. "You can show yourselves out."

"You'll be hearing from us again, Mr. Anderson, and our offer will not be so generous next time." The front man confidently nodded at Chase. He tossed his business card on Chase's desk before leading the way out.

Chase was seething as the men finally left. He stood and walked the few steps to the window, looking out at the docks. There were plenty of other towns, many hurting for business, who would benefit from cruise-line stop, or even a "generous" buy-out. Whatever their motives, they weren't respectable businessmen. They were awfully confident – how many businesses did this bullshit work on? He'd have to call Aiden and see what they could do about their thinly veiled threats to shutdown McAllister Fisheries.

He was positive that Dylan was up to something other than business, and Chase couldn't shake the feeling that it involved Maddy. There had been a strange, viciousness about him that Chase hadn't seen very often. Something was not right about that man. Thinking of that asshole with Maddy was more than he could bear. The way Maddy had reacted when he even mentioned Dylan to her yesterday. There was a lot Maddy wasn't telling him.

Preparing for battle, Chase closed his office door and plopped down into his cushioned chair. He immediately called Aiden. He knew McAllister Fisheries could withstand the storm but wanted his legal expertise just to cover his bases. Maybe he could wheedle some more information about Maddy out of him while he was at it.

14

THE FOLLOWING TUESDAY MORNING, Maddy popped into Flotsam Antiques. She'd been restless. She knew Chase was avoiding her, and she didn't blame him. Her intentions were quite clear, and she hadn't waited to hear his response, fearing he'd refuse her.

The ball was in his court now. But he was taking his sweet time deciding. She hoped the delay wasn't him waiting around to let her down easy. Maybe Payson would be able to help her brainstorm how to move this along. Her poor imagination was running wild, and she was running out of batteries around the house.

She knew sleeping with Chase would change things, but it was officially too late. They hadn't even had sex yet and the dynamic had already changed. She couldn't get him out of her mind.

The shop was quiet aside from the cheerful bells ringing as Maddy entered the shop. She immediately noted a new leather chair, some new shipwrecked treasures in a glass display. Payson always had a new supply of treasures of all price ranges, so even those here on a budget may find a small souvenir to remember their vacation. Payson surfaced from the back at the sound of the bells, brushing dust off of her hair and dress. Seeing it was just Maddy, she took a moment to dramatically shake the dust bunnies out of her hair.

Maddy laughed, "Is it time to do your annual dusting of the back room?" She knew her friend was meticulous about the storefront, but the back was a bit of a mess.

Payson feigned offense, "You're so funny. I just got in a shipment of vintage wine and cider bottles from France. The owner recently passed away, and her grandson was doing some housekeeping and found some great old pieces like these. These were in the attic and hadn't been dusted in centuries."

"Ooo, can I see?" Maddy was practically jumping up and down.

Payson led the way back. Payson knew the way through the dark storage room well enough to not trip, but Maddy stumbled a few times. "Really, why don't you clean this crap more?" She narrowly avoided knocking over a Tiffany-style lamp.

"I do, I just keep getting new shipments. Maybe you should come help me on your next day off, when you're not wearing a pretty white eyelet dress. Gorgeous, but not very practical. What's the occasion?"

"I'll fill you in on that later." She about dove into the old wooden crates that held said dusty old bottles. "I love these! Save me a few? Maybe I'll take some in payment for helping you organize this dump."

Payson pulled a few from the crates and started setting them on the table. "It's a deal. I'll pick out some that will go on your mantle as bud vases or candle holders. You may want to wait a week though; he's sending some chests of vintage clothes."

"I can't wait. I'm so glad you moved here; my décor was so boring before you arrived." Maddy looked around the storage room. "I've got some ideas on how you can organize better. Can you order some heavy-duty shelving and I'll come by and help you put it together?"

"It's a date. I need to upgrade anyway; these are still what I could afford when I first opened. Now, explain, why are you dressed so pretty and here so early on your day off?"

"Thank you," Maddy spun a little circle to show off the fun dress. "I bought this last year at the farmer's market. Remember, Tori was selling these? One of her handmade specials. Anyway, I found it in my closet this morning and realized I'd never actually worn it before. It's my day off and I wanted to feel pretty. And, I was thinking you should take a break and come play with me... at least for the morning. You deserve some time off. I'm restless and need some quality time with my best friend," Maddy smiled hopefully at her friend.

Payson shook her head in amusement, shaking more dust out of her long auburn hair. She eyed her friend suspiciously, "Wow, your mom's been gone for what, not quite a week, and you're already lonely? Don't you usually bum breakfast from her?" Payson started for the front, neatly dodging the flotsam on her way out. "Fine, you talked me into it. Town is awfully quiet today, and I haven't taken a day off in weeks."

"See? I'm doing this for you. It's your day. Want to take a walk on the beach?" Maddy moved toward the front door, gesturing for her friend to make the final step outside. She went out on a limb and turned the sign to *CLOSED* before Payson could change her mind.

"Let's grab a snack for the walk. Muffins and a mocha? I'm starving." Payson grabbed her stomach dramatically. That girl did love her carbs.

"Stressed? You only binge on carbs and espresso when you're worrying about something." Maddy followed Payson out the door and helped her lock up. The morning chill hadn't worn off yet, and some gray clouds threatened in the distance. Maddy slipped on her denim jacket to fight the chill, glad she'd thought to bring a coat.

They crossed the quiet avenue and headed toward Moe's Morning Mug. There couldn't have been more than ten people on the entire stretch of Beachside Avenue this morning. Must be the threat of thunderstorms this afternoon, but the clouds hadn't dropped more than a sprinkle or two so far.

"Not really... Maybe a little overwhelmed..." she paused outside of the coffee shop. "Ok I'm ridiculously stressed," Payson gesticulated wildly with both arms flailing in surrender, suddenly pacing in front of the coffeeshop door. "I talked to my sister last night. She's dropping out of college and wants to come work for me. Cara has worked so hard. She only has one semester left. She wouldn't say what's going on either."

Payson had two sisters, and it had been just the three of them since their parents passed when Payson was in high school. Her older sister, Jen, was married with two kids and had a successful career as a museum curator in Boston. She and Payson had worked hard to put Cara, their youngest sister, through college.

"I'm so sorry. We'll figure this out. Let's get your carbs and caffeine and take that walk. You'll feel better once we talk it through." Maddy linked her arm under Payson's and guided her into the coffee shop.

Moe's door chimed as they walked arm-in-arm through the doorway together. Gilly, Moe's teenage daughter, greeted them from behind the counter with a perky, "Hey ladies. What can I get ya? The usual?" With barely an affirmative nod from Maddy, Gilly got to work.

Like the rest of town, the coffee shop was nearly empty. The smell of freshly baked muffins and cookies filled the air. There was a bakery further down Beachside that carried the best pastries, but Moe still made his own deliciously old-fashioned baked goods that soothed the soul. A gas fireplace in the corner warmed the room. Some cozy couches and side chairs flanked the fireplace, and the rest of the shop had mis-matched tables and chairs scattered throughout. There were a few favored tables at the back of the shop that had a spectacular view of the beach.

They made friendly conversation with Gilly while waiting for their treats. Gilly had just graduated from high school and hadn't decided what to do about her future. She'd dyed her hair a brilliant shade of blue, pierced her nose, and stayed on to work for her dad for now.

Payson was clearly deep in thought, so Maddy gently placed the drink and treat in her hand and guided her through the back of the shop and out the patio door to the beach. "Thanks, Gilly, see you next time," she waved on the way out.

Maddy savored the first few chocolatey sips as they walked across the patio toward the sand. Before stepping onto the beach, each briefly set their cups on the nearest table. They synchronously slipped off their shoes and walked along the beach in their bare feet, not caring that their feet would be numb with cold shortly.

Once in their rhythm, Maddy offered, "Maybe you could pop down to Boston and see what's going on with her? You could see if Natalie can run the store for two or three days."

Payson didn't answer at first, methodically blowing across the lid before each small sip. "I really need to. This would be asking a lot more of Natalie than I have in the past. I know she can handle it, but I feel like it's a big favor to ask."

Payson handed Maddy her muffin in its bag and made the call. It didn't take long. "Ok, Natalie's on it. That was easy. That girl is too dang nice to me. You'll help with any major deliveries while I'm gone? I can try to leave this afternoon to talk some sense into my wayward sister."

Swallowing the huge bite of blueberry muffin she'd stuffed in her mouth, Maddy responded, "Of course. I'll be glad to help. That was nice of Natalie. I told you she doesn't mind helping when you need it."

Payson nodded, "I know. I just hate to ask. She's such a sweetheart, but she's so reserved. I hate to bother her."

"I think she's just really shy. I like her; we should invite her out more." Maddy nodded at her own suggestion, resolving to make an effort to make friends with Natalie.

"Good plan. Now, I'm going to put my worry for Cara and the shop behind me for a few minutes and am going to worry about you for the duration of our walk." Payson eyed her friend over her coffee cup.

"Me? I'm great. Why would you worry about me?" Maddy nearly choked on her last bite of muffin.

"Because, dear friend, it's Tuesday morning, and you've already gone for a run, showered, dressed in your prettiest sundress despite the gloomy day, done your hair, talked me out of work and agreed to sugar overload. This is normally your project day at home. What's up?"

Dang, she'd gone the first 25 years of her life without a good girlfriend. Payson had become ridiculously good at reading her. She couldn't get away with anything. "First off, it's nothing wrong... but I was going to ask for some advice on how to get laid."

Payson managed to swallow her sip of mocha before she either choked on it or it sprayed out of her nose, then she let the roaring laugh out. "Wow, you're never dull."

"Seriously, I'm terrible at this. Terrified. Totally terrified... of sex or anything close to it. But, I think I'm ready to try. You know I have an unpleasant and just plain stupid history with sex. You may be right that it might be good with someone I trust. I'm ready to try, but I don't know how to seduce anyone."

"And why do you think I am well versed in the art of seduction? Go ask Aiden, he gets around enough."

"Wow, I'm so not asking Aiden. He'd flip out and lock me away in a tower. Dad's not even as protective as he is."

"Fair point."

"You've dated a heck of a lot more than I have. I've been with all of two guys. You know how the first relationship went. My second attempt was so damn... timid. Which had been my plan, to find a sweet, timid boy, but it was downright boring. He was afraid to even touch me. I even gave him a few more chances, but there was absolutely no spark and certainly no orgasm on any of these occasions."

Payson laughed mirthlessly. "Maddy, my dear friend, you do need a quality lay. Not with a creep or a lame duck this time, but someone decent. Someone that appreciates you. Someone that knows what he's doing."

Maddy allowed herself the moment of self-pity. They reached the end of the beach, just before the start of the fishing docks, and turned an about-face, continuing back the way they came. "You're right, but I can't help but feel terrified that maybe it's me. Maybe my vagina or my clitoris or my pheromones are broken. I don't know," she pouted.

Payson grabbed Maddy by the elbow and looked her right in the eye, blazing mad. "I don't ever want to hear that kind of talk from you again. I have no doubt your girl parts and your pheromones are perfectly normal. That's the shit Dylan told you, isn't it?"

Maddy nodded, avoiding eye contact.

Heart breaking, Payson continued, "You know it's not true. You're a passionate woman... you enjoy your... solo time, right?"

Maddy blushed, "I do. I know my head is fucked up thanks to Dylan. I know it's not true; I know he was a manipulative creep. But I'm still scared. I really want it, but I'm terrified. How do I do this?"

"You trust Chase, don't you? The way you talk about him, I know you do."

"Yes, I trust Chase completely." Maddy didn't hesitate. She'd never had any doubt she could trust him completely. Even when he was trying to get himself kicked out of school or arrested, or pushing her away, she knew she had only to ask and he'd be there for her. She'd just been too stubborn to ask.

"And, you've enjoyed your time with Chase so far? You spent the whole day with him, right?" Payson studied her friend's face, looking for clues. Maddy failed at hiding a goofy grin. "Ok, I'll take that as a yes. Did you kiss him?"

"Yes, and it was incredible. I've never felt anything like it. We made out in his truck. Second base? Third base? I've never really understood that baseball analogy. Regardless, we had a very nice time. Then, I sort of... propositioned him. I practically ran out of the truck before he could answer, afraid he would say no. But then, *nothing*. He's been avoiding me. It's been a week now." Maddy filled Payson in about all the details: the great day in Portland, then the steamy moment in the truck, her declaration-slash-invitation, his using Aiden as a chaperone the next day, then radio silence from Chase.

"Yikes, that is a tough one." Payson picked up the pace and Maddy had to run a few steps to catch up. "You're a sexy woman, and he pretty much told you he wanted to jump your bones, gave you a hot, steamy make-out session in his truck. However, he's in a tough spot and won't take this lightly. He is your brother's best friend and your father's business partner and probable successor. And, he's been one of your best friends since you two were kids."

Their cheeks were flushed from the brisk walk. Her toes were officially frozen. She managed to not chatter her teeth when she responded. "I know all of that. I'm taking this seriously too. My parents adore him. I wouldn't want him to feel like he'd let them down by taking advantage of their daughter. But I'm the one trying to take advantage."

Maddy watched the dark clouds rolling in, rain approaching from the distance.

"And, he's trying to re-shape his reputation and establish himself as a respectable member of the community." Payson pointed out, gesturing with her nearly empty coffee cup as she spoke. Realizing the cup still contained a few sips of coffee, she finally gulped the rest of the now-cold espresso. "Sorry Maddy, you've got a lot working against you here. It's clear he wants you, but he would be putting a lot on the line for just one night."

"Dammit, Payson, you're supposed to be helping me here," Maddy pouted. This was not going the way she had planned.

"Ok, well, the guy's in a tough spot. Why don't you spend some more time with him and see where it leads? Let nature take its course, so to speak. If you two are already having trouble keeping your hands off each other, the opportunity is going to arise without you even having to try. You'll see where it ends up; I suspect this will end much better than you think. Don't rush it, or you'll feel bad and he'll hesitate. Your self-esteem does not need that." Payson shoved the last bite of her muffin in her mouth triumphantly.

"I am feeling a bit guilty now. But I guess if it's just letting nature take its course, there's nothing I can do." She shook her head dramatically, laughing at herself. They brushed off any stray muffin crumbs and tossed the empty cups and bags into the nearest trash can. "Now, as previously mentioned, I do look great today. Maybe I'll go visit Chase at work and see how he responds. You know... nature."

From the window of Moe's, Dylan sat festering, ignoring his untouched and now cold coffee. Slut. How could she walk on the beach in that short white dress laughing and chatting?

He worried about her. She was vulnerable. She'd hidden in Seattle when she'd run away from him, but he'd found her and watched her then. From a distance.

Just like he'd always watched her.

His mind flashed back again to the episode in Chase's truck; he'd had a perfect view from his hiding place in the bushes. The whore dove onto that asshole's lap, climbing all over him and letting him touch her. This time, she'd learn. He'd make her realize she was his alone. No one else would take care of her the way he could. Protect her from the world.

He knew he'd made a mistake all those years ago, causing her to run away. He'd warned her what would happen if she tried to leave him. A decent woman would have come crying back when her future had fallen apart. But not his Madelyn. She'd run away like a wounded bird.

Next time, he'd show her how much she meant to him by keeping her close. He'd have to keep better track of her. He reached into his pocket and jingled the keys he'd fortuitously found when he'd snooped her house.

15

Maddy finally waved goodbye to her friend after their snack, walk, and Payson's quick packing. Payson leaned out the window as she drove away, "You'd better have gotten laid by the time I get back. You know, nature."

The avenue was thankfully, still mostly empty. Maddy felt empowered after her talk with Payson. She wouldn't pressure, just see what happened. She strolled down the length of Beachside Avenue to Chase's office. Funny, when had she begun to think of it as Chase's office, and not her dad's?

She stopped outside and straightened her dress and hair. Mustering up her courage, Maddy let herself in the back door to the office. She used to work around the office or on the docks every summer, wherever they'd needed an extra hand, and still had a key.

Brent greeted her with a smile as she reached the top of the stairs. "Good morning, Brent, how's the day going?"

Brent was a sweet guy, a few years older than Maddy. He was happily married with a baby on the way. Handsome, with a few gray hairs that had only recently made an appearance on his sideburns. A Seaview transplant, his wife had dragged him here from the midwest. "It's a quiet day around here, thankfully. What are you up to this morning?"

"I'm enjoying my day off and was hoping to drop in on Chase. See how he's holding up with Dad out of the country." Brent eyed her suspiciously. Maddy realized the excessively feminine sundress combined surprise visitation when her father wasn't there might look a bit suspicious. Maddy hoped her prim smile reduced the desperate-for-a-booty-call look she may have donned.

Brent blushed. Nope, she likely looked quite obvious. "Chase was here for a bit this morning, but just left about half an hour ago. He wasn't sure if he'd be back. Said he had some personal business."

She thanked Brent and made her way back downstairs. Personal business? As she walked back out onto the quiet street, she remembered the day. It was Chase's dad, Henry's birthday. She should have realized it would be a tough day. He hadn't seen his dad since he left, and he had returned a few months after he'd passed. No funeral was even held, as he hadn't had many friends in the end. Chase had put on a brave face, but of course he would mourn.

Maddy strolled the mile-long walk back down Beachside to her house and hopped in her jeep. She didn't even hesitate, driving straight to the cemetery. It was a guess, but she suspected he'd be paying his respects.

He couldn't have gone to his dad's house, as it had been torn down about two years ago when Henry had passed out after having loaded firewood haphazardly in the fireplace. He'd woken up enough to pull himself out alive, but the house had burned to the ground. Maddy suspected Chase had sent back money for Henry's housing, as he was quickly placed in a nice assisted living facility.

The cemetery was as quiet, as town had been. Maddy parked her jeep next to Chase's truck. She pulled on a flannel shirt with her denim jacket, anticipating the increasing chill in the air, as the wind had picked up with the approaching storm. Wishing she had thought to bring an umbrella in case those dark clouds opened up, she trudged on.

She hoped he wouldn't mind the interruption. Of course, her lustful thoughts had quieted, and instead she worried for her friend.

Chase stood stoically a hundred feet away. He silently looked down at the headstone, his body stiff. Maddy quietly walked up to join him. His body jerked as she arrived, as if she'd caught him unaware.

As he looked to Maddy, she noted his eyes were moist with unshed tears. His jaw was clenched tight. She softly slipped her hand into his and leaned into his side. His gaze turned back to the headstone. Maddy hadn't seen the headstone yet. Simple, nothing eloquent written, just name and date. She guessed there hadn't been much to say.

Minutes ticked by as the pair stood in silence. The wind gently stirred the simple bouquet of assorted flowers that sat in front of the headstone. Chase broke the silence. "I didn't bring those. Must have been Aiden for your mom. No one else would have thought of it."

"Despite Henry's failings, my mom knew he loved you, so she loved him for that." Laura had always seen the best in everyone, even Henry. Maybe that was why she'd been such a beloved judge. She followed the letter of the law, but always understood the people it affected.

Chase inhaled slowly, calming his thoughts. "How'd you know I was here?"

Maddy leaned her head on his shoulder. "I stopped by your office, but Brent told me you'd left early and wasn't sure if you'd be back. I'd forgotten the day at first, but knowing you weren't one to leave work early without a good reason, it didn't take long to deduce where you'd gone."

"Thanks. Thanks for coming." He put his arm around her waist and pulled her in close.

Maddy basked in his warmth against the cold wind. "How are you holding up? You hadn't said much about your dad when you got back, so I didn't want to pry."

"It's ok. I'm doing better than I thought I would." Chase paused, looking around at the trees surrounding the cemetery. "I was so mad at him for not pulling it together. For not seeing that I needed him. He'd started to drink when my mother left us. She'd already been so distant I hardly noticed she was gone. Damn, what a terrible mother she must have been for me not to care that she'd left. Dad had to work two jobs to make up for the loss of income, maybe that was the problem. I don't know.

"I just know I saw less and less of him, and he drank more and more. We'd moved to Seaview when he'd run out of work back home, or at least had burned enough bridges. He'd gotten a job on a construction crew up here. Didn't last long. I thought I'd fall apart. I was so lost." Chase kissed the top of her head, still holding her close. "But then I met Aiden and you, and your parents of course. I knew I'd be ok."

Maddy felt a hot lump forming in her throat, eyes blurring with tears of her own. "You fit right into the fold pretty nicely. It was hard watching you go through those tough years. My parents felt so torn, knowing they could only do so much to help you."

"Hey, just spending those one or two nights a week with your family was amazing. I couldn't abandon my dad though; I knew he needed me. I was so angry at the world for what I couldn't control. It was finally your mom, you know..." Maddy's eyebrows raised in question. "...Why I could leave. She worked with various social programs to keep

Dad housed and fed so I could leave without worrying that he would wind up dead on the side of the road. She and Frank bought my damn plane ticket out of here."

"I didn't know she did that. I knew you sent a lot of money back over the years, for medical bills and caregivers. He knew. Mom kept him updated on how you were doing; she'd give him copies of the pictures you sent."

They stood together for what felt like forever. When the rain started to fall, Chase let go of her waist and took her hand in his. "I'm ready, let's get out of here." She let him lead her back to their cars.

"Need some space, or would you like to come on over? I'll make you a sandwich and we can sit on the deck and watch the storm brewing over the waves," Maddy offered.

"That sounds perfect, I'll meet you there."

For the second time since Chase had been back, he followed her into town at a respectable distance. She glanced in her rearview, wishing she could see his face. She hadn't been sure how he would react when she arrived at the cemetery, but now she was glad she'd come.

A short while later, Chase and Maddy sat side by side, curled up together on the porch swing, watching the waves and the quiet beach, as promised. The rain picked up, and the temperature had dropped. Still, it was pleasant to be outside, under the covered part of the deck. Maddy had brought out blankets to keep warm.

She'd started the morning with a plan to seduce Chase, but she had comfortably accepted that today was not the day and enjoyed the quiet with him. Chase's long legs stretched out and rested on the railing, gently rocking them. Maddy leaned against him, his arm around her shoulder.

Chase slowed the rocking of the swing. It was time for truths, and maybe, just maybe, she'd open up about what had happened while he'd been away. "Maddy, I need to know. What happened... with Dylan? I hate that neither Aiden, nor I were there for you when you needed help. Not that you weren't perfectly capable of taking care of yourself, but I wish I'd been there. Dammit, what kind of brother was Ronan?" Ronan had been friends with Dylan. But, how could Ronan let his own sister go out with such an asshole?

Maddy took a few slow deep breaths. "First of all, don't you dare blame yourself for not protecting me. I made my choices and should have protected myself better. You know Ronan was in his own world, just waiting to get out of this town, maybe even more than you. I don't even know what country he's in these days. It wasn't until we got to college that it became so much worse, when none of you were around."

With a sigh, Maddy scooted further away from Chase on the swing. He watched her shift a pillow behind her back and she swung her legs up, now sitting sideways on the swing, tucking her feet under him. Her feet were freezing. Chase pulled the blanket over them both and tucked the blanket around her goose-bumped legs.

Not wanting to push her beyond her comfort, he listened patiently. He looked out at the beach and watched a couple jogging past. They synchronously waved cheerfully. Whoever they were, Chase politely waved back.

Finally, she continued. "You and Aiden were on a path to self-de-struction. I appreciated that you didn't drag me along when it got rough, but it wasn't just you that pulled away. I'd decided to become a judge like Mom and wanted to be sure I had a nice, clean reputation. I added more and more classes at the community college through running start so I could get a jump on my future. It took a while before Dylan finally made his move.

"He was quite the gentleman, very devoted. He'd escort me to class, call me beautiful, brought me flowers. Breaking me in was a slow process. It started with small criticisms. 'Maddy, you wouldn't look so tired with a little make-up... you should wear a push up bra, so you have more curves... of course you're not as smart as I am because you're a girl...'"

Chase silently cringed, having some idea of where this was leading.

"My self-esteem gradually worsened: I was 'frigid' and 'homely' and, I 'wasn't capable of orgasm,' so of course I was so lucky I had someone understanding like Dylan to be with. I 'wasn't smart enough to make my own decisions', I was 'socially inept so I shouldn't talk much' in social situations...

"I knew better, but it's hard to realize you're drowning when you're being pulled under so gradually." Maddy paused to collect her thoughts. She maintained a blank expression, eyes dry. "Every time I tried to pull away, he'd lavish me with praise and tell me he couldn't live without me. He threatened suicide a few times so I wouldn't leave. I put up with him for way too long. Eventually, mid-way through our freshmen year at college together, I'd had enough. He hadn't."

Chase could feel his face heating with anger. His fists clenched. He imagined tearing Dylan apart limb from limb... dick first. He'd tack it to the old oak tree in the center of town square, a warning for all other dickheads.

Knowing there was more, Chase tried to calm down for her. Her courage was incredible. She must have felt so alone, her family and friends so far away.

He gently took her hand. "Maddy, you don't have to say more if you don't want to. Just tell me what you need."

She sniffled and avoided eye contact, only briefly letting emotion show. Recovering quickly, she continued. "Thanks, but I can do this. It's part of who I am today.

"I started to secretly plan transferring schools the following semester. I applied to several pre-law programs at universities across the country, and was set to get in. My grades were excellent. I had always been a model student. I had great recommendations. But I was so scared. I knew he would find out; he always found things out. And, he did," Maddy paused, pulling her arms further in, face impassive. Chase's heart ached watching her stoicism as she told her horrible tale.

"He didn't say anything to me, not directly. He pretended he didn't know anything, so I didn't realize he'd found out my plan. He'd taken pictures of us, mostly of me. Very pornographic. I hadn't even known he was taking them. He sent those photos to all the schools I had applied to, with inappropriate notes of the things I was willing to do to be accepted into their programs. My rejection letters came next; some simply stating I wasn't a good fit for their program, others more direct. I knew he'd track me down and ruin any chance I had at a career in the public eye.

"One afternoon, while he was at class, I packed up my things and snuck out the back door of the dorms. He must have anticipated and was waiting for me at my car. I was lucky. No broken bones, but I sustained some pretty big contusions all over my body. It took weeks to recover from the concussion."

"Oh Maddy, I'm so sorry. I wish I'd been there for you." Chase leaned over and wiped the single tear that had fallen down her cheek.

"Don't blame yourself. Aiden blames himself already, which I think is why he's still so protective of me. My parents tried to get me to come back home, but I refused. I moved to Seattle where I could start fresh; transferred to University of Washington. I already had a lot of my required coursework done, with all the running start I'd done in high school, so I still would graduate ahead of schedule. I got a job doing clerical work at a police station. I trained hard in martial arts. There was no way I would let anyone have that power over me again, emotionally or physically."

She turned toward him and finally looked him in the eye again. Her icy blue eyes were full of fire; he adored that about Maddy. "Most importantly, I started to like myself again. Nearly immediately, I found I loved the police department; stopping violence as it happened rather than long after the fact. So, I changed my major and studied criminal justice, worked my way to detective with the Seattle PD. And, eventually, I came back here."

Chase raised her feet and slid toward her on the bench, setting her legs back on his lap. He wrapped his arms around her and rested his chin on her head. "Thank you for telling me. Please, don't be mad if I'm a bit overly protective." Maddy nodded, her hair brushing against his chin. He pulled away and looked her in the eye, "I'm serious Maddy. I know you can handle yourself, but please don't go anywhere near him. Do you have an alarm system in your house?"

"I've made enough mistakes when it comes to Dylan. I have a security company coming out tomorrow to do a complete install. State of the art. I started researching and put in the order the day I ran into him in town."

Neither knew how long they sat together after that. The sun eventually started to set. It had been an emotional day for both. Maddy walked Chase to the door. Wanting more, but knowing it wasn't the time, Chase pulled Maddy in and pressed his lips softly against hers. It was tough to pull away. She leaned against the open doorway and watched him drive off into the blustering wind.

16

A FEW NIGHTS LATER, Maddy was stuck at work. She hated night shifts. But, criminals seemed to prefer the night. At least, they did tonight. Nothing too intense so far. She'd quieted down a few high school kids out for a late night on the beach. Ticketed a tourist that couldn't figure out his GPS to get to his hotel, so he'd been swerving all over the road.

Around midnight, things got more interesting. Quinn buzzed through, "We have an alarm going off at McAllister Fisheries. Maddy, Ian, are you two able to respond? You're all that's on tonight."

Turning her SUV around, Maddy headed straight to the scene. "You got it. I'm about 5 minutes out." Maddy radioed to her counterpart to confirm.

Ian's voice echoed back through the radio, "I'm closer to 10 minutes out. Lights blazing or make a subtle entrance?"

"Let's go for subtle tonight; I'll scope it out. Hopefully just some birds." A short drive later, she parked around the corner from McAllister's. For food safety, they generally didn't have bird issues, keeping a tightly sealed system with high quality alarms.

She grabbed her gear and hopped out of the SUV. Using caution, she pulled her gun from the glove compartment. Never could be too careful, even in Seaview. Trusting a gut instinct could keep you safe. Her gut was screaming tonight.

The street was clear, not a soul in sight. Maddy dashed across the street, eyes scanning for activity. Back against the wall, she edged along the wall until she reached the nearest window. She subtly leaned around to glance in the window.

Nothing.

She silently crept along the wall until she reached the door. Dammit, ajar. Stupidity was really not her thing; she held her position and waited for Ian to join her.

She didn't have to wait long. Ian's dark silhouette dashed across the street, his feet silent and movements swift. Within moments, he joined her, each against the wall on either side of the door. Silently, Maddy motioned to the slightly opened door. Nodding in agreement, Ian motioned *after you* with a friendly gesture. Rolling her eyes, but enjoying the silent banter, Maddy pushed the door open slowly, sidearm drawn and ready.

She heard him before she saw him. "Fuck, ouch." A few feet more, and she caught glimpse of him. A very tall, lanky man, dressed all in black, was behind a refrigerator, pulling at wires and shaking his right hand as if he'd been shocked.

Ian snuck in the far door, armed and blocking the other exit. Maddy cleared her throat. "Sir, you're under arrest. I'd appreciate it if you–" he turned and bolted. He made it a few steps before he saw Ian, stopped abruptly and raised his arms in submission.

With a smart alec response, Ian chuckled, "Nice to see you too, asshole. On the ground." He glanced up to Maddy, "Warehouse secure?"

The illegal electrician laid on the ground as directed, without hesitance. Too easily. Ian quickly cuffed him. Suspecting more, Maddy kept her eyes moving as he made the arrest.

She'd been through enough drug busts in Seattle, she knew to ensure every hiding place in the building was cleared. One of her first nights out, a guy that had trashed his brain cells from years of meth use came running out from under a desk in an abandoned warehouse. Screaming, he hadn't realized a major drug deal had been going on that night, he'd simply forgotten where he was and took a nap in the wrong place.

"Ian, stay on this guy." Maddy stepped back, drawing her weapon and listening carefully.

Nothing.

Silently, she crept towards the dark office stairs and listened. Something wasn't right.

If others were present, they'd be upstairs, and maybe waiting for her at the top of the stairwell. Maddy pulled back out of the building and stealthily raced around to the back of the building and unlocked the back door, making her way up the employee staircase to sneak up from behind.

Tiptoeing in the still darkness, she peeked in the window of the fire door at the top of the stairs. No one in sight. Slowly, silently, she opened the fire door and made her way into the office. The door creaked quietly at first. Cringing, she hoped she hadn't given away her position.

The front office was clear, not a soul in sight. Gun ready, she cleared the room before moving into the wide hallway to the other offices. The dark was almost oppressive, only a small trickle of moonlight available to light the way. Her ears tuned in to the slightest sounds; she thought she heard a shuffling from the far end of the hall when she'd come in, but nothing now.

An arm shot out of the dark supply room and knocked her gun out of her hand. Swiftly, she dove backward, avoiding the lunging attack that followed close behind, a Bowie knife slashing at her. If she'd been slower, or off her guard, he'd have sliced her neck with a quick flick of his wrist.

She ducked and bobbed, driving a kick straight into the emerging perp's gut.

With an "Oof," he swiftly grabbed her leg mid-air and tossed her into a nearby desk.

Furious, she flipped her legs up and nailed him with a roundhouse kick. His head crashed into the wall as he tumbled.

Bouncing back up, the huge man grinned at her, pulling out a .22 and aiming it between her eyes. Some people felt the .22 was not powerful enough to do much, but those were folks that hadn't seen the holes they made in skulls like she had.

"You have the right to remain silent," she began.

The burly giant grinned, his teeth and eyes glowing in the shadowy room, "Come on sweetheart, I've got the upper hand here."

With a shrug and a smirk of her own, she countered, "We'll see. I'm just getting this out of the way; let me finish, okay?"

Sidestepping around her, he kept the gun trained on her. "Don't move a fucking muscle; I'm getting out of here before your pal starts looking for you."

Maddy waited as she was told, holding her ground until the right moment. He backed away toward the door she had come up through, the moon's reflection off the gun a handy locator in the darkness. Reaching behind, he opened the creaking door and stepped slowly back as she did as she was told. She wasn't stupid, getting shot was not on her to do list for the night.

Nor was she letting him go. As soon as the door clicked, she sprinted flat-out down the main stairs, out the front building and reached the back of the building just in time to watch him making a run towards his car. No way, not tonight.

Continuing her silent sprint, she reached him well before he reached the car and threw her body on him, tackling him to the ground.

With a howl of pain as he hit the pavement face down, he tried to spin the gun towards her. Anticipating the move, she dug her knee into his spine.

As he instinctively tried to throw her off of him, she cracked her elbow into his eye and knocked the gun from his grip. Stretching his arm beyond her reach, he went for the gun. Rolling off him, she kicked his gun completely out of reach and turned back him.

Cussing, he came at her with a closed fist. His angry response worked to her benefit, and she used his momentum and threw him over her hip as she ducked.

His huge figure crashed into the concrete with a dull thud. Without a blink, he kicked his leg out straight into her gut. Her body flew back several feet and she hit the ground.

Dammit, he wasn't going down easily. Wincing, she grabbed her bruised ribs, waiting for him to get closer. As he neared, she flung her legs around like a helicopter and knocked him to the ground.

Immediately, she leaped back to her feet. He grabbed a smaller knife from his boot and rose to the ground, knife swinging like a windmill. With a swift kick of her foot, she knocked away the knife, spun around and threw her cuff on one hand, twisted, and had both hands cuffed before he could recoil.

After a swift kick to the backside, he was on the ground howling.

Now, with both hands behind his back, he was significantly limited. "Want to give up now, or keep going?" Maddy smiled. She knelt down and picked up his fallen sidearm. His shoulders hunched, giving up.

Siren blasting, lights blaring, Andrea's rig sped into the area. Maddy nudged the perp until he rose to his feet. As instructed, he hobbled to the waiting rig and ducked into the backseat.

Ian raced back, his own rig now loaded with the other perp. "Got him?"

"Of course. Didn't feel like lending a hand?" She panted breathlessly, smiling all the while.

Ian shrugged, "Thought I'd let you have a little fun first. Come on, let's get these guys booked and finish up. I'm hungry."

"Fun? Maybe. Guy was a fucking gigantic martial artist with a fist bigger than my skull. You got the wormy electrician that rolled over and showed his belly. Let's trade next time, my ribs are killing me." She dramatically grabbed her side and limped. Laughing, he nudged her until she gave and shoved him back.

Andrea, her boss and chief of police, dashed over to check on her officers. "You ok?" After seeing Ian had hardly broken a sweat, she checked Maddy for injuries like a worried mama bear.

"I'm fine." Maddy answered with a smile, shrugging off the attention but appreciating it all the same.

With a smile, Andrea looked down at the injured perp on the ground, "That all of them?"

Maddy bantered back, "Was this not enough? This big guy put up a hell of a fight," she grinned back, "but seriously, I believe this is it, but I can't say for sure. We'll head in for a final sweep."

Glued to his front grill as instructed, Chase tried not to imagine all of the horrible things that could be waiting to jump Maddy inside. Once he'd been notified that the alarm had been triggered and police were on the way, he'd quickly tossed on some clothes and tore out of the garage, fearing the worst. The chief of police had arrived a few moments before he had and warned him that he'd better not take even a step away from his car or she'd arrest him for interfering.

When Maddy walked around the from the back of the building, alive and well with a grin on her face, although her hair and uniform a bit disheveled, he'd never felt such an overwhelming sense of relief. He knew she was no slouch; she wouldn't have made detective so quickly back in Seattle if she weren't an exceptional cop. But still, it was hard not to be scared. Or tear down the front door of his own office to get to her and pummel the jerks that hurt her.

Now, he was forced to watch her go back in, weapon drawn and body on high alert. Not wanting to affect her concentration, he stood incredibly still at the front of his truck. Occasionally, he'd see she or Ian cross by the window. Finally, after what seemed an eternity, she and Ian came back out, looking quite a bit more relaxed.

"All good, chief," she hollered over the Andrea, who stood by their SUVs that contained the perps. "Building, docks, and boats clear."

"Nice work officers. Ian, you've got one in your rig, Maddy, you've got the other. Go process these guys. I'll start the investigation here and interrogate once I'm finished, but I may call you over if I need anything." Turning to Chase, she headed his direction. He watched as Maddy gave him a quick wink and drove away, all efficiency as she got the job done. "Mr. Anderson, I guess you're in charge tonight?"

He nodded, "That's me. Frank's out of the country. What can I do?"

"You can come with me. Let's do a walk-through and see if you notice if anything has been disturbed." He followed as directed. Halfway up the stairs, she stopped to ask, "You have security cameras?"

Chase nodded, "Sure do. The only access is locked up in Frank's office." He led the way. Immediately at the top of the stairs, he saw some destruction from the arrest. A head-sized indentation in the wall near Brent's desk. Paperwork scattered on the floor. The desk shifted out of place and the computer monitor on the ground next to it. "I'm glad I saw everyone walk out of here ok, or I'd be worried."

Andrea agreed, "I'm glad Maddy was on tonight. As well trained as my officers are, she's one of the few who could have gotten this done without any shots fired." Passing a huge Bowie knife on the way toward Frank's office, Chase took a deep breath to calm the rage that was boiling up inside. He had little doubt Dylan was behind tonight's activities, after their comments in the office, and the break-in was on one of the few night shifts Maddy had worked lately. He shared as much with Andrea.

"I'll look into that avenue. Keep me posted if you think of anything else. I'd like to get full statements from you and your crew, see if anyone else has seen or heard anything."

As he unlocked the closet door in Frank's office, he nodded in ascent. "Sure thing."

He turned on the locked computer and loaded tonight's security footage. Watched as the break-in occurred, the two he'd seen Maddy and Ian come out with. The first headed toward the nearest refrigeration unit and immediately began finding the right wires to dismantle. The second headed straight upstairs to the office.

He selected the main office camera and enlarged the picture. With purpose, the man headed straight for the storage closet where they held printed back-ups of data, budgets, tax files. Setting up better electronic storage had been on his agenda, which was now taking a big priority, aside from boosting security in general.

Within minutes, before the asshole had made much progress, Maddy entered the picture. He'd seen a pretty straightforward arrest on the smaller picture for the downstairs camera, but was more focused on her stealthy trek up the back stairs to sneak up on the upstairs perp. Shit, this was like watching a nightmare unfold.

Maddy was incredible in action. He'd never seen her like this. She disarmed the perp with a swift, effortless move. Used her own momentum to throw the asshole across the room. As terrifying as it was to watch, he didn't worry about her so much now. Not stupid though, the second the gun was trained on her, she waited him out and moved damn fast down the stairs to catch him off-guard from the other side.

She hadn't been kidding, she could take care of herself just fine. Running a hand through his hair, he slowly exhaled, getting control of his emotions.

At his side, Andrea was proudly grinning. "Yep, we're lucky she was here tonight. I think I'll ask her to start a training program for our other officers."

17

Maddy was just turning off the shower and heard her phone ringing from the bedroom. Crap, her parents. She'd asked them to call the second they were settled into their "villa." Of course, they called when she was away from her phone. She tossed her towel around her, but knew it was fruitless, she'd soak the floor anyway. She leaped at the phone, saw her mom's number on the screen, and managed to answer in the nick of time.

"Mom, are you there?" She was breathless as she answered.

"I'm here. What are you doing? You sound out of breath."

"I heard the phone ringing as I was getting out of the shower. I suppose I could have just called you back... that actually sounds much more reasonable now that I think about it. Guess I was looking forward to your call. Well? Are you totally jet-lagged or have you acclimated? Is it beautiful?" She wrapped her towel around her and sat on the edge of the bed, looking out at the sun warming the beach.

"This country is incredible. We stayed in Rome the first few days, so the jet lag is already much better. It's incredible. We have a spectacular view of a vineyard. The people are truly amazing. So kind and welcoming."

Laura went on to describe their trip so far. "I lost a bet with your father and was stuck riding in the middle seat on the flight over. The woman next to me was delightful but talked for two hours straight. I had to put on my headphones and close my eyes and pretend I was asleep, and she still didn't get the message," she stopped to laugh, and Maddy heard her father grumbling in the background. "So, when your dad got up to use the bathroom, I told her how much he'd love to hear about her business plans, and I switched spots with him. I could hardly sleep at that point for laughing at my cleverness." Maddy loved the visual of her parents. Her mom had a wicked sense of humor, and her parents still managed to joke so well with each other.

"Devious, Mom. But, well-played. What was the bet?"

Laura paused, "I... I'll tell you when you're older sweetheart."

"Mom, as much as I'm happy you and Dad maintain a healthy sex life, I really don't need details." She inwardly cringed, blocking the threatening visual.

"That's not what I meant. It was about you dear. Nothing unkind. Love you. Have a good day. Ciao," and her mother barely waited for her ciao back before hanging up. Now that was odd.

Her parents were a bit strange. The last few months, they'd been strongly hinting that she should consider giving dating another try, and she suspected it was related. If only they had any idea where her brain was these days.

Mom, Dad, I'm thinking of having epic, mind-blowing sex with Dad's business partner.

That would go over well.

She shook her head, amused at herself. Maddy remembered she was still soaking wet and went back to her morning routine. Still a bit sleepy from her double night shifts, she brewed a large pot of coffee and got ready for the rest of the day, now that the morning had been mostly wasted sleeping off the past two nights.

Still in a fatigued fog from her late night, Maddy rubbed her eyes and got ready for her day. She was not counting on having a productive day; the day after was always rough. Last night hadn't exactly been a typical Seaview night either. Not quite like her nights in Seattle, but she was a little sore from the beating she'd taken last night.

No word yet on who'd hired the perps, but there was little doubt that Dylan was involved. His goons hadn't said a word. Maybe after a night in a cell.

She slipped on an easy maxi dress and flip flops, skipping make-up or doing her hair. She poured a cup of coffee and headed out the door. A trip to the farmer's market for some fun groceries sounded relaxing, and she could grab an easy breakfast while she was there.

She hopped in the jeep and drove up the hill to the farmer's market. The market was mostly open-air, with a few permanent fixtures in the covered section. During the summer, especially on the weekends, the place was a madhouse. As she pulled into the parking lot, she was grateful it was only Friday and there were a few open spots.

Grabbing her shopping bags, she hopped out and headed straight to her favorite produce vendor. The market was absolutely gorgeous this time of the year, with massive gardens surrounding it, full of color. Maddy took her time picking out a variety of fresh fruits and veggies.

Magnificent smells emanated from the food vendors, making her remember she hadn't had breakfast yet. She grabbed a yummy breakfast sandwich to soothe the angry growling in her belly. As she munched, she perused some of the craft vendor offerings and found a pretty handmade wooden salad bowl and tongs that would make a perfect housewarming gift for Chase. Pleased with her own thoughtfulness, she stopped next and picked up a tablecloth to cleverly wrap it in.

Maddy was just heading for the exit, refreshed after a successful shopping trip, when her heart leapt into her throat and started pounding so hard it echoed in her ears when she saw him. Chase stood, maybe fifty feet away, paying for some produce he'd just purchased from the same vendor she had visited on her way in.

She allowed herself to stare, appreciative. His crisp white t-shirt hugged his broad, muscled shoulders, and his tattered jeans hung low on his hips. Despite the heat, he wore sturdy work boots. His sandy blond hair was chronically tousled, his jaw accented by his just-beyond stubble beard. How did he manage to always have that dark, sexy look to him even when he was smiling and chatting with the cashier?

As he turned and started walking her direction, she knew the moment he spotted her. His walk morphed to a strut, more purposeful as he closed the distance between them, his intensely dark blue eyes locked with her own. The corner of his mouth turned up in a subtle smile, his eyes twinkling in amusement.

Maddy didn't bother to hide her own smile, not that she could have held it back if she tried. "Well, well, well. Fancy meeting you here," she said once he was close enough. They stopped just far enough away to maintain an appropriate distance.

"I stayed at the office with Andrea until she'd finished collecting evidence, then hung around the office to answer a lot of questions. I needed some fresh air and just heard we have a farmer's market now; thought I'd check it out and stock up on some groceries. Pretty nice place." He shrugged and looked around.

"I try to get my produce here every week in summertime." She gestured to her grocery bags.

They sat there a bit awkwardly for a few moments, smiling but having no idea what to say to each other. The last time they'd been alone together, they'd poured their hearts out. The time before, they'd frantically made out before she'd propositioned him for a night of no-promises sex. She started laughing, the awkwardness was indescribable; she was so thrilled to be near him but had no idea how one approached conversation after their last few interactions.

He looked at her like she was nuts. "Maddy, you are a mystery. I'm struggling to figure out what on earth to say to you, and you're having a giggle fit."

She calmed down enough to tame her laugh to just a smile, "I'm laughing as I have no idea what to say to you." She took a few deep breaths to hold back another giggle from escaping. "Oh, I got you a housewarming present. I was going to stop by and deliver it later this afternoon."

He peered down at her bags; fortunately, his surprise was covered. She hid the bags behind her back so he couldn't try to peek. "Why don't I grab us some sandwich fixings, and you can stop by for lunch and bring me my present. And, I'd like to hear about those fancy moves you used on that asshole that broke into my office."

Crap. He'd watched the security video; she'd forgotten her father had installed those after a break-in a few years ago, which had resulted in a dead-end investigation with no good evidence and a whole lot of damaged product. "How much did you see?" She hoped he didn't think ill of her. Over the years, she'd run into enough sexist assholes who were intimidated when they realized she could kick their asses without breaking a sweat. Not that she would, of course.

"All of it," a mischievous smile crossed his face, "want to try some moves out on me later? I'd love to spar sometime."

Thrilled that he seemed to actually admire her skills, she couldn't hide her relief. "You got it. No sprouts."

The look of confusion on his face was adorable. She couldn't say that she intentionally tried to throw him off but enjoyed it regardless. "What?"

"On my sandwich. No sprouts, but I'm good with pretty much anything else." She swayed her hips innocently as she smiled.

He shook his head, his sexy slow smile forming. "You got it. I'll see you at my place." She enjoyed the view as he walked away toward the bakery stall at the end of the market.

Rather than going in through the garage door, Chase met Maddy outside to walk her in through the front door. Knowing Miss Hanson would be glued to her window, peering through her blinds per her usual whenever he came and went, he waved politely. As usual, the blinds abruptly shifted as she hid, pretending that she hadn't been staring.

He was starting to enjoy the routine. At least he had a neighbor he interacted with. Good progress.

He suddenly felt a bit nervous as he unlocked the door and let Maddy walk in the door before him. Would she approve? He'd put a lot of thought into putting his home together, which is why it was still so sparse.

"This place is gorgeous. The floors are amazing. I would have moved in just for these spectacular wood floors." She didn't hesitate walking in. She hardly paused as she stepped out of her flip flops and walked into the house, her gaze missing nothing.

"I'm glad you like it. I rented it from an ad online; it was a bit scary moving in without having seen the place first." He sighed in relief and followed her into the house. He tossed the groceries on the kitchen counter and watched her continue her self-guided tour of the house. Leaning against the dining room arched entry, he watched the show. Her sense of wonder was... refreshing.

Her hips swayed and the long, narrow dress accented her spectacularly fine ass as she walked. She'd let her hair go wild today; he had to restrain himself from pulling her against him and burying his hands in the wavy mass of hair. Her face was freshly clean without a trace of make-up; she looked hot with it but was a goddess without.

She strolled toward him finally, adding an extra swing to her hips and a shy grin on her face. Maddy handed him her gift, wrapped creatively in fabric. "The wrapping is a tablecloth, fyi. They didn't have any wrapping paper or gift bags at the market today, so I improvised." She nervously held her hands behind her and backed against the dining room table to watch him open the gift.

He grinned at her, slowly opening his present. Under the blue linen tablecloth was a smooth, wood-grain salad bowl with matching fish-shaped tongs. Sturdy pieces, classy but not delicate. "Thanks, this is awesome. I like the fish."

He walked toward her and reached around her, setting the bowl on the dining room table. Then, again, silence. He pushed through. "I need to thank you, and Ian, for last night. I checked out the office this morning, spent a few hours cleaning up and looking for anything stolen. Looks like you got them before they did any serious damage. Some broken furniture in the front office – you ok?"

"I'm good. He resisted arrest, but I got him."

"Was that your skull or his that dented the wall? The cameras didn't capture the specifics in the dark... just bodies flying." Chase gently stepped closer, his hand feeling the back of her head for injury.

"That was his skull."

"And these bruises on your arm?"

"I did get a few bruises, nothing serious." He studied her from head to toe, looking for other bruises. "Really, Chase, I'm ok."

"Are you sure? No bruises here?" He kissed her forehead sweetly.

She managed a soft, "No."

He continued his gentle ministrations, "Here?" and he made his way lower, kissing her neck, cheeks, finally landing on her mouth, gently pressing his lips to hers, then pulling away slowly. Her sigh about undid him. Mouths inches apart, he smiled, "I've thought about your... suggestion, by the way."

Eyes fluttering open, she breathlessly responded, "And?"

Without answering, he kissed her again, gently teasing. He nipped at her lower lip. Drew his tongue gently along where he'd nipped. Her body pressed tightly against his, her hips pressed against his own. His hand slid into that mass of brown hair finally, and he deepened the kiss. Quickly, he lost control as their bodies frantically touched, mouths inseparable. He paused long enough to suggest, "Tomorrow?"

She pulled away, "Tomorrow?" Her look of disappointment was priceless, fully stroking his ego.

"After the beach party. For now..." He slid down the straps of her dress and grasped her breast in his hand. A bit rougher than he meant to in his haste, but she gasped and pushed further into him. His hands teased through delicate lace of her bra; her response was incredible, unrestrained, sensual.

He slid her dress all the way down, and she stood before him, her hands gripping the table behind her, wearing nothing but a flimsy, white lace bra with matching wisp of a thong. Words flew out of his brain; he was sure his mouth must be gaping open.

Moving close again, he slid his hand down along her smooth abdomen and teased his way into her panties. Shocked, she flinched. "- Sorry."

She looked like he'd burned her, but she tried to smile to cover her panicky response.

"Don't be sorry, I'm sorry. You ok? I... are you ok?" He didn't know how to respond, but knew he'd pushed too far, thinking of her traumatic past.

She shook her head. "No, it's ok. I just... I, uh... I've never..."

He nodded, understanding sinking in. "Maddy, I gathered you've had pretty terrible sex. Hasn't anyone ever..." Dang, now he felt like a shy teenager, trying to get out the right words. "Maddy, I don't want to hurt you. Ever."

She nodded, "I know. I want you to keep going."

"I have an idea. You are going to stand there, gorgeous as you are." He leaned in, gently pressing his body against hers. He whispered gently into her ear, his breath warm against her neck as he kissed her gently. "You let me know what you like, but the second you say stop, I'm stopping."

"Ok, I want you to keep going," she managed to respond. Maddy mentally kicked herself for being such an idiot. She was desperate for him, wanted him so badly. The moment he'd moved under her panties, she freaked. All the terrible sex had come flashing back. It had never been... forced, well, she guessed it had in a way... she really didn't want to think about that right now. Regardless, it had certainly never been any good. Terrible really.

Chase started from the top again, kissing her with such compassion she nearly cried at his intense caring. His kiss deepened; the passion was intense. Heat started to curl through her body again, extending deep to her core. As he kissed her, his hand grazed her breast.

His caress began gentle but accelerated with her breathing as she responded to him. She felt him reading her response. Knowing he was taking it slowly, at her pace.

His tongue glided down her neck. He kissed slowly as he moved down. Sliding her bra out of his way, his tongue circled her breasts and finally, as her breathing quickened, he took the peaked nub into his mouth and suckled until she cried out in pleasure.

As she was distracted, his hand again slid into her panties. He cupped her soft curls, this time her breath hitched with pleasure. Heat and pressure built within her as he rubbed her clit slowly at first, increasing his pace with her breathing.

As the orgasm ripped through her, she cried out, making a sound she'd certainly never heard herself make. Her hands gripped the table tighter, struggling to hold herself up as her legs quaked beneath her.

She felt him smile against her neck. "You liked that, then hang on."

He knelt in front of her. Before she could object, knowing where this was going and terrified, he gently nudged her legs apart further and pressed his tongue to her sensitized center. She gasped, overwhelmed but unafraid. His tongue circled slowly, pressing as he laved against her swollen nub. The orgasm tore through her, stronger than the last one. She cried out; he slowed his warm licks until her breathing calmed.

She looked down as he pulled away with a huge, satisfied grin on his face. She could hardly hold on her legs were so shaky. Seeing her shocked, but very sated, tired body struggling to stand, he stood and held her close against him. She buried her head into his neck as she slowed her breathing.

"Ah, hang on," He pulled slightly away and adjusted his pants. Selfishly, she was glad he had enjoyed himself. He saw her smile down at his bulging erection, "Uh, yeah..." He looked embarrassed, which was ridiculous, which heightened when she started laughing. "Hey..."

She shook her head at him, still clutching his waist, "No, I'm just so glad you're not grossed out."

"Grossed out? Are you kidding? You taste so good. I'm going to need a really long, really cold shower and hope I'm not completely blue." He finally laughed with her and stood holding her in close. How long they stood that way, she couldn't have said. It felt so right to just hold on to each other.

"Chase?"

"Yeah?" He replied sleepily as his head rested against her own.

"I think I'm going to head home now... You want to come over after the beach party tomorrow?" She was too afraid to look at him, in case he said no.

"Oh, hell yeah." He managed to pull away and pick up her clothes. She quickly put her underwear and dress back on. Cheeks flushed, she smiled at him as she walked across the large living room to the front door. Again, he leaned against the dining room doorway, the corner of his mouth turned up as she quietly left.

18

Seaview was bustling come Saturday. The town had a huge anniversary festival every August. The hotels had been booked for months. Shops were all-hands-on-deck, busting to the gills with tourists. And sales. Sidewalks were standing room only at best. The beach looked like a hurricane had come through and neatly deposited towels, umbrellas, and picnic baskets across it.

Maddy had been on duty since 5 o'clock that morning. But she'd been uncharacteristically awake since 3:30 in the damn morning. She'd been awoken by repeated chimes from her phone notifying her of incoming texts. In her sleepy haze, she'd tried to ignore it, but then worried it could be important and rolled over to check her phone.

Twelve picture messages had buzzed in sequentially. Her parents toasting at a cafe table in front of rows of grapevines. Her mother posing with her hand cleverly pointing to the colosseum in the background à la Vanna White. Her father wearing some rather tiny European swim shorts in front of a sparkling azure sea–that was a visual she didn't need so early in the morning. Maddy couldn't help but smile and enjoy the series of pics her mom had sent. She took the hint and called her mother.

"Good morning honey," her mother softly answered, as if expecting her daughter's sleepiness on the other end.

"Good morning my world travelling mother. Not that I mind hearing from you, but do you have any idea what time it is?" Maddy's voice croaked through the phone. She rolled flat on her back and stretched her tight limbs, slowly accepting wakefulness.

"I sure do darling. I remember you saying you were taking the early shift today. So, I thought I'd catch you before you left for work." Her mother was awfully chipper. If Maddy weren't so glad to connect with her, she might be irritated. Maybe.

The woman was tough to be irritated with. Unless you'd done something stupid. Like get caught sneaking back into the house at two in the morning. She winced at the thought. Her judgely-ness always had punishment to meet the crime. Such as taking advantage of her being awake at two in the morning and assigning several chores to be done before dawn.

They had been playing phone tag for days, and she'd been missing her parents terribly. Leaning over, Maddy switched on her bedside lamp, savoring the last few minutes of coziness under the covers. "Tell me everything about your trip. It looks like you guys are having an amazing time."

"We are, it's just incredible here. Your father's attempts at Italian are pretty terrible, but we've met some wonderful people that have helped him with his accent and shoddy grammar. Not that I'm one to talk, I haven't advanced beyond 'ciao,' which only gets you so far."

Her mother spent the next ten minutes telling her about every detail of their stops, and the magnificent inn overlooking the Mediterranean where they were spending the rest of their trip. She made her mother promise to take her along next time. "Of course, you'd just love it here. We're missing you so much. Next time, let's make it a family trip and drag you and Aiden along."

"Sounds like a great plan. I'll download an app to learn Italian." Maddy was liking this plan very much. She was suddenly wishing she'd had an espresso machine so she could start her personal immersion program. "Did you hear from Ronan? I know you were hoping to catch him while you were across the pond."

"I thought I'd sent you the picture, darn it, must not have gone through." She could hear her mother scrolling through her phone, discovering the failed send. "Yes, he met us in Rome. He couldn't tell me anything about what he's up to, of course, but at least he spent the day with us. He looks so handsome with the beard he's grown. A bit like a mountain man though. He's got a ponytail. I would never have picked him out of a crowd with the eccentric new look." Maddy could hear her mom fighting bursting into tears on the other end of the line.

"I'm so glad he took the time to come see you. He loves you mom. You know Ronan, he's always been absurdly driven, and I suspect he's crazy busy with whatever it is he's doing over there."

"I know. I held it together; I didn't cry until after we'd parted. I may have hugged him too many times, but he put up with me. I think... I think he's about ready to come home."

"Did he say anything?"

"No. He wouldn't. I could just tell. He looked tired. Weary. Like he used to when he'd get back from one of his old punishing exercise regimens." She heard her mom sniffle and clear her throat. "Let's move on for now. I'm not going to dwell on that right now; I can't. We'll just see what comes of this."

Maddy finally dragged her butt out of bed, rumpled camisole and panties just hanging on as she padded across the cold wooden floor toward the coffee pot. She struggled not to yawn as her mother changed subjects. She wasn't bored, just finding her bearings.

"How's Chase settling in at work? Dad doesn't want to ask himself. He's trying to pretend he's not worrying; he wants Chase to know he trusts him."

"Chase is doing great, Mom. Everything is running beautifully. Did you hear about Dylan's mission for a hostile takeover to bring in the cruise ships? And the break-in?" Maddy managed to keep her voice calm but couldn't hold back the bitterness in her tone. She set the coffee pot to brew and leaned back against the cabinet.

"Chase, of course, has kept your father posted. I don't like that Dylan's creeping around. Aiden's reporting in, too. You be careful, ok?" Laura couldn't hide the worry in her voice.

"Yes, I'm being careful. I just had a security system installed. I'm sure he's not a threat to me, however. I've hardly even seen him. Last time he came near me he wound up in jail. He's not stupid. He's not going to risk his future again. Or his genitalia, as this time I'm castrating him if he comes near me." Maddy tried to reassure her mom, but if she could just reassure herself. She focused on the gurgling sound of the coffee pot brewing away.

"Please call me if anything changes. Anything."

"Will do. Can you text me the details of your flight home? I'm on pick-up, right?"

"Yes, thanks. I'm not sure our extra luggage and ourselves will fit in your Jeep, or Aiden's fancy little car. Why don't you rope in Chase to drive with you? We can throw the luggage in the back of his truck." Her mother's helpful suggestion was awfully suspect. She couldn't know, could she?

Maddy played along. "Good idea, his truck is pretty spacious."

Her mother made an odd sound on the other end of the phone. Almost like a satisfied *Hmm*. Before Maddy could ponder what that meant, Laura moved on, "Are you all going to the Seaview Beach Party tonight? I'm so sad we're missing it this year. I still remember the first time your father took me. I was staying at the cabin; I had decided to spend the summer there on a break from college. That was the night your father and I... well, you don't want those details. But let me just say, that was one magical night." Her mother's voice had gone all soft and distant.

Maddy laughed, she was pleased to know that her parents enjoyed a... healthy relationship. "Thanks for sparing me the details. I had actually wondered why you two always headed back first, leaving us to walk back by ourselves."

"Maybe you should give it a try, Maddy."

What? Maddy was a bit confused, "Pardon?"

"An evening at the beach is certainly romantic."

"Mother, where are you going with this? I'm a bit... I'm not sure ..." The coffee pot puffed as it sucked the last of the water out of the reservoir, sounding as exasperated as she felt.

"Maddy, I love you. I know you're terrified of trying at a relationship again, maybe even of sex–"

Maddy groaned. Damn, she was afraid that's what she was getting at. "Mother, you know I can talk to you about anything, but–"

"Don't you 'Mother' me, missy. I'm serious. I want you to be happy. You are a wonderfully passionate person. Just... consider giving things another try. With someone you can trust."

Whoa boy, slow down. Was her mother psychic? It was a well-established fact that Laura McAllister had eyes in the back of her head. Maddy was becoming increasingly sure her mother was even more mystical than that.

She heard her dad clearing his throat in the background. He had clearly just joined her mother. She hoped he was coming to the rescue, and not here for the double-team.

Her dad grabbed the phone. "Maddy. Hi. Miss you darling," he rushed through his greeting. "We won't push you on relationships, that's entirely up to you. But..." he drew out the pause, clearly not comfortable with the direction this one was going. "Maddy, honey. It's time to think about... Remember what I'd encourage you to do when you fell off your bike?"

Maddy rolled her eyes but knew what he was getting at. "I'd get right back on, despite the tears and scraped up knees. And you'd cheer me on."

"Exactly. See you soon honey." Her dad ended the call before she could. She sat and looked out to the dark ocean, finally pouring herself a cup of much needed coffee. Gently blowing the steam from the top.

She was ready. But maybe not ready to talk with her parents about it and certainly felt a little weird thinking of them cheering her on about her sex life.

Chase didn't need her messing with his future, now that his future was looking so bright. She was a disaster. Maybe she should try a stupid online dating thing like Payson, who was so convinced it would work. Then, it would only be a total stranger she'd mess up. Her heart ached at the thought of even considering anyone other than Chase. Well, that was an interesting revelation. A bit possessive of her. Dammit.

Her phone buzzed again with another picture message. Her mother was incorrigible. She read the text before looking at the pic, *I know what you're thinking. Stop worrying and let it happen.* Nosy mother; lucky she liked her so well or she'd have to avoid her indefinitely.

She opened the attached picture. It was from her mother's retirement party. Her mother had made it her mission to capture all her memories on camera, stating she was preparing to bore the eventual grandchildren with photos.

As she looked down at the photo, she laughed out loud. Dang that woman. The photo was of she and Aiden having a heated debate, with Chase standing at her side and joining right in the debate, his hand subtly on the small of her back, almost protectively. Her parents didn't miss a thing; she should have known. How long had they known?

Feeling like she had their permission, she relaxed a bit. This whole 'let nature take its course' business might just be a bunch of bullshit. She'd been drawn to Chase since they were kids. And she'd been fighting it for just as long. Maybe it was time to stop fighting. For a night. Anything more than that was a bit scary to think about still, but becoming less daunting by the moment.

19

Parade duty was officially her least favorite job, the day had been long and hot and busy. No one else had wanted it either. This year, they'd held a lottery to decide who had to work the tough shifts for the festival weekend.

But they tried to make it fair.

Maddy took the twelve-hour parade / crowd control shift, but then had the next two days off. Today was the busiest day of the festival. The crowds would start thinning out tomorrow and heading home.

The weather was perfect on the beach, but the street was sweltering. She reminded herself that everybody loved a parade. Just not her, at least, not when she had to work. She was relieved when the parade was over, but now she had her work cut out for her.

She'd already had to make one arrest for a drunk and disorderly that had nearly been runover by an ostentatious Sponge Bob float. Most of the crowd had been pretty well-behaved today... compared to last year. As the revelers dispersed, Maddy had cleared the avenue one last time and re-opened Beachside for traffic.

Grateful to be done with parade duty after a long-ass day, Maddy nearly skipped back to the station to finish her office duties before starting her weekend off. She made her way through a crowd heading toward the beach, thankful they were using the crosswalks again.

A hand grabbed her arm and jerked her to a stop as she stepped onto the curb. "Excuse me," Maddy demanded as she turned toward the perpetrator. She froze, a hard lump forming in her throat as she realized Dylan had her arm and was squeezing firmly. His eyes were dark, lips pulled tight.

She tried to pull her arm away, "Get your hands off of me."

Dylan appeared to remember where he was and relaxed his grip, but still refused to let go. Maddy wanted to run, but her training kicked in. This might be a good chance to get information about why he was really in town.

She didn't pull away anymore, but stayed silent, waiting for him to speak. Silence encouraged a confession more often than direct questions. "My dear Madelyn. I enjoyed watching you at the parade. You sure could handle yourself with that drunk. I'm so proud of you."

Maddy silently glared at him. He didn't seem to notice, "I'd like to reconnect with you. We were so good together."

She couldn't resist poking at the bear, "When were we good together? Was that when you were belittling me? When you were assaulting me? When you were trying to ruin my reputation and my future?"

Rather than getting riled, he smiled back at her, "But Madelyn, I have so many lovely pictures of you. I look at them every day. We belong together. If you disagree, I would be happy to share them with the chief of police."

Maddy smirked back, knowing the threat wouldn't take him as far as it had last time he'd sent out dirty photos of her. "Go ahead and try. Any evidence you can submit against yourself will only worsen your business attempts in town. I sure would appreciate if you provided the chief with evidence to support my request for a restraining order to start, and certainly if I decide to press charges for blackmail, defamation of character, or maybe assault," as she looked down at her arm, there were finger-shaped bruises forming. "Drop those photos off anytime."

Hoping she'd won this round, she pulled away and attempted to walk casually toward the station. As she had hoped, Dylan didn't make any attempt to stop her.

The station was quiet, as most of the crew was still out in the streets. She'd been on duty nearly twelve hours now. They'd staggered their shifts to maximize coverage. Her shoes squeaked as she walked along the freshly waxed taupe linoleum floor of the reception area. She waved to the receptionist, Darlene, as she walked past.

She normally passed right in through the key-coded door, but today it took a few tries to enter the code correctly as her hand shook. She'd been on shift since before dawn and was already exhausted by the time she'd run into Dylan.

Trying to keep her voice steady, she shouted to her counterpart that was just coming on shift as she strolled past him, "Ian, I'm out for the day." She didn't hesitate to walk straight into the chief's office. If anyone stopped her and noticed she was on the line of falling apart, she was afraid she would lose the last threads of control she was desperately clutching.

"Maddy. Nice parade, wasn't it?" The chief asked, hitting send on her email before she looked up. Her tone changed when she saw Maddy's distressed expression, lips pressed tightly together and eyes watery.

Andrea was in her early fifties, fit, and wore her gray hair in a spunky short ponytail. She didn't put up with any crap, which Maddy adored about her. In this case, she was also grateful Andrea was a downright good person and had raised four polite, caring grown kids of her own. Andrea's face softened, turning more into mom-mode than chief, "Are you ok? What happened?"

"Andrea, can we talk? I have a bit of a situation." Maddy closed the chief's door and took a seat in one of the worn leather chairs in front of the desk. She hated to reveal so much of herself, but knew she needed to be completely honest. She knew Andrea had her back, but she also knew Andrea would need the whole story.

Taking a deep breath, she pushed her emotions to the back burner. She described her history with Dylan since high school, the photos, the assault, and his threats to make the photos public again, the interaction just moments ago. His rather suspect plans for Seaview. "I'd like to keep my personal life as private as possible, but I know what he's capable of and wanted to keep you in the loop."

"Oh Maddy, I'm so sorry you went through all of that. He could never compromise your employment here. I agree, if he does send in any inappropriate photos, he is more likely to incriminate himself than you. I suspect those would be only to get your attention. A demonstration of power. Why don't you call your brother and arrange for the legal protection you need? It sounds like you went through all the appropriate legal channels before, so you should have a good case against him."

She leaned on her elbows, looking Maddy in the eye, "I know you want to keep this private, but the team needs to know so they can keep an eye on him. We're already investigating him after speaking with Chase Anderson about the break-in and the buy-out offer they'd received. Don't go near him alone; don't go anywhere alone. I'm going to shuffle the schedule around a bit. You'll be with a partner full time; I know Ian won't mind."

Maddy considered arguing that she could take care of herself and didn't need a partner. But she wasn't stupid.

Andrea paused, as if contemplating sharing this with Maddy, "I have a bad feeling about him. I've seen him around town. He's charming and friendly, but there's something... off about him. Like none of us are good enough to share the same air that he breathes."

"I know what you mean. He was arrogant when he was younger, and I watched that transform into something more. Something darker, just before I left. Thanks for being so supportive, really. I'll be careful. I just want to put this behind me once and for all."

Maddy left the office feeling much better. She knew she could defend herself, but she wasn't taking any chances. His grip on her arm had been intense. That look in his eyes. There was something very disturbing in his expression, a hollowness that she had seen only a few times.

Like when he'd bashed her head against her car the day she'd left him.

She called Payson while she finished her work for the day. "Hey Payson. Want to walk home with me? We can get ready at my place and head for the beach party together. I could use some company on the walk."

Maddy loved living so close to work, right on the beach in town, but walking the near mile alone, already freaked out, was not appealing. She might as well start the buddy system, even though she was still armed and in uniform.

Payson was more than happy to join her and met her at the station an hour later. She mercifully didn't ask any questions as they headed out together. "Natalie's watching the shop until closing in an hour. You were right about hiring her on more hours per week. She agreed to 20 hours most weeks but is willing to work full-time hours when I am willing to take a vacation, or on weekends during the peak of tourist season, like today."

The pair walked down the busy street, not talking much until they hit the beach. Payson slipped off her heels and walked barefoot as usual. They must have looked quite the pair, Maddy in her black police uniform and Payson in her bare feet and breezy floral sun dress. Not wanting to talk about Dylan until she got home, Maddy asked about Payson's trip to Boston to see Cara, her sister.

"You were right; I'm glad I went. She got her first D. My goodness, it was like the world had ended. She was so afraid she'd never get a decent job with such a terrible grade on her record. It was philosophy for crying out loud. Cara's a scientist and apparently did not get on well with her head-in-the-clouds professor." Payson rolled her eyes as she lovingly talked about her younger sister. "Where that girl came from, I'll never know. I got more than my share of D's in school."

"With her panic, I assumed she'd gotten arrested or something."

"Not Cara. I love her to death, but oh my she's dramatic. I'm hoping she'll grow out of it someday. Maybe a little life experience will put things in perspective."

They continued to chat as they walked. Maddy was grateful for her friend's lightheartedness on the walk home. Payson kept things light, knowing Maddy wasn't ready to talk about things yet, but sensed something was up. They walked up the steps from the beach to the house, but rather than entering through the slider on the deck like they normally would, Maddy led them around to the front door.

Payson was surprised to see Maddy unlock the deadbolt and head in to disarm the new alarm system. "That's new. What's up?" Re-setting the alarm for home-mode, she filled Payson in on the run-in with Dylan, her agreement with Andrea to not go anywhere alone. She slipped off her shoes but couldn't manage to sit still quite yet. "I'm so sorry Maddy. You seem pretty shaken. I'm glad you called so you didn't walk home alone."

"I appreciated the company. Andrea is totally on top of things. She's alerting the team and assigned Ian to be my full-time partner until things calm down. I don't mind; we work well together. I'd like Dylan to try something when I'm on the clock. Make a nice, easy arrest," Maddy paced the living room, plotting.

"Your history and his threat weren't enough to do something today? He left bruises on your arm, Maddy." Payson looked up from her place on the couch, her face in a plotting scowl as well. Payson's eyes followed Maddy's path back and forth across the room.

"Some of these bruises are from an arrest night before last. But, yeah, some are new. It was an ugly legal battle before, and he didn't learn a damn thing. Today, he had this crazy look in his eye. I don't think the slap on the wrist he'd likely get right now would be enough to even phase him. I want him to go away for a long, long time. So, I need to play my cards right."

Payson couldn't stand to watch her friend so upset; she walked over and pulled her friend into a hug. "Don't do anything stupid. Please, be careful," Payson begged of her friend.

"He's not going to rule my life ever again. I'm not stupid and will protect myself. I'm going to get changed and try to calm down before Aiden gets here; he's overprotective as it is. Aiden and Chase are planning to park here, hang out for a bit, then we can all walk together to the beach party." Maddy put her shoulders back, head held high, and headed to her bedroom to change.

20

Chase pulled into Maddy's driveway, parking next to Aiden's slick sports car. Maddy had invited them to park at her place and walk to the beach, as they had done when her grandparents owned the cabin. Parking on Beachside would be a disaster tonight.

He couldn't help but feel a bit nervous. Keeping his distance had been tough. Rather than clearing his mind of her, it had gotten worse. Her offer that night in the truck had been... more than tempting. It had been bad before, but now he didn't even have to close his eyes to get lost in increasingly creative fantasies of her.

He'd barely held on to his shred of control yesterday at his place. Totally unplanned. She'd tasted so good. Those moans of pleasure still echoed in his head. The cold shower after she'd left had barely helped.

He finally turned off the engine and slammed his head against the steering wheel, groaning out loud. Dammit. He'd wanted her for so long. One night, that's all she'd asked for.

What if he wanted more? Over the years, he'd had plenty of one-night stands. She was not a one-night stand. She was... everything.

He understood she was terrified to ask for anything more. Terrified to want anything more.

That day at the cemetery he discovered how much he needed her in his life. Full time. When she finally opened up and told him all about her nightmare of a relationship with Dylan, he'd had trouble not murderously driving straight to Dylan's house to kick the shit out of him. Not that he knew where Dylan was staying. His emotions were all over the board when he was around Maddy these days.

Eventually, Chase reigned in his racing thoughts enough to climb out of the truck. Payson opened Maddy's front door to let him in. "Hey, Payson," he nodded as he walked in the door. As he entered, he heard Aiden shouting and pacing the living room in front of Maddy, arms gesturing wildly. She sat on the plush couch, leaned back, arms folded across her chest.

Payson stopped him before he could tear into the room and defend Maddy, whispering "Give him a moment. I think he's winding down."

He nodded and walked toward the arguing pair more slowly, like he was trying to calm a growling bear. Maddy glanced to him and rolled her eyes. He winked back.

Aiden realized his friend was behind him and swung around. Still shouting, Aiden looked to Chase, pointing his finger at Maddy, "She's not going tonight."

Maddy calmly rose from the couch and walked into the kitchen. She casually returned and set a handful of beers on the coffee table. She politely invited her guests to have a seat in the living room, playing the polite, imperturbable hostess.

Maddy sat on the couch and opened her own beer. Payson obediently took a seat in a living room chair. "Aiden, I appreciate your concern. Really. I'm not going to be foolish." Maddy then turned to Chase to bring him up to speed, "Dylan stopped me after the parade.

He left this creatively hand-shaped bruise on my arm," she gestured to her arm where faint finger-imprints visible.

She continued on calmly, as if the bruises were nothing, "And, he threatened to release some nude photos of me–again–if I don't see reason and... shack up with him. My legal counsel here requests that I obtain a restraining order and never go out in public again. I'm considering my options but have not agreed to his recommendations at this time. I have agreed to hire my own attorney, but not tonight."

The corner of Chase's mouth turned up. He loved her grace under pressure. Almost as much as he enjoyed watching how she could fluster her brother. She would have been a great attorney. Although, she was an amazing cop, and that would have been a sad thing to miss.

Chase popped the top off his beer and stood next to Aiden. "Maddy, he might be right," but before she could pounce on him, he continued, "Please, when you're off duty, don't leave the house without one of us. Your parents will be back soon and can help, too."

To make peace, Chase sat down next to Maddy on the couch. Without thinking, his hand fell to her bare knee. Realizing his mistake, he pulled away abruptly. He quickly looked to Aiden, fearing he'd been caught with his hand in the cookie jar. Aiden was still pacing and had been looking the other way. Close one. He glanced to Payson who had clearly seen.

She raised her eyebrows at him, and the corner of her mouth turned up into a sly grin. Aiden was about to rant again, when Payson put her feet up to block his path. "Aiden, sit," Payson commanded like a seasoned general. "Let's let Maddy decide what is best for her. She told us all what happened right away. She had me walk home with her. For now, she has agreed to not go anywhere alone. She already installed a fancy alarm system." He begrudgingly sat back down and opened his beer.

"No offense, Payson, but you don't look like much of a bodyguard." Aiden was sure on a roll. He was in full-on big brother mode. He shook his head judgmentally while taking his first swig of his beer. Sitting on the edge of the leather chair.

Maddy was about to jump to her defense when Payson interjected, "My muscles may not be as impressively bulky as yours, but I know some basic self-defense. Most importantly, Maddy can kick his ass while I call for help," she added with a smile at Maddy.

Maddy was clearly done with the debate. While the others watched for her reaction, she tipped up her bottle and gulped a large last swig of beer and abruptly rose from the couch. Gasping for a big breath after the large swig, she inquired in her best hostess voice, "Who's ready to go?"

Without waiting for an answer, she hopped up from the couch, grabbed a jacket and her flip flops, and headed for the front door. She grabbed her keys and phone from the entry table. She motioned for the others to go out the door first. "Well, I need to set this pretty new alarm. Everybody out."

The other three quickly obeyed and marched out the door. Chase made sure he was the last one out. As he passed Maddy, he stopped directly in front of her, leaned down, behind the cover of the open front door, and gently touched his lips to hers. The contact was brief, but intense. There was so much passion he could feel even with the brief contact. Chase knew he wouldn't be able to stay away any longer. He ran his hand through his chronically tousled hair as he stepped outside, joining the others.

Maddy and Payson led the way down the beach, laughing together about some shared joke. Chase and Aiden trailed behind as they walked down the beach toward the festival. The sun was starting to make its descent to the west, casting long shadows across the beach.

Salty ocean air swirled around in the warm sea breeze. The heat from the day kept the sand just on the comfortable end of hot.

He tried paying attention to his friend but couldn't have said what he was talking about. He managed an occasional "uh-huh." Watching Maddy's long legs walking barefoot on the beach, hips swaying in the short cotton sundress, flip-flops in hand.

"What do you think?" Aiden asked.

Gorgeous. Sexy. Amazingly long legs that would wrap around him perfectly. Wavy brown hair that his hands ached to bury into. A hearty laugh that echoed deep into his core. Wait, what? "What?" Chase managed to respond, completely lost.

"Man, are you hearing anything I'm saying? You're in your own little world today. Not sleeping much?" Aiden shoved his friend in the shoulder playfully.

"Sorry, no. I'm not sleeping much," although he didn't tell Aiden that he couldn't sleep because he was overwhelmed thinking about Aiden's sister. He lied, "I'm just thinking about how to set up the new fishing tour."

Aiden shook his head in disbelief, laughing at his friend. "Man, you're just like Dad. Head always stuck on the boat." Man, his friend was dense.

They arrived at the beach party in time to see the beach volleyball tournament coming to a close. A crowd surrounding the winning team jumped and cheered. Families were packing up their picnics, taking young children home for bed. Others were lighting bonfires to welcome the night.

The foursome joined some old friends at one of the larger bonfires. They roasted hot dogs and marshmallows, reminiscing with people he hadn't seen in years. Chase remembered moments like these when he was younger. Days like these made up for so many lonely days at home.

Chase sat at Aiden's side, burying his toes in the warm sand. Chase enjoyed the downtime with his old friend.

His eyes, however, were only for Maddy. She laughed and visited with others, introducing Payson to some old friends that were in town visiting. Aiden nudged his side. "What about you?"

Chase realized he'd been watching Maddy again and hadn't been listening. He picked a response, "Sure."

"Earth to Chase. Come on, when was the last time you got laid? I know you haven't since you've been back. It's like you've been in your own little celibate bubble," Aiden teased, "What'd they do to you on that rig? Some woman leave you broken hearted?"

Wow, Aiden hadn't noticed Chase making the moves on his sister the past few weeks. Lucky. He knew Aiden would kick the shit out of him if he knew even half of the thoughts that passed through his head. Most of those thoughts involved Maddy naked and doing very erotic things to him. He coughed to hide his smile. "I guess my mind has been... otherwise occupied."

"You've been watching Elena for the past hour. Didn't you and she have a thing senior year?"

What? He looked around, finally spotting Elena. He hadn't even noticed she was here. He realized Elena was standing and talking with Maddy. They'd had a very brief but mutually satisfying interlude in her parent's basement senior year. She was still gorgeous, but he wasn't the least bit interested.

Aiden went on, "She's been checking you out all night, too. I think she lives in those apartments across the street."

Chase shrugged nonchalantly.

"Come on, Chase. You need to get out there, with Elena, or whoever might float your boat. I holed up when I first got back too, but it's time to get back out there again. Promise me you'll make a move.

Tonight's looking like a good night." Aiden's voice drifted, his gaze was elsewhere. Making plans for himself.

He grinned and toasted his friend. "Aiden, you have my promise on that one. It has been way too long." Aiden was going to kill him when he found out exactly what Chase was promising.

Chase gulped down the last of his beer and hopped to his feet. Heading toward Maddy and her friends, he walked around the fire and approached the group. "Ladies. Enjoying your evening?"

Payson nudged him in the arm. "You and Aiden done gazing into each other's eyes over there?" Man, that woman was wicked, but she could put about anyone at ease with just a look and a joke. "Come on, Sean's grabbing a football from his truck. A friendly little round of touch football?"

He shook his head with a smile, "Aren't we all getting too old for touch football?"

"Depends on who's doing the touching," Payson teased again with a wink.

Damn, he couldn't get away with anything around her. Elena jumped on board and recruited a number of their old friends, Aiden included. She even managed to rope in newcomer Natalie, who was notoriously reserved.

Sean raced down onto the beach with a few other guys and set up a few spotlights and cones for the game. Chase hadn't ever played competitive football, but he'd always enjoyed the game. He ran over to help them with set-up.

Elena and Payson got to pick teams. Elena nabbed Maddy first. Wait, what?

Shit. He forgot about Maddy's football skills. She had a mean spiral and an outrageously competitive spirit. It took a few more rounds before anyone picked him. Didn't surprise him; there were several guys from their high school team present. At least he wasn't picked last.

Glad he kept in shape; the game was surprisingly intense. He hadn't laughed that much in a very long time. Payson couldn't throw worth crap, but she was surprisingly fast in her delicate flowered sundress. No one had been able to catch her so far. She made a great teammate and was somehow as competitive as Maddy. No wonder they were such good friends.

Sharply calling his name, Payson tossed a lateral as Aiden came close to catching up to her. He smoothly caught the clean toss and headed for the goal. Out of nowhere, he heard Maddy run at him from the side. With a battle cry worthy of the ancient highlanders, she threw her body against him with incredible force. Apparently, the game upgraded to tackle when Maddy switched to defense.

As he flew to the ground, gripping the ball tightly in his extended hand to make the TD, his other arm wrapped up Maddy and pulled her in close, protecting her from crashing into the sand. She was fucking crazy. As they crashed into the sand together, she curled into him, allowing him to break her fall. Neither wanted to move at first, laughing and enjoying the closeness. Until they realized where they were, with all of their friends watching.

"Woohoo!" Payson ran toward them, grabbing the ball out of his hand. "6 points," she hollered as she danced around with the ball.

Maddy jumped up and brushed off the sand. With a huge smile, she gave him a hand up. "Nicely done Anderson, but game's not over yet," she taunted. She caught the ball Payson had tossed to her to start the next play. With a wink back to Chase, Maddy strutted back to the line of scrimmage. It was on.

Next play, he went in for the sack. Maddy did a smooth juke as he got closer, but foolishly moved closer to the incoming tide. She was only a few steps ahead, going for a running play.

Water splashed at their feet as he subtly drove her closer to the water in her efforts to escape him. As she neared the endzone, he caught up to her and grabbed her, throwing her over his shoulder.

Anticipating his move, she tossed a quick backward pass to Aiden to finish the play. Chase didn't give a damn; she had been the goal anyway. But he should have known better than to think he'd caught her. From over his shoulder, she rotated her body around him and dragged him down with her, right into the oncoming wave.

Both were encompassed in the crashing sandy, salty wave. The huge wave was totally unexpected. They were briefly caught as the undertow tried to pull them out to sea. Chase held Maddy close as the wave tossed them around, waiting for the calm. When it came, he pulled her out with him. The crash had been intense; he'd expected her to panic.

He should have known better. In all his years in some intense ocean waves, he'd known some experienced divers that wouldn't have handled the surprise swell with such ease. She'd relaxed her body as the wave had overcome them and the undertow tried to pull them out, but held on tightly to him, trusting him to pull them out of it. Her bravery, her trust was... humbling.

Standing straight as the wave receded, Maddy grabbed his hand and led him out of the water. He lagged behind, helplessly enthralled. She looked back at him and gave him a seductive smile. Shit, she was incredible. Others looked on, making sure they were ok.

Releasing her hand, he pulled off his soaking wet shirt to ring it out. Not wanting to attract too much attention to their bond, he hollered, "Did they get the touchdown?"

As always, he could count on Payson. She hopped over to him and gave him a big high-five. "Nice tackle. He caught it but was no match for my amazing speed," she paused, looking to Aiden's shrug. "That's a game, we win!" His team cheered, giving their own high-fives and hoorah's. He joined in but couldn't help but keep glancing back to Maddy.

She pulled up her dress to a not-quite indecent level to ring it out. His gaze landed on her thighs, quietly hoping she'd forget where she was and pull the dress up just another inch. The wet dress clung to her everywhere. Glancing around, the others were drifting apart, either settling back into their spots by the fire or heading home. He watched Aiden leaving... and not alone.

Watching from a nearby bonfire, Dylan felt his rage boiling under the surface. He maintained a pleasant face, making boring conversation with old friends from school in a veiled attempt to win them over. Everyone was so fucking happy. Life was just peachy. What the fuck?

They welcomed Aiden and Chase into their midst, forgetting all the trouble they had caused in this town before abandoning it. Cheering them on in the rather crass football game. All the while he, Dylan, a respectable businessman with a real vision, had to charm his way into the fold. This town didn't share his vision. He'd make them.

When that bitch had turned on him and he wound up in jail, he didn't sit and pout, biding his time like a kicked puppy. He made some good friends, solid connections.

His father certainly had broken more than a few financial rules in his own rise to power, so Dylan's bending a few laws to set his life in order had only been natural. After getting out, he'd started buying up small businesses, then breaking them down to expand his own wallet. Filling the pockets of his associates, building a solid organization.

Now, he needed to make Maddy his again. He had waited years, until he had powerful connections, so he could make a grand entrance back into town. Fucking Chase had arrived a day after and stole his thunder. Everyone talked about Chase Anderson, how much he'd grown up, his plans to strengthen the community. He'd take care of Chase.

And he'd make Maddy watch. She'd never turn against him again. His colleagues questioned his move to take over Seaview and win back his girl, but he'd earned their unquestioning loyalty. They knew better than to defy him.

He'd made mistakes with Maddy before, and dammit he'd made a mistake again today. He shouldn't have stopped her in the street. He just couldn't think clearly when she was around.

He still had several tools at his disposal, including a foolproof back-up plan if she didn't fall into line. Better than those morons that had gotten themselves arrested. He'd have to step it up a notch. And be sure they knew Maddy was not to be touched. As soon as that lout was released, he'd answer to Dylan for hurting her.

Dylan ignored the inane conversation around him to watch Maddy. She was wearing a very short sun dress. Despite the ridiculous game, despite her dunk in the water with that asshole... he wished he could have taken pictures of her ringing out the bottom of her skirt, wet and clinging to her long legs.

He was so angry at himself for his mistake today; he knew it would cause a huge set-back. He wanted her, needed her. Waiting for her to come around was going to take too long.

Time to step things up a bit. He pulled out his phone and texted Nielsen. *Time to make our next move. Bring in the team. Start with the boats.*

21

MADDY WALKED UP THE beach toward Chase, soaked, feet covered in sand. It felt great to laugh with friends after such a long day. She hadn't felt so carefree in a long time. Who knew football was such a great stress-reliever? She waved goodbye to Payson as her friend headed back to her apartment above Flotsam Antiques. Where was Aiden?

Maddy said goodnight to old friends. Finally alone, she walked straight toward Chase who had completed his farewells. She stopped in front of him, putting her hands on her hips. Their eyes met as he looked down at her. Soaking wet bodies just centimeters apart. She'd never felt so... desired.

"Where's Aiden?" Maddy asked, grinning up at Chase.

"He left. With a girl," Chase responded. "He thinks Payson is walking you home tonight and that you're planning a girl's night tonight. I may have let him think I planned on going home with Elena tonight." Chase laughed and shook his head, "Your brother is a smart guy, but not when it comes to his little sister. I was practically drooling over you, all evening. Shit, I can't stop thinking about yesterday. And tonight," he paused, taking a few deep breaths.

He shook his head to clear his thoughts. "Anyway, I didn't want to let him in on my actual plans for tonight, as I suspect he would have ruined our plans. So, I let him think I was checking out Elena." He grinned at his own cleverness.

She laughed as they walked hand-in-hand down the beach. "You're so clever," she rolled her eyes. "That boy is a bit dense. But, works out in my favor tonight. Nice tackle, by the way."

Chase shook his head, wincing, "Payback's a bitch, but I really didn't mean to land us in the water. I am sorry about that," he paused, looking her up and down, appreciating the wet dress clinging to her.

Like her, she suspected, he was feeling completely overwhelmed, imagining what was going to happen when they got home.

After an absurdly longer-than-usual walk back to her cabin, they'd finally arrived. He followed her in the front door and patiently watched her adjust the alarm for the night. Maddy suddenly felt nervous.

She'd been thinking about this for too long. So many fantasies built up, but now what? She wasn't any good at this.

Looking over her shoulder, she gave Chase her best come-hither look, and strolled into the bedroom. That was about as brave as she got. What was she going to do with him when he followed? She stopped next to the bed and turned toward him, watching him walk towards her like a tiger stalking its prey.

He walked slowly, his eyes locked with hers. He stopped when their bodies were just inches away. They weren't even touching and Maddy was on fire with anticipation. The heat at odds with her freezing cold, soaking wet dress. He looked down and grazed his hand along her cheek. "Maddy, I want you so bad. I've wanted you for so long."

Maddy could hardly concentrate. Looking into his eyes, she became spellbound by his steady gaze. "Please," she begged, her breath catching. Chase grasped her hips, his grip scorching against her ice-cold body. He pulled her in close.

His smiled victoriously as his lips finally met hers. He pressed his lips gently against hers, slowly teasing. Maddy's heart raced at his gentle touch. Heat curled through her as his tongue invaded and began an erotic dance with hers.

She gasped as he deepened the kiss, his hands gripping her sides and pulling her hips against his own. He slid her wet cotton dress slowly up around her hips. His warm hands caressed her bare skin as he continued to kiss her deeply.

Chase finally ended the kiss and pulled away a few inches. He pulled her dress further up her abdomen, gently caressing her wet skin on the way up.

She couldn't stand the waiting. Remembering his mouth on her breasts that night in the truck, nearly coming at his touch, his mouth on her yesterday afternoon, her wanton response as she cried out in orgasm.

Goodbye hesitance. Farewell shitty memories.

Feeling emboldened, she slipped off her dress the rest of the way, tossing it aside. Hearing it land with a wet slap against the floor. She unclasped her bra and brought his hands to her breasts, no longer feeling shy. He groaned with pleasure and quickly obeyed.

He ravenously grasped her breasts in his hands, teasing her tight nipples with his thumbs. She moaned as he increased pressure, encouraging him further. He leaned down and ran his tongue across her breasts, setting her afire. Heat overcoming the cold. He wrapped his mouth around her taught nipple and sucked... hard.

Liquid heat radiated out from her core, setting her on fire.

"More," she desperately pleaded. He quickly obeyed, and moved slowly downward, trailing kisses as he slid her soaked panties off. He backed her down onto the bed, mouth never leaving her body.

Tongue trailing up her inner thigh, leaving an electric hum in his wake, he drew closer, circled, then pressed firmly against her core. She cried out and her body trembled, quickly remembering the orgasm he'd given her yesterday. And his own response. Her hips instinctually rocked as his tongue laved and rubbed her core.

Her soft cries turning frantic as he increased speed and pressure. She couldn't hold back as the orgasm built, and finally ripped through her. Tearing her apart in a blissful shattering. Tenderly, he kissed his way back up her abdomen, taking a quick nip at her breast on the way up. With pure male satisfaction, he grinned up at her.

Maddy laughed back at his smugness. He sat up to his knees. His body was incredible, his abs ripped from years of intense physical training. He unzipped his soaking cargo shorts, looked down at her and hesitated, silently waiting for her response.

Maddy sat up on her knees to get closer to him. Brushing her sensitive breasts against his chest. Needing to be close to him, she pressed her body against his, pressing soft kisses along his neck. His frantic pulse raced against her lips.

Following instincts, her hands trailed down his body, caressing his incredible abs as she moved south. She slowly pushed his shorts over his hips, sliding her hand down his sopping wet briefs. Grasped his already throbbing iron-hard cock, cold from the ocean-water but burning in her touch regardless.

Chase groaned in response as she ran her fingers along the satin shaft, exploring. Without warning, she grasped near the base firmly, immensely enjoying his sharp intake of breath. "Damn, Maddy. I'm already just barely hanging on."

Pulling back from her, he stood and stripped off the rest of his wet clothes. He grabbed a condom from the cargo pocket of his shorts and tossed his clothes aside, adding them to their pile of salt-water soaked clothes. Chase stood in front of her, his eyes serious now. "Are you sure?"

Maddy's eyes locked onto his, she ran her hands down his taught, muscled arms, his skin hot under her touch. "Yes, I want this."

Chase watched as Maddy lay back down on the bed, her incredible body bare before him. Appreciatively, he stood for a moment and drank her in as her gaze held his own, daring him to make his move. He had been sure she'd be nervous, after all she'd been through.

But, she hadn't been the least bit shy. Her orgasm had rocked through him, maybe affecting him more than her. He hadn't anticipated such an unbridled response; he was again amazed at how she didn't hold back, in anything. He slid on the condom and lowered his body over hers.

Allowing himself a moment to savor, he pressed his sheathed cock against her core, rocking against her. Breathlessly, she begged, "I can't wait anymore, please." Neither could he. Slowly, he slid inside. She was so tight around him, so hot.

He groaned in pure pleasure and rocked slowly as she adjusted to him, trying to take it slow for her. She grasped his hips and pulled him in deeper, pleading for more. Her eagerness drove him on. She kept pace as he pumped faster and harder. She cried out his name as she climaxed, stirring his own.

Sated, they breathed heavily together, his body crushing her underneath him. "Sorry, I meant to take that slow," Chase apologized as he rolled off of her, dragging her with him so her head rested on his shoulder.

Her body began to tremble and shake. Uh-oh. He had gotten carried away; he'd meant to be gentle, but she'd been so wild in his arms, he lost control. He felt like a complete ass for making her cry.

Then she started to laugh out loud and he looked down at her face. She was lost in a laughing fit. "Uh, Maddy, you ok?" he smiled hesitantly.

"Yes, you ridiculous man. I'd never been laid properly. That was... incredible... wow. When can we go again?" Maddy managed to control her laughter, sporting a huge grin as she waggled her eyebrows at him.

Chase found himself laughing with her. "Give me a moment, I'm not a machine." He hopped up and headed for the bathroom. He returned to find her still laying naked on the bed, the sheets completely tossed off the bed. A goofy grin still pasted on her face. She lay on her side, watching him walk toward her.

She looked so hot, her cheeks still flushed, a gleam of sweat covering her lean body. Those breasts. Damn, she was more amazing than he could ever have expected.

He reached down and tossed the blankets back onto the bed and slid in next to her. Without pause, he moved straight in and kissed her deeply. "If I'm only getting you for one night, I'm making the most of it. You ready to go again?" Hand already between her legs, teasing for a response. "I think I could go all night... Shit, I only had the one condom."

Again, she laughed. Maddy leaned over to her bedside table and tossed a box of condoms at him. "I've been wanting to jump you for weeks. I'm prepared."

Before Chase could respond, she nudged him onto his back, ripped open a condom and slid it over his already hard length. He about came as she gripped him. He found he enjoyed her bossiness. Her new sense of empowerment when it came to his naked body. He'd created a monster... a sexy, insatiable monster.

"Don't move," she commanded. Slowly lowering herself onto his erection, she straddled him, riding him like a warrior goddess. Holy shit she was hot. She took him deep and rocked her hips.

Overwhelmingly touched by her trust in him, her uninhibited passion, his heart took a nosedive. He'd let her think one night would be enough, but he knew himself better than that. Maybe she did too.

Sitting above him, her hips rhythmically grinded against him. She was so close. On an impulse, he took her hands and placed them on her own breasts, guiding them under his own as he caressed. Caught in the moment, she caught on quickly and took over, pleasuring herself atop him. For a moment, he watched as she sensually caressed her own breasts, grinding her hips against him. Fuck, she was so amazing.

His own hands glided down to her hips, moving her faster and harder against him. With a cry, she squeezed him tight; he kept the rhythm and held her peaked with pleasure until he couldn't hold back his own anymore, until they came together, exhausted and satisfied.

Sunlight streamed in through the narrow opening in the curtains hours later. Maddy lay on her side, Chase's body spooning her own. She smiled inwardly, remembering their night. Her initial shyness had flown right out the window, when she finally accepted that she was completely safe with Chase.

He had been so attentive and thorough. She should be embarrassed for jumping on him and riding him like that, but somehow, she wasn't. They'd finally crashed hard and slept for a few hours. Sometime during the night, he'd woken her and taken her again in the moonlight.

She quietly slipped out of his arms and made her way into the bathroom. Maddy turned on the water for her shower and brushed her teeth while the water heated.

Her poor brain was a sex-hazed mush, her thoughts never straying far from his incredible body, those outstanding abs, his smug grin after he'd brought her to yet another orgasm, the way he ensured she felt safe and satisfied. She nearly choked on the toothpaste, she was so distracted thinking about the night before.

Stepping into the steamy shower, Maddy faced the hot spray, closed her eyes and let the water soothe her sore muscles. A cool draft wafted over her as Chase stepped in behind her. Now acutely aware of his every move, she anxiously awaited his touch.

Wordlessly, he stepped close behind her, reached around her to grab the soap, and started creating a bubbly lather over her body, taking extra care to ensure her breasts were squeaky clean. Maddy chuckled at his persistence. From behind her, she could feel him smiling at his own cleverness.

Turning in his arms, Maddy faced him and took the soap from his hands. "Your turn." The soap glided smoothly across his hard, wet body. As she moved down to stir his interest, she noted he was ready for her. The soap slipped from her hands as he picked her up and took her against the shower wall.

22

Maddy couldn't help the dopey grin that was stuck to her face. She slipped on a comfy pair of distressed jeans and a camisole while Chase finished up in the shower. She left a spare toothbrush on the bathroom counter for him and headed to the kitchen to make coffee.

As she crossed the living room in her bare feet, the doorbell rang. Who would be ringing her doorbell this early on a Sunday? Well, not that early. They'd been up all night, so they slept in. Maybe if she just ignored it?

Whoever was out there put a key in the lock and slowly opened the door. Shit. Maddy suddenly regretted giving Aiden a key and the alarm code. He entered arrogantly, his own dark hair mussed from the night before.

"Morning, sis," he greeted her with a sleepy grin.

Maddy silently willed Chase to stay in the bathroom. "Morning," she nodded back, trying for nonchalance.

"I see Chase's truck is out front still." Maddy froze, but before she could panic, Aiden laughed, "I just had to make the damn walk of shame down the beach. Thought I'd snag some coffee and sit out on your deck and heckle him as he tries to sneak back to his truck. Poor guy had been twitchy, it had been so long since he'd gotten any. Maybe he's loosened up a bit. Come on." Aiden started for the kitchen to poor his coffee, when he saw movement coming from Maddy's bedroom.

Maddy suddenly forgot how to swallow... or even breathe when she saw Chase coming out of her bedroom without a shirt, his freshly washed and dried cargo shorts hung low over his hips, and a toothbrush sticking out of his mouth. It was pretty obvious when he saw Aiden and realized they were busted. He pulled the toothbrush out of his mouth and swallowed his mouthful of toothpaste.

Poor Aiden's head turned so fast back and forth between his best friend and his sister as he struggled to make the connection. He scrunched his brow in confusion. His mouth opened and closed like a fish out of water as he struggled to find words. No longer the glib lawyer.

Chase spoke first, managing to break the silence with a cautious, "Good morning."

Aiden's fists clenched at his sides and Maddy could almost see the steam escaping from his ears as he fumed. His feet planted firmly to the ground. He was caught in a desperate battle to maintain his cool. Through gritted teeth, he managed to ask, "What. The. Fuck?"

Maddy saw when her brother snapped. This time, he didn't pace back and forth, but he marched straight up to Chase. Both stood tall with their chests puffed out like angry gorillas. He stopped about a foot away and looked ready to pummel his friend.

Chase held his ground, looking equally scary. His own fists clenched at his sides, the muscle in his jaw tensing rapidly. Chase was about to speak, when Aiden let loose. "What the hell man? That's my baby sister. She's been through enough and doesn't need you messing with her life right now." He shoved Chase's shoulder.

Chase didn't take the bait but held his ground.

Maddy stormed to her brother and whacked his deltoid. She took pride in her ability to respond calmly and articulately. That was completely gone all of a sudden.

She raged, "Are you nuts? Messing with my life? I make my own decisions and don't need your hovering, protective big-brother-meets-caveman attitude. Yes, I've had some record-breakingly terrible relationships, but you're just as bad off. I didn't ask you why you came home when you did; why you buried your head in the sand for months. Back. Off."

She stormed into the kitchen to make the coffee. Maybe it was the late caffeine intake causing her headache, but more likely it was her headache of a brother. She knew he meant well. Certainly, she had never intended for him to find out this way.

Not that there was a good way to tell him she had a wild, erotic night with his best friend. Although, if they kept it to the one night, he'd never have needed to know at all.

The thought of not being held in Chase's arms again was downright heart-wrenching. Fighting her own internal battle and Aiden's appropriately furious response, Maddy tore off to the kitchen to make that coffee.

Shit. Chase hadn't meant for Aiden to find out this way. What a way to tell his friend he'd had the hots for his sister.

Although, it was *really* lucky he wasn't here fifteen minutes earlier when they'd been in the shower. His body pressing hers against the tile. The hot water running over them; her slick, pliant body wrapped around him. Her crying out his name as she came in his arms. He shook the image out of his head. Not a good time to get a hard-on.

"Aiden, I am so sorry you had to find out like this. Please, stay right here, I want to talk to you." Chase raced back into the bedroom, put down the toothbrush, swallowing a thick minty glob, and pulled on his black t-shirt. Aiden had followed him and was now leaning against the bedroom doorjamb, arms crossed. He hadn't lost the I'm-going-to-tear-you-to-pieces scowl, but at least he'd waited to hear him out.

Chase walked up closer to Aiden, his arms held out forward in peace, hoping to calm the situation. Hoping Aiden would keep it down so they could talk out of earshot from Maddy. Chase imagined she was still furious. Although, she'd looked more scared than angry, and Chase knew she wasn't afraid of Aiden. He suspected she'd been much more scared of herself and their night together.

Aiden spoke quietly, "It was my sister you were watching last night, not Elena, wasn't it?"

Chase sighed, hoping he could convince his friend this was a good thing. Hopefully a really good thing. If he didn't blow it. He'd need some help from Aiden in that regard.

"I know how this looks, but it's not like that. Last night was the first time we..." He left the next few details out, sparing his friend the visual. But he might as well go all in. "And, I sure as hell hope it's not the last." His expression pained, he awaited his friend's response with bated breath.

Aiden softened a bit, maybe remembering his friend was not a complete asshole. "How long has this been brewing?" He pointed his finger back and forth between Chase and Maddy across the house.

Making sure he could still hear Maddy moving around in the kitchen, Chase lowered his voice to barely a whisper, "Forever... Aiden, please, be ok with this." He sighed, trying to find the right words. "She's still pretty skittish about anything serious. Please don't scare her off. I can't lose her." Chase could hardly swallow for the lump in his throat.

Aiden's expression was quickly becoming sympathetic. Like Chase had done, he listened for Maddy's movement in the kitchen before speaking. She was still tearing about the kitchen furiously.

Looking Chase right in the eyes, searching, he whispered softly, "Do you love her?"

Chase couldn't say it out loud, not yet, not before he'd even admitted as much to himself. Lips pursed tight, he nodded an affirmative.

Aiden's demeanor took on a dramatic change. He grinned and pulled Chase in for a manly hug and slapped him on the back, nearly knocking him over. "Good thing for you. I'd really hate to kill my best friend. You'd fucking better take good care of her or I'll kick your ass. If you can even convince her to keep your sorry ass around."

"As if you could kick my ass. Pansy-assed lawyer. But, if I do hurt her, I'll be begging you to kick my ass for me." The pair laughed companionably, glad to be back on the same page.

Maddy's shout from the kitchen was a welcome interruption. "Coffee's ready. I hope you two are still alive and unscathed."

Chase let out a big breath he hadn't realized he'd been holding in. He followed Aiden into the kitchen. Maddy handed each of them a steaming cup of coffee, black for Chase and with cream for Aiden, as each preferred. She stared at each in turn, looking back and forth between them suspiciously.

Aiden spoke first, "We're good. For now," he playfully eyed Chase with a feigned threat. He set his coffee down and pulled his sister in for a tight hug. Chase didn't want to interrupt, so he took his coffee out to the deck.

Maddy could hardly breathe with Aiden's arms squeezed firmly around her. "Maddy, I'm ok with this. You're both my best friends. But please, please don't hurt each other," he begged. "I'm not giving either of you up. I know you're scared, but don't hurt him. I don't think he'd survive it if you broke his heart."

"Him? What about me? What about all the crap that I've been through that you threw in his face a few minutes ago?" Maddy demanded as she wiggled her way out of his hug. Not that she wanted to draw attention to her own issues, but Aiden had sure taken a sharp about-face.

"Your skin is thick as a damn polar bear's hide. Nice try." Aiden raised his eyebrow at her in friendly challenge. He picked up his coffee and gulped down a big first sip. "I'll head on out. I need a shower myself. I'm stealing this coffee cup."

Maddy stopped him. "Wait a minute. Why were you making the walk of shame?" He ignored her. "This is a small town. I'll find out eventually..."

Aiden paused long enough to wink at his sister, then strolled out the front door, locking up behind him.

"Hypocrite." She rolled her eyes. Maddy grabbed her own coffee and headed to the deck.

Wordlessly, Chase shifted his coffee to his other hand as she joined him on the swing. He drew her in close against him; she curled her legs up and snuggled close. They companionably sipped their coffee in silence, soaking up the heat from the sun, warming the chill from the morning air.

Their one night had turned her world on end. Night over and she still wanted him, rather desperately in fact. And not just his body. Just sitting here like this, relaxed, silent, close... it was extraordinary. Not needing conversation, just co-existing in such satisfying harmony. Conversation was good with him too. Laughing with him, teasing, walking, talking, sleeping, eating... all amazing.

A firm clunk echoed through her chest. She was surprised he didn't hear the loud crash. The sound of her heart. Tripping, falling. Crap. What was she going to do?

23

Chase drove to work Monday morning, feeling ready to take on the world. He'd gone home just long enough Sunday afternoon to grab a change of clothes, then straight back to Maddy's. She hadn't invited him exactly, and he didn't ask. Both just... let it happen. And oh man, did it happen. And happen again. And again.

He knew he looked like a complete idiot with the smitten grin pasted to his face. They'd spent the rest of the weekend in bed. Having amazing, mind-blowing, earth-shattering sex. He'd enjoyed the non-sex parts, too. Maddy snuggling up against him, her need to be near him. Talking about the past and present, joking around. He'd even enjoyed cooking with her, which was usually a very solo activity for him.

As he hopped up the back stairs, he saw Brent arguing with the lawyers from the other day, with Dylan leading the pack this time. The rest of the office crew were peeking out of their office doors. Brent's voice was uncharacteristically raised, "I'm telling you, you'll have to wait for Frank to return. He's back next week and can take a meeting after he gets back."

Chase stepped in, hoping to diffuse the situation. "Gentleman. I believe I made our position clear when you were here last. We're not interested. Please see yourselves out, or I will contact our attorney, and quite possibly the police."

Dylan's face lit up as he jumped at the idea. He stepped up closer to Chase, sneaky smile on his face. "Why don't you call the police? I believe I saw Madelyn patrolling not far from here this morning. I'd sure love to see her; I'd like to hear all about her... interesting weekend. I hear she stayed in all weekend. Poor thing must not have felt well after the beach party. She'd gotten awfully... wet playing in those waves."

Chase seethed. Hearing Dylan call her Madelyn made him nauseous. It was one more power play, calling her by her formal name, that no one else called her, was sort of a declaration of intimacy. He'd seen Dylan eyeing Maddy during the festivities. He knew Dylan had watched them leave the party together. Now, he knew Dylan had been doing more than watching from afar.

Before Chase could come up with a response that didn't involve his fist, the oldest of Dylan's trio, the one who had done all the talking last time, Nielsen, interjected. "Please, none of us wants to involve the police –"

Chase couldn't help but interrupt, "I'll bet you don't want to involve the police. I wouldn't want to either if I were responsible for hiring thugs that have been arrested for breaking and entering, destruction of property."

Without missing a beat, Nielsen continued, "We heard about your break-in, and I'm so sorry that you're having to deal with that unpleasantness. We had nothing to do with it; please hear me out. We are truly presenting a great business opportunity for you and your crew.

Fisheries is a dying business around here. Your boats are in serious need of updating.

"Please, review the offer. I believe you will find it more than generous. We'd like to hold a meeting, open to the public, to present our proposal to buy out your property, and others with some upgrades to the waterfront, in detail. We've reserved the local grange hall, Thursday night, 7 o'clock. We'd like you to be there. You will be free to ask any questions. We're hoping to convince you this is the best thing for the town's future."

The man held out his business card to Chase. Chase shook his head, stepped forward and took the card. "Mr. Nielsen. We have no intention of selling out, for any reason. You can tear this place apart, but we're still not selling. I see that you're not leaving until you understand that. How about this, you can hold your meeting. I'll bring my own presentation so you can see where interested parties stand, and so my people can see where this company is going. I'll see you Thursday."

He watched as the men walked out the door. Chase turned to the office crew. "Well, you heard them. They want to tear down this building and put up a dock for their planned cruise ship stop. Then, they'll put in their own shops and run our local businesses out of town. Talk to your friends and family. We'll need their support if this gets ugly. We already suspect they sent those goons that were shuffling through the office and messing with our electrical system, which would have cut some of our critical refrigeration downstairs. I'm willing to bet that's the tip of the iceberg on what they're capable of."

Latasha, from accounts receivable, approached him first. "Chase, he's not wrong about the boats. Two of the boats couldn't launch yesterday and another this morning. Engine trouble, leak, broken fishing equipment. Maybe they're here, now, because they know how badly we need updates." A few others came closer, nodding in agreement.

Before Chase could respond, he heard Steve coming up the stairs. "I heard the whole damn thing. Load of baloney." He looked to the office crew, expression firm, "When's the last time we couldn't launch a boat, for any reason? Never, that's when."

He turned to Chase, "It is time to call the police back in. My boat's just back in for repairs; if we hadn't been as thorough as we are, we wouldn't have caught the flares jostling right next to the new fuel leak. Just waiting to ignite. Doesn't make a damn bit of sense. I smell foul play, and it reeks."

Chase nodded, in complete agreement. He had no doubt that Dylan wasn't playing fair. Now, he was endangering his crew. Chase answered questions as he made his way back to his office.

He didn't want to disturb Frank and Laura, but he didn't have a choice. Next week couldn't come soon enough. In the meantime, he needed to prove to Frank, the employees, and, mostly to himself, that he could handle this.

Steve couldn't have timed his entrance better. He wouldn't have lasted long without his experienced voice calling bullshit in front of the office staff. Sitting at his desk, he made a plan. He'd have to put off the new tourist boat for a bit. Safety, security, and repairs came first.

If their current safety checks hadn't been so effective, they could have been miles out when they ran into trouble. Dialing up a nearby security firm, he hired some emergency security guards and surveillance equipment. Subtly. He'd like to catch these assholes in the act.

24

MONDAY MORNING, MADDY BREEZED into work, cheerful and bearing coffee and bagels for her partner. She practically floated into the office area, still glowing from her weekend with Chase. She passed into the office area that was getting over-crowded with desks purchased from varying decades as the department expanded over the years.

For a small town, they had a pretty good-sized police department. Maddy passed her own scuffed wooden desk and sat on the corner of Ian's 1950's-era faded pea-green desk. Ian had eyed her suspiciously, "Maddy, you are awfully perky this morning. I thought you'd be upset about being chained to a partner until this bullshit with Dylan Mayberry blows over."

Maddy just smiled at Ian as she handed him the treats she had brought him. "Thanks for agreeing to be my partner. I am incredibly irritated that my routine is being altered due to an asshole I thought I'd been rid of years ago. But I appreciate you agreeing to partner up and wanted to show my thanks."

Ian accepted the treats appreciatively. He tore into the bagel with gusto. Cheeks full like an eager chipmunk, he began, "I checked in with Andrea already. We're on foot patrol today. Let's start with Beachside and circle outwards, sound ok? No calls or anything needing our attention, so I thought we'd go looking for trouble."

Count on Ian to look for trouble if none was to be had. Not that he always found it, or wanted it. But he had a good attitude about it. "Sounds like a plan," she grinned back at him, looking forward to the day.

The day started out pleasant, but that didn't last long. Maddy and Ian strolled out the front door, nodding to Quinn, who was in charge of the front desk and phones today. "You two take care out there. Peaceful so far." She smiled from under her coke-bottle glasses.

"Will do. Have a good one." Maddy nodded to the receptionist.

They walked out the front door, a blast of hot air taking her breath away as they stepped outside. When had it gotten so hot out? She'd wheeled and dealed enough with Andrea when she'd first started to get pants and shoes that breathed better than the old starch and leather, but the dang uniform was still thicker than she'd like, especially on hot days like today. Sliding her shades on, she scanned the streets. "Peaceful, but not quiet."

Pulling his shiny aviators on, Ian nodded in agreement. "Let's stroll by Flotsam on the way by, shall we?" He grinned at his partner.

"Nice try, Romeo," knowing Ian had a thing for Payson, but more for fun than anything. Ian was a few years younger and more than a few years less mature. "I already saw her this morning. I brought her a muffin before bringing you your bagel." She took off heading north.

"Such a spoil sport. Someday she'll come around and realize we're meant to be," he dramatically gripped his hand over his heart. Unconvincingly. "North, huh? Headed somewhere specific?"

"No, just wandering."

"Not hoping we can check in on McAllister Fisheries and your new boyfriend?" He waggled his eyebrows at her.

"After the break-in, it would be wise to check on McAllister Fisheries and ensure they had a safe weekend. And what gossip mill have you been tapping into?" News couldn't have traveled that fast, could it? Too damn small of a town to keep anything quiet for long.

"I happened to be driving by on my patrol when you got in from the beach party. With a Mr. Chase Anderson. Looking awfully cozy."

Maddy blushed. Dammit. At least it wasn't via grapevine. "Ok. It's not a secret or anything, I just hate being the object of gossip. Why do you think I ran away for so long?"

With a sympathetic punch to the shoulder, Ian was at least remorseful for the tease, "Sorry Maddy. We do have a hell of a gossip mill around here. I have not spread any gossip, just sharing a first-hand report to a first-person party."

Rolling her eyes at him, she kept strolling. When they finally got to McAllister Fisheries, and they saw Dylan and his goons coming out of the office, looking awfully pleased with themselves.

Shit. She quickly ducked back behind a nearby parked SUV. Hopefully, they were far enough away that they weren't spotted. As much as she wanted this over, she wasn't feeling it today. Talking to Dylan when she was too angry and ready to tear him apart... it wouldn't be very professional.

Ian read her signal immediately. He stayed close but kept the trio in his sights. And was pleasantly ignored as they hopped into a generic black sedan and cautiously pulled out onto the road, driving the opposite direction. Maddy let go of the breath she'd held in. "It's ok Maddy, he's gone."

"Thanks." She nodded in appreciation and continued on the prior trajectory. They strolled past McAllister's and veered east. About two blocks up, they stopped abruptly as they heard raised voices coming from the alley.

Not a dark, scary alley or anything, those didn't exist in Seaview. Not many alleys in general. Just a space between the old, unoccupied candy shop and a tall vacation house.

The pair silently crept closer, staying out of sight. "Don't you fucking tell me what's my business and what isn't. I saw you behind the restaurant with that local fuck. You're mine for the week. No play for anyone else."

Smack. Whoever was talking must have struck the other person. A woman's voice, with a thick midwest accent growled back at him, "Then you'd better pay me better. I promised you one week. That's it. One week. I never promised you monogamy or some shit like that."

Okay. Not a normal Seaview domestic dispute, that was for sure. Maddy and Ian eyed each other, waiting for the conversation to progress.

The gruff male voice started back in, "Bitch, I'm paying you a thousand dollars. A thousand fucking dollars for your company for a week. Don't you go blowing any other assholes just 'cause you get restless. I'm stuck in this tiny-ass town until this job's over. I've hired you to entertain me for the week, that means what I say, when I say, and who I say. If you want your cash and your ticket back home, you'd better behave yourself."

The voice paused. Maddy knew this wasn't heading anywhere good but went with her instincts and waited; it wasn't time to pounce yet. They needed more to go on.

Patience paid off. Fantastic. Sick bastard just couldn't stop. "Baby, you make up for it and give me the goods. Now."

"Fine. Just, fine. Behind the dumpster or someone will see."

Ears perked, Maddy waited until just the right moment. She inched closer, straining to hear. Yep, disgusting groans and... eww, sucking. "Yeah, baby, that's it. Suck it." Gross.

Maddy signaled to Ian that she was making her move. They confirmed the area was secure and moved in together. As expected, a bit of prostitution was going on right around the corner. The woman was on her knees delivering a nice early morning blow job for Mr. "In town on a job."

Maddy was eager to find out what that job might be, as she suspected a quick blow wasn't what he was in town for. "Good morning sir. I see you've found a lovely little spot to engage in a little business. However, you are, if you hadn't noticed, right out in public. If you both will just come with us, we'll get this little matter sorted out at the station."

Expletives flew out of the man's mouth, faster than the scantily clad woman spit out his dick. Without acknowledging his rapidly softening dick that was now flopping around, he paced back and forth before giving up for arrest.

Ian interjected, "Hey, pal. You're already looking at a number of charges here. Try putting your little friend away before you rack up any other charges." Like Maddy, Ian winced as he was subjected to the show.

Reading the pair their rights, Ian cuffed them while Maddy called for back up to drive the less-than classy folks back to the station for processing. "And you thought this was going to be a boring day," Maddy teased Ian.

He chuckled. "And I was hesitant about having a partner. I'm so glad I didn't have to witness that alone. Now, whenever you piss me off, I get to bring this special moment up and let your poor brain remember that... vivid image."

Rolling her eyes, she directed the perps to the main road as help arrived in the form of two SUVs for transportation. Back at the station, the perps were processed, and the mountain of paperwork completed. Andrea called Maddy and Ian back to her office. "Nicely done. I'm looking forward to reading your report."

Ian laughed, "I made sure to include every juicy detail for you."

Andrea winced, "Thanks Ian, I can always count on you to brighten my day."

She pointed to the matching guest chairs in front of the desk for Maddy and Ian to take a seat. "Maddy, do you mind running the interview? I'd like to know what he's doing in town for so long that he felt obligated to import paid female companionship. Why he was found so close to McAllister Fisheries, and why he was there right after Mayberry and his crew had left the area."

Maddy smiled, glad to have something meaningful to do. She'd done her share of interrogations for the Seattle PD. "You got it."

Lacking similar experience, Ian jumped in, "Can I join? You can be good cop and I'll be bad cop?"

Appreciating his eagerness to help, Maddy motioned him to follow. "How about you stay in the back and don't talk? Wear your best poker face while I do all the talking?"

"Fine. But next time I get to be bad cop." Ian practically hopped as he followed her to the back.

It was difficult to even look the sick bastard in the face after his little scene in the alley. Wearing her own best poker face, Maddy sat in the chair across the table. "Mr. Lang, I'd like to know what you're doing in our little town of Seaview, all the way from Chicago?" She smiled innocently at the perp.

He sneered, staying quiet at first. "I'm not saying nothing without my attorney."

"That's just fine Mr. Lang. You can wait for an attorney," she stood to walk out of the room but paused. "I ought to mention, your sweet lady friend didn't want to wait for her attorney, she bartered a deal and has a lot of information to share about you. And your boss," she went out on a limb, assuming he wasn't here of his own volition. "I'm looking forward to speaking with her in more detail. If you'll excuse me." She put her hand on the door, knowing he would object.

"Ok, ok. Hang on. I'll talk now. I'd sure like to avoid any... attention regarding my lady friend. Let's just let her be our little secret." He shuffled nervously.

"What are you doing in town Mr. Lang? What can you tell me about your boss?" Maddy got right to the point this time.

Avoiding eye contact, he started, "I... I'm doing a little work in town. My boss hires me to do little jobs for him here and there to lower the price on his business ventures."

"What property?"

"Some old fish plant, docks. And some bar. Crazy if you ask me. A lot of other docks without all the fuss."

"Why do you think he chose this spot?" Maddy already knew the answer but wanted to hear it from him. To confirm her fears.

"Some broad. Some bitch he's after. Says she owes him bigtime. Paying double his normal fees as it's so important to him. I been working for this joker for a few years. He pays decent, normally has a good head for business, but he's way off on this one.

"I don't mind giving him up if it means saving my ass, since he's already fucking this whole deal up. Coulda made a shit-ton of money too, got this cruise ship company on the line, ready to buy him out once he lays the groundwork. Fucker is blowing it, all because of this bitch. Which is why I only hire temps."

She knew she should wait, let Andrea take over, as she knew Andrea was listening in and chomping at the bit. She'd already skirted the line interrogating when her father's company was likely in the mix, but when she was a major part of the plot, she ought to get out. The guy was so riled up, he wasn't likely to stop now. And she didn't want him to. "What did Mr. Mayberry ask you to do to the docks?"

"Mayberry's talking through that Nielsen guy, never talks to me directly. I only seen him once in town, but I know he's in charge. Has been since he and Nielsen served time together. The brainy one. Nielsen says we're to be subtle, that they're already on to us. Just get in, do just enough damage to slow them down. Drive down the price."

Man, this guy was easy. She didn't even imply that he was getting any sort of deal for spilling the beans. Not her fault that he assumed that all on his own. "Who's the bitch Mayberry's after?"

"He won't say. Says we'll ruin it for him."

Before she could go further, Andrea pulled her out. As instructed, Ian had stayed silent in the corner, looking intimidating. He followed her out as well.

Maddy was immediately apologetic. "Sorry, I know I shouldn't get too close to this. By the time I confirmed who he worked for, I was afraid to end the interview, or he'd stop talking."

Andrea nodded. "I know, you did the right thing. We got enough to go on. I didn't want this going further than it needed to. Needed to get you out of there before you got yourself in too deep and we lost our footing."

"I know. I shouldn't have pushed."

"You're right. You shouldn't have. But I'm not sure I would have been able to resist either. You did good. We have a pretty stellar witness. Stupid, but stellar."

Nodding in agreement, Ian chimed in, "We got lucky. Bigtime. We saw him with his goons in the black sedan shortly before I wrote down the plates, maybe it'll get us somewhere."

"You're on. Run it, track them down. Maddy, I want to ask you some more questions about Mayberry. Come on into my office." Andrea was all business now. They didn't get many interesting cases around here. This one was a little too personal to be interesting, unfortunately.

Maddy filled Andrea in on what she knew about Dylan. Which turned out to be a lot. His obsessively high achievements in school: 4.0 GPA, membership in all the right clubs and sports. His father's questionable business practices. His mother's frequent travelling, was never around, no one knew what she was up to. Her relationship with him, how it ended. Andrea had already heard a lot of it but was drilling her on the minutiae now. Maddy was exhausted by the time she was done.

Maddy went into the locker room to change after her shift. Grateful to change out of her uniform on the hot day, she changed into ankle length skinny jeans and tucked in her breezy button up top.

She had agreed to not going anywhere alone. Ian had kindly agreed to escort her to Flotsam Antiques on his way home where she'd planned to meet up with Payson. Maybe his offer was self-serving, but she didn't care. He was a good sport regardless.

On the way, he filled her in on the info from the plates he'd run. Which was nothing. No information. Registered to a fake name at a fake address. Unlikely they'd use those plates again after Lang's arrest.

Payson was assisting a customer, so Maddy took a moment to relax and peruse the shop. She admired a few new pieces that had come in. There was a reclaimed wood side table that practically had her name written on it. She sat on the brown leather chair next to it and rested her eyes for a moment. Just a few moments of rest and she'd be good to go. Five minutes, that's all she needed.

"Boo!" Maddy about jumped out of the chair when she discovered Payson had snuck up behind her and booed in her ear.

She glared at her friend. "You are a truly horrible human being! You scared me to death."

Payson laughed, "Looks like someone needs more sleep. Stay up too late all weekend?"

Maddy's vision went all soft when she thought about her amazing weekend, suddenly forgiving her friend for scaring her. "Yes, I sure did. Thanks for asking."

"Uh-huh. Can I say I-told-you-so? Nature knows what she's do-ing." Payson nudged her friend playfully, then walked around the wagon wheel coffee table to sit on the floral settee across from her.

"In this case, yes, you can." Maddy didn't mind the occasional told-you-so, especially when it was meant affectionately.

"Yikes, I think you may be turning into a complete sap," Payson teased. " I have a date of my own tonight, so I'm ditching you. Chase agreed to keep you company as soon as he's off work."

"Really? And who is the lucky guy? Meet him through another online dating service?" Maddy replied with an eye roll. Her friend had been on a quest to find Mr. Perfect since before Maddy had met her. She'd had a remarkably terrible string of blind dates and had resorted to online dating last winter, but she still refused to give up.

"Hey, I'll have you know this one shows promise. He's a banker. Thirty years old. 5'10", black hair, blue eyes. Enjoys walks on the beach and drinking wine by the fire in a snowy ski lodge." Payson nodded stubbornly and put her hands on her hips defensively.

"Sorry, I shouldn't have been sarcastic. I really hope this one is *the one*." Maddy felt for her friend. Their love lives had run in completely opposite directions since meeting each other. Payson had a regular, but terrible dating record. Maddy hadn't dated at all.

"I'm not optimistic, but worth a try. Who knows?" Payson sighed, resigned. "Let's get you home so we can both get ready for a hot night," Payson teased.

Downright sweltering outside, they decided against walking. Payson drove her home. Maddy waved back to Payson when she made it safely inside the house. She turned the alarm to home-mode and headed into her bedroom.

The bed was a disaster after 48 hours of fairly constant inhabitance. She worked up a sweat pulling off the sheets and starting a load of laundry. Old cabin meant no air conditioner. She opened a few windows to catch the breeze off the ocean, adjusting the alarm accordingly.

According to Payson, Chase hadn't hesitated when she had called him requesting that he babysit Maddy tonight so she could go on her hot date. Although Maddy was not thrilled about the term 'babysitting,' she was glad he wanted to come over. A night apart had been his idea. He'd been trying to give her space, which she hadn't wanted, but hadn't argued as she wasn't ready to tell him yet that she didn't want to give him up.

He would be here in a few hours, and she wanted everything freshened up and ready for a relaxing evening... or hopefully a not so relaxing evening. Maddy calmed her overactive libido and put crisp white sheets on the bed, tidied the blankets, fluffed the pillows.

She stood in the doorway, hands on her hips, and admired her handiwork. Nothing was quite so inviting as clean white sheets and a plush down comforter, facing out the window toward the ocean...

What the...? Something caught her eye on the far wall. Just above the curtain rod was a circular dark spot she hadn't noticed before. Huh.

A spider? She wasn't afraid of spiders, but certainly she didn't want one crawling on her while she slept. Or while she was awake for that matter.

And, she wasn't convinced it was a spider. She walked just to the side of it and pulled a chair over to get a better look. Her heart stopped when she realized what it was.

A camera. Forcing air in and out of her paralyzed lungs, she slowly lowered herself off the chair. Tiptoeing, foolishly trying to avoid detection, she focused on moving one foot in front of the other as she escaped the tainted room. Before she fell into a complete panic attack. Breath in 2, 3, 4... shit, she sucked at meditation.

Grabbing her phone from the entry table, she called Andrea as she lowered herself slowly to the floor before she passed out. "Andrea, it's Maddy. I... he... there's a... spy-cam... in my bedroom." She forced herself to breathe in and out.

Maddy could hear Andrea getting up quickly from her desk. "I'm on my way. I'm bringing Mike with me. He's good with tech stuff. Stay where you are." Fearing she'd lose it if she spoke out loud, she nodded, knowing Andrea wouldn't wait for her agreement.

She sat frozen on the floor, legs pulled in tight, afraid to move while she waited for Andrea and Mike. Now she knew where the spare keys had gone.

The terrifying revelation crashed over her in a tidal wave. That day in Portland; she'd rushed out the door so quickly she hadn't locked up.

It was the next morning that she'd noticed her spare keys were missing. Had he installed the camera that day, or come back later?

She hated to think of him coming in multiple times. She'd have to change out all of her keys. At least she had the new alarm system. The security company was top notch; he'd have to be ridiculously skilled to get past it.

The doorbell startled her, interrupting her freaked out, overwhelmed brain. Andrea had made good time. After confirming who was at the door with the video monitor, she let her boss and coworker in. Andrea pulled her in for a quick, sympathetic hug, then got straight to business. "Where is it?"

Maddy pointed to the bedroom, "Above the curtain rod."

Without more than a nod in greeting, Mike got straight to work. Within minutes, he had removed the camera and moved on to sweep the house for any other surveillance equipment. While he worked, Andrea took down her story.

"I know it was Dylan, but I can't prove it."

Andrea looked her in the eye, "We'll figure this out. I agree, Dylan is the obvious suspect, but we will stay open to any possibilities. We'll get the evidence when Mike analyzes the camera. Until that time, I don't want you leaving the house alone, and when you are home, the alarm is set and connected directly to the station if anything triggers the alarm." Maddy nodded in agreement, shivering despite the heat.

Andrea continued to pick Maddy's brain and talk over the possibilities while Mike finished his sweep. It had taken nearly two hours, but finally Mike came out of the guest bathroom. "Maddy, I can assure you, this was the only device. I did a full sweep. I know my stuff, I did a lot of tech work in Chicago," he looked her in the eyes as he ensured she was convinced. He'd worked for the Chicago PD before "retiring" to their little seaside town.

Maddy nodded, "Thanks, Mike. Can you tell me anything about the camera?"

Mike sat on the chair across from her. "It's pretty basic. Anyone could find it online. No audio. Video only. I suspect it has limited Bluetooth capability. From what I've seen in similar devices, I'd say the perp had to be within 100, maybe 200 meters to pick up any signal. I'll do some research and confirm." He collected his gear and headed out, passing her another sympathetic look before heading for the door.

"Hang on Mike," Andrea stopped him. She looked to Maddy. "You said Chase should be here any minute? We'll hang on until he gets here. You going to be ok?"

Maddy again nodded. "I'll be fine. Not my first rodeo, unfortunately. Different strategies, same asshole. You'll let me know if he sends you anything incriminating or tries to get in touch with you?"

She continued, knowing Andrea would need more details, and feeling grateful she had a boss she felt comfortable enough to be so open. "As he escalated last time, when I didn't respond how he wanted, he started undermining my pillars. My reputation at school and my plans for the future, communication with family and friends. He knew how much those pictures wouldn't just ruin my chance at working in the law, but knew how deeply they would upset me. I was very... reserved about my own body; mostly thanks to his insults."

Bastard. He was freaking obsessed with showing her and others... her. Knowing how private she was and how much it would bother her. Maybe he felt powerful holding that over her. Or, maybe he was just a freaking creep.

Andrea replied, "Maddy, look me in the eye. We will handle this. I will keep you fully in the loop. You call me if you even smell something funny, got it? You go anywhere I'm not expecting, you call me first."

Grateful yet again for her incredible boss, Maddy promised to run everything by Andrea. "Really, thanks."

They heard Chase's truck pulling in, so Andrea and Mike took their leave. Maddy got up to walk them to the door, disabling the alarm to let them out, "Be careful," Andrea said as they left. Maddy stood in the doorway. She watched them wave to Chase as they hopped into their Explorer. Chase's concern was almost palpable. He watched the Explorer drive off and looked back to Maddy with question.

"Hey there. You ok? What was that all about?" Chase asked as he walked in the house, setting the home-alarm himself after locking the front door. He followed Maddy into the kitchen, setting a bag of groceries on the counter.

Before he could say anything, she threw herself into his arms for a desperately needed hug. Later she'd consider freaking out that things were moving so fast between them, but not now. She needed him, and it just felt right. His powerful arms wrapped around her.

She basked in his warmth. Inhaling his scent, somehow always like a fresh sea breeze, and something indescribably masculine, so very Chase.

Pulling her in tight, he kissed the top of her head. His legs braced apart, leaning against the counter and holding her tight against him. Waiting for her to speak, when she was ready. It was too much.

For the first time, she allowed a few tears to seep out. Then a few more. Her body trembled. If he hadn't been holding her up, she would've crumbled to the ground. His hand gently rubbed her back, soothing as best he could.

With a sniffle, she pulled back. She grabbed a paper towel and dried off the tears. Done with the crying jag, she crumpled up the paper towel and threw it forcefully in the garbage. Stupid paper; it fluttered gently to the trash. Argh. She wanted to throw something, tear something, scream and rage.

25

"Ready to talk about it?" With her sudden shift to angry, Chase stayed put, trying not to look too sympathetic. He knew her too well. The anger helped.

She filled him in, not letting the tears come back. Her hands kept busy to distract from her whirl of emotion. Maddy uncorked the bottle of wine he'd brought, pouring them each a glass. She told him all about the camera, Mike's impressions, Andrea's promise to investigate.

"Why can't he just move on? Why cameras? I'm working on a complex about it, but I'm resisting. I don't want to give him the satisfaction. Maybe I should call Playboy and do some pictures, let him know it's not the way to get to me. Not sure I have the breasts for Playboy. Find one that doesn't mind a barely-B cup."

"Honey, you have amazing breasts; Playboy would be stupid to turn down your naked body." He folded his arms in over his chest. "I think it is his way to show you that you can't escape him. That he's always watching. One more way to prove to you he holds power over you."

Gripping her by the hips, Chase pulled her in close again. Looking down at her, he kissed her gently on the forehead. "You're incredible. You'll get through this. I'm here for you, this time, if you want me. What did you do to escape him before?"

Without waiting for her response, he continued, "You made a freaking great escape plan. Yeah, he found out, and you made him pay. Shit, Maddy. Despite the trauma, the legal shit you had to go through, uprooting your life and transferring schools, you still graduated early. With honors. And made detective in record time."

Her poor ego wasn't going to be able to take much more of this; she just may explode. She grinned back up at him as he continued boosting her mood. "When you were ready, you came back home. Stronger than ever. Made an incredible home," he paused, the corner of his mouth turning up as he continued to describe her, "Turned this tiny police department on its heels, modernizing their protocols and even the dang uniforms. Now you've been asked to train your fellow officers in hand to hand combat. I watched the security tapes from the night of the break-in; you have some serious power. Physically and mentally."

"And you..." *Make me feel whole again.* He paused, not wanting to push too far, but knowing he needed to finish the sentence, "kicked my ass in football." Pressing his mouth to hers, fire coursing through him. Tongues tangled in an epic battle. Scooping her up, he took her right there in the kitchen.

As the sun set, Dylan pulled into his favorite spot, in front of an empty cabin a few house's down from Madelyn's. He turned on his phone, deciding to scroll through some of his favorite moments while the Bluetooth connected. Madelyn slowly undressing, Madelyn coming out of the shower. His personal favorite was of her pleasuring herself, breasts bare and legs spread wide.

After enjoying a few moments of his and Madelyn's personal time, as he considered it, Dylan knew it was time to focus. He had to do some creative editing to cut Chase out of some of the images from over the weekend. Disgusting bastard. How could she do those things with him? Whore. He'd have to teach her a lesson. Soon.

He pulled up the app on his phone to see what she was up to now, connecting to the Bluetooth camera. Nothing... signal lost. She'd found it.

In a rage, Dylan threw his phone against the windshield and punched the wheel repeatedly. He didn't notice his knuckles bleeding. She'd installed that alarm system. He knew a few guys that may be able to get passed it, maybe. Top notch guys. He'd make a few calls.

But, they wouldn't move fast enough. He needed to move faster. If she'd found the camera, after she'd already arrested three of his guys...

Controlled breaths in and out, he steadied himself. He was flexible. He was smarter. Appreciating that his phone hadn't broken in his rage, he called the station.

"Seaview Police, how can I direct your call?"

"Hi there, this is Detective Stanton Phillips, I work for the Georgetown PD. I have a telephone meeting with Madelyn McAllister tomorrow at 4 o'clock regarding a recent arrest she made. I have some information she will want to hear regarding Mr. Lang. I have to reschedule; I'd like to speak with her or one of her associates now if they have a moment?"

The receptionist replied, "I'm sorry Detective Phillips, but Officer McAllister is unavailable right now, I'll pass along your message. What's your telephone number?"

He gave her the number to his drop phone, hoping he could get someone on the phone. Maybe if he shared some information as another detective, he could find out what all Lang had told them.

Dylan hung up. Dammit. Lang was a fucking moron. Couldn't keep it in his pants long enough to finish the job. Without a doubt, he'd rolled over and showed his belly. Who knew how much he'd said? Dylan had to assume the worst. Which is why Lang was only given need to know information... ever.

26

Both were quiet after the quickie in the kitchen. Satisfied, but quiet. Maddy ran her hand through her hair, adjusted her clothes, and dashed off to the bathroom to freshen up.

Chase let out a sigh. Not sure what that was. Incredible. Every time was somehow more intense, more amazing. Despite how much he wanted her in his life, indefinitely, he was a bit terrified. Never had he felt so connected. So... overwhelmed by someone else.

Shaking his head, he tried to clear his thoughts. He poured some olive oil in the sauté pan and got cooking. Distraction. Cooking cleared his head nearly as well as diving.

Maddy walked back into the kitchen, casual as can be. Like the moment in the kitchen hadn't thrown her quite like it had him. In front of him at the island, he tossed together a salad. "Sit and relax. We'll worry more tomorrow; are you working?"

Maddy sat at the bar and sipped her a glass of crisp white wine. Delicious smells started to fill the kitchen. "You are a bossy man, Chase Anderson. Nope, I usually can count on Tuesdays off, then I work Wednesday and Thursday."

She tried to relax and enjoy being waited on. Had she been alone tonight, she would have heated a frozen pizza and called it a night. Chase, on the other hand, changed the tune of the evening.

"Maddy McAllister, my intention is to spoil you rotten with good food and drink, enjoy this beautiful evening with you on the porch swing, and then..." He paused and leaned in, their faces only a few inches apart, "and then, make you scream my name in pleasure... again and again."

"Ok," she responded, eyes dreamy. He laughed, clearly pleased he'd emptied her brain so completely.

The moment was quickly ruined as Maddy's phone rang. It was the station. "This is Maddy," she answered, immediately suspicious. Chase stirred dinner, but kept his eye on her, awaiting her response.

"Hey, Maddy. It's Quinn," the receptionist hesitated before going on. "Maddy, I just got a very strange call for you. Do you know a Detective Stanton Phillips from Georgetown? Said he had a meeting with you tomorrow that he needed to reschedule. Something about information he has about Lang."

"Quinn, I don't have any meetings scheduled; you know my schedule better than I do."

"I know, that's why I'm calling. I think he was fishing for information. I told him you were unavailable but wouldn't tell him anything more. He gave me a number, to what looks to be a pay-by-the-minute phone, and asked that you or one of your associates call him back."

"Thanks Quinn, you did great. Do you think you could recognize his voice if you heard it again?" Maddy suddenly felt like a police officer, and it helped. If she could keep this business, she'd feel more empowered.

"Absolutely Maddy. There's one other thing. He asked for Madelyn McAllister. No one calls you Madelyn." Maddy knew one person that called her Madelyn.

"Quinn, is Andrea still at the office?"

"No, she's gone for the day."

"I need you to write down the entire conversation exactly as you remember it. I'm going to call Andrea and let her know. Thanks for calling, I think your suspicions are on target."

"Thanks, Maddy. You be careful." They disconnected. Quinn had worked for them for the past six months. She was great, had incredible instincts. Maddy was trying to talk her into applying for officer training next time something opened up.

She called Andrea right away to relay the message. As expected, Andrea was on it. Andrea promised to head straight in and see if Quinn could identify the voice, although they knew it would be Dylan's.

Maddy hung up and glanced at Chase, knowing he'd been listening, even as he added freshly chopped rosemary and garlic to the pan. Chase held her eyes for a moment, then silently returned to the stove. He combined the remaining ingredients and set the pan to simmer. The lobster gnocchi dish smelled amazing. Her appetite was rather touch-and-go with all the stress, but she'd find room.

Chase turned back to her and sat down at the bar with her. He sipped his own wine, as if considering his words carefully. Maddy knew it couldn't be good. Today had been filled with too much bad news, all Dylan. "Maddy, I might as well add one last Dylan update to the mix before dinner." He told her about the lawyers, the upcoming meeting.

"I understand his business plan, but it's stupid. There are other, struggling towns on the coast that would jump at the opportunity to build up their community. Our harbor is relatively calm, but not an ideal cruise stop." Maddy was furious.

It was clear Dylan's intentions were devious. He was much more likely to tear apart the community than add to it. Maybe she was biased, but her father had spent decades building a strong company to support the town, as other industries had come and go. As they'd seen other fishing towns dwindle to dust.

Chase shook his head, just as exasperated. "That's just it. Economically, he could do much better elsewhere. This is personal. He's got those two attorneys with him that do most of the talking. I have all of our people informed and ready to come to the meeting as well."

"Why did you even agree to the meeting? Why did they arrange a meeting? Dylan and this Nielsen were both named by Lang."

"Exactly. I already called Andrea. They don't know Lang named them. She's keeping it all under wraps, waiting for them to make a move. I agreed to the meeting in the hopes they'll slip up. Besides, I'm losing ground with some of the crew; I see how their plan works. They must do this a lot. We have a lot of internal dissent right now. I plan to make a counter presentation to earn back their trust."

"Well, Mr. Anderson, I'm sensing you have a strong business plan to counter with. And, you're letting them know that you are invested in their future. You're presenting them with all of their options, Dad would appreciate that. Even if Dylan's ridiculous plan is not really an option at all." Maddy would enjoy seeing him in action.

She knew her dad was a good judge of character. Selecting Chase as his successor had not been just for Chase's benefit. Chase would go to bat for the company, no hesitation. He had enough charisma that others would follow him. She thought for a moment, taking another sip, finger raised as she collected her thoughts. "Hang on, I have a thought." She pulled up her phone and re-dialed her boss, knowing she would be back at the station to talk to Quinn soon. "Andrea, have we run checks on where Dylan has been the past few years?"

"Of course. But, we haven't found much so far," the other woman responded.

"How about the goons he has with him? Says they're from a firm called Briggs and Johnson. Can we investigate the Briggs and Johnson attorneys they sent with Dylan? Maybe find out who they represent? What work they've done for Dylan in the past? Are they connected with our lovely pair of out-of-towners that Ian and I arrested? Lang only mentioned Nielson and Dylan, but wasn't able to connect more dots for us. I'm wondering if we can put the whole picture together and make a move before the meeting Thursday. If Dylan called pretending to be a detective in Georgetown, maybe there's a real detective in Georgetown that might be helpful. I'll bet they've already turned some heads with their atrocious business practices."

"Maddy, I like your thinking. Now try to get some R&R; I'll see you Wednesday." They disconnected.

This time, Maddy stood and walked around the island, stepping up to Chase. She put her hands under Chase's chin and pulled him in to face her. She pressed her mouth to his, soothing away his worries, which she knew were as deep as her own. Someday, she was sure his kiss would stop stirring her so deeply, but as of yet, it seemed to pull her in more each time they touched.

Pulling away with a laugh, she suddenly felt famished. "Dinner smells good, let's eat." He laughed and followed her as they dished up and took their meal to the deck. Watching the sun set, they ate and relaxed.

27

DYLAN STORMED INTO HIS motel room, slamming the door behind him. Bitch. He knew she was up to something. He'd watched as she and Chase sat out on her porch swing that night. Snuggled up and making out half the night like a couple of horny teenagers. It had taken the last of his willpower to not confront her right then and there.

Taking over her father's business, amassing a fortune as he took over the small town should have been enough to make her see reason. Things weren't going as he planned. They still had the upcoming meeting, which would keep Chase, and likely Aiden busy. He'd scheduled it at a time he knew Maddy would be working, unable to make the meeting. While everyone was distracted, he would be able to make his move.

Nielsen and Cochrane were on hand if he needed their help until then. He put them in charge of the meeting. He called Nielsen, "Hey, I have a small change in plans."

Nielsen's steady voice responded, as usual, without hesitance, "I'm here."

"McAllister Fisheries has made it clear they won't go down without a fight. Lang blew it. He's been arrested for prostitution of all things. I need you to call in the support team, let's step up our efforts. If the meeting doesn't end with the deal we want, send them out to the processing plant. Be as creative as you'd like. Maybe sink a boat or two, just make it look like an accident."

Again, if Nielsen had any objections, he didn't voice them. Good help was so hard to find. "I'll contact everyone tonight so we're ready to play hardball."

"Not before the meeting. I'll keep campaigning. Stir up some distrust in Chase Anderson. Several were eager to question him when we were there last. If we can demoralize, then bring in the support team, we'll get that place at a steal."

Dylan responded, his mouth salivating as his plan was finally coming into fruition. Not as simply as he'd hoped, but he would prevail. "Another thing. Madelyn has a new security system. Send in our best. I want full surveillance."

Nielsen didn't need it spelled out for him. "Done."

"Perfect. I'm going to play with her a bit, bring her to her knees. She'll be key to the plan. Whatever we do at McAllister Fisheries, it won't be enough. Anderson and McAllister will do anything to keep her safe. The night of the meeting, you're on your own. I'll take care of her and send the message. If they won't sell out, even if their business is crumbling before them, they'll sell out for her."

Uncharacteristically, Nielsen questioned Dylan, "Are you sure she'll be the compliant mouse you're hoping for?"

Dylan gritted his teeth at his insubordinate subordinate, "Not that you need to know, but she'll be an easier target if she's already down. Which I'm working on. Taking her out of circulation at work. Surveillance in her house. Drive her away from Anderson."

Nielsen back-pedaled, "Of course."

Dylan disconnected, eager to move along with his plan. He wished he'd be able to see her face each step of the way.

28

Wednesday morning, Maddy's doorbell woke her from a delicious dream. Chase had left for work an hour prior, locking up and setting the alarm when he left. Maddy had stayed in bed, exhausted from the night before.

Aiden was due to check in on her soon. Payson a few hours after that. It was exhausting, never having a moment to oneself. She had negotiated a few hours in between visitors, citing her alarm as a pretty good defense.

Maddy sat up in bed, still naked and even a little sore from the night before. She threw on jeans and a t-shirt, pulled her hair back, and rubbed the sleepiness from her eyes as she headed for the front door. Andrea.

Maddy adjusted the alarm and opened the door for her boss. Andrea stormed in. "Maddy, let's sit. Do you have coffee made? I have an update for you."

She went into the kitchen to pour coffee for them both. She led her boss to the couch and sat, prepared for anything by this point. "Go ahead."

"Quinn was able to officially identify Dylan as the caller the other night, not that we're surprised." She paused. "And, there's another thing." She handed Maddy the manila envelope she'd carried in with her. "These are just copies. We're running the originals. God, I feel like I've horribly invaded your privacy, but we need the evidence."

Maddy opened the envelope and pulled out a stack of photos. Her stomach rolled as she went through the pile. The first she had seen before. It was from the set Dylan had sent to the colleges she had applied to. The second was a security camera shot of her sobbing after Dylan had beaten her all those years ago when she tried to leave him. The next of Maddy in Seattle at her martial arts studio. She'd had no idea he'd followed her all that way.

Pausing, she tried to fight back the tears, "I had no idea he'd tracked me to Seattle. He was in jail when this was taken." Maddy gagged when she saw the next one; it was her in her bedroom, having a very private moment alone in her bedroom. He'd love that. Sick bastard. He wanted to capture personal moments, and well, he succeeded.

She flipped to the next picture. "It's from last night, isn't it?" Andrea was sympathetic but didn't beat around the bush. The photo was of Maddy and Chase. Last night, they'd sat out on the porch swing for hours, talking, laughing, trying to feel normal.

Clearly, they'd been watched; she wasn't surprised he had been watching, that wasn't the most disturbing part. In the photo, Maddy and Chase snuggled on the swing, looking out at the dark ocean... but someone had drawn a red X across Chase's eyes. "Have you talked to Chase?" Maddy managed to ask.

"I assigned two officers sent to protect him. We're taking this as a very serious threat. You'll both have police protection 24 hours a day."

When she got to the last photo, she stared for a minute, slowly realizing what it was. In the photo, Lang's hooker was sucking off Chase. With a choking sound, she dropped the pile and rushed to the bathroom. She'd had enough. She hadn't eaten breakfast yet, thank goodness. She splashed water on her face, noting her ghost white complexion in the mirror.

"Maddy, stop. Wait. Look closer," Andrea urged. Showing her the picture again.

"I do not want to see that closer." She stormed past Andrea, stomach churning. Eyes burning.

"Maddy. Trust me. Look closer," and Andrea shoved the picture in her face. "Look at the outlines. The setting." Curious, but still mortified, Maddy finally studied the picture. "It's edited. That's not Chase. Just his face. The lighting is all wrong. You can see outlines. It's a decent edit, but definitely false."

Maddy breathed slowly in and out. Stupid relaxation breathing. Never worked, but worth a try. "Ok. I see that. Give me a minute."

"This was very intentional. You freaked. Which was what he wanted. To cause distrust. Don't let him." Andrea stood by her patiently. Maddy stared at the photo another minute.

"I'm sorry. You're right. I feel stupid." Her stomach slowly stopped churning. Nausea fading. Humiliation turning into anger. At Dylan. Again. "That first picture. Dylan sent that, among a few others, to the colleges that I had applied to for the pre-law program. It would be in the files from before. That should help confirm Dylan as the perpetrator." Maddy managed to sit back on the couch next to her boss.

Andrea smiled. "And that's why I hired you. You're a good cop. I'll call Boston PD and pull those records," she paused, sipping her now-cold coffee as she collected her thoughts.

"Still working on the background checks. As the pictures indicate, Dylan tracked you to Seattle, and I'm wondering if he followed you there after he was released. We have a lot of gaps in his timeline. We're slowly putting it together. Business associates, acquisitions. I think he's been busy. Maybe not legally, definitely not ethically. We have a lot of digging to do. There are still a lot of gaps. I want an airtight case."

"Where did he spend the years in between? In Seattle the entire time? Closer to his parents? The attorneys?"

"So far we know that Briggs and Johnson is a reputable law firm out of Boston. They represent a number of businesses, including Dylan's. Mike will be looking into the attorneys that have been showing up with Dylan specifically. I have the business card they gave to Chase. We'll keep digging. I know Nielsen has a record, but nothing recent."

"Thanks, keep me posted." Maddy sighed, her entire body feeling heavy. "I'm more worried about Chase. I hadn't imagined Dylan would go this far, but those photos... I'll freely admit I'm terrified. He's building up to something. Before I was assaulted, he had gradually tightened control. Shrunk my circle. You know I'd feel better if I could have a hand in the investigation."

Andrea shook her head. "You know you can't. We need an airtight case. You've said that Dylan can be quite cunning. I have plenty of work to keep you busy. You're off today and you're taking tomorrow off, and I want you to get your head together, but you're back on duty Thursday as scheduled. During that meeting. I don't want you near it."

"I want to help. If I can find it on the internet while I'm off duty and send you ideas, that's not violating anything." Maddy sighed, leaning back on the couch and putting her hands in her lap.

"You know I'd like my best officer on this one," Andrea said with a friendly wink. "You are to send me every bit of information you have; every suspicion or even vague memory. But, no official leg work here. On this case, you're a victim. Airtight case. But protect yourself."

A knock at the door startled her. She hopped up from the couch, nearly knocking over her coffee. She checked the security cam. Chase, thank goodness.

Chase was relieved to find Maddy at home, safe and sound. He'd panicked at work and had to come see her. Couldn't even say why. Bad feeling. Weird. He normally had a level head. Had to in his previous line of work. But sometimes it paid to trust a gut feeling.

He'd been on his way out the door when two officers had stopped him. Said he was to have protection. Before he freaked, they'd made sure to tell him Maddy was fine, but he knew she may be safe, but wasn't fine.

Deep under water, you often couldn't see more than a few inches in front of you and couldn't afford not to listen to your gut. Hadn't led him astray so far. He pulled her in tightly as soon as he walked in the door, needing to feel her close. She was still warm and rumpled from their night together but was... off. Different.

"Chase, you ok? You're back early." Maddy pulled back just enough to look up at him.

"I'm fine, thanks," her look turned suspicious. "How are you?"

Andrea interrupted, startling Chase. He'd been so caught up in Maddy, he hadn't realized she was there. Already feeling silly for having fled work to check on Maddy, he kept a calm demeanor, hoping to maintain a façade of unflappability.

"Chase, I'm glad you're here actually, we have some new information for you. As threatened, Mayberry sent pictures to me directly. He's a smart guy, but I'm not sure he's so good with people, or he'd have realized the photos were incriminating for him alone and would have no effect on Maddy's employment."

Chase's jaw clenched in response; he was surprised he didn't have angry dragon-smoke puffing out of his nostrils. Andrea continued, "Chase, there's more." Andrea looked to Maddy in question, waiting for permission before sharing the photos. Maddy handed him the packet of photos, her expression grim.

He quickly rifled through the photos, feeling increasingly... rabid. Furious. What the fuck? What was this guy's problem? Why would he distribute such personal photos? He has to be completely off his rocker.

This made no sense. The photos of Maddy were intimate; he'd know how much that would bother her. He shuffled right past the picture with his eyes crossed out. Not surprised there. Fucking psycho.

The last photo caught him off guard. Chase was grossed out just looking at it. He wasn't a back-alley blow job sort of guy, so the photo was just... disturbing. Before he realized his thoughts were no longer isolated to his head, he found his thoughts expressed aloud, "Agh. Gross. Who is she and why is she doing that to me and why didn't I know about it?"

Maddy almost laughed, glad his reaction had been similar to her own, just more humorous. "Photoshop." She headed back to the living area and crashed back down onto the couch.

Chase shook his head, trying to find the humor with her as he followed her into the living room. "But it's so graphic. And vile. Eww." The more he stared at the photo, the more obvious the photo editing became.

A deep laugh boiled up from his gut. "Could you image him spending hours, trying to connect my head onto some other dude's body. Staring at that image for hours? Sick perv." No longer able to look at the picture, he stuffed the pile back into the envelope. He looked to Andrea, "Why do you think he sent these to you?"

She considered before speaking. "I don't know for sure, but I have a few theories. He used these as a tool before, to keep Maddy from being able to leave him. Cutting off her options. It would make sense he's trying it again. Driving her away from you. Scaring you both. Making Maddy feel insecure. She's a private person, and he has completely invaded her privacy. Maybe wouldn't want to go back to work and face us if these are floating around."

"Didn't exactly get what he wanted, did he?" Chase sat in the armchair across from Maddy, leaning forward and resting his elbows on his knees as he faced her.

Maddy laughed humorlessly. "No, he sure didn't. Before, the photos completely trashed my career plan, my reputation, and inspired me to move across the country. I wasn't going to be able to pursue a career in the public eye, which ruined his dream of our being some sort of power couple. My dreams changed for the better. His, not so much. Ruined his own future more than mine. And, again. This time, he has incriminated himself more than hurt me. He just doesn't get it."

The chief leaned in, continuing the debate. "His plan... sucks."

Chase shook his head. "Those photos sure got a lot of attention last time," he moved to sit by Maddy. "After you removed the camera, he had to have been seriously pissed off. You have a top-of-the-line alarm system; he's not getting back in. His plans for Seaview aren't going the way he wants either. He's getting desperate."

"He pissed me off with the photos, but they don't have the power to ruin me anymore. The threat against you, however, that *really* caught my attention." Maddy leaned forward to sip her now-frigid coffee, but her hands were shaking so hard anyway she had to put it back down before she spilled. So much for appearing unperturbed.

Andrea started to speak, but then shook her head. She stood and walked to the door, grabbing her keys. She stalked back over to the living room and leaned on the back of the empty chair. "Maddy, you tell me anything, absolutely anything you think may help. I'm going back to the office to find out where he is. Find out where his home base is. Track this asshole down. We have plenty of evidence now; I shouldn't have any trouble getting a warrant. Then, I'll put out the word to arrest him on sight."

Maddy nodded in assent. "His parents sold their home in town as soon as he left for college, but I believe they still own a few rentals around town."

"Thanks, I'll check those out. And Maddy, it's time for that restraining order."

"I couldn't agree more." Maddy rubbed her eyes and sighed, emotionally exhausted.

"Call if you think of anything. I'll ensure protection for both of you until we catch this creep. Don't leave the house without an officer. Either of you. I don't like where this is going. I'm calling in for back-up from the county sheriff's office."

Chase stood and walked Andrea to the door. "Thanks Chief."

She patted him on the shoulder warmly and walked out the door.

After locking up and setting the alarm, Chase turned back to Maddy. He hated seeing her like this, so distraught. Her face was sullen, eyes moist. "Hey, can I get you anything?"

Maddy stood and took the coffee cups to the sink. Ignoring the tremoring in her hands. She poured the leftover coffee into the sink, watching the dark liquid flow down the drain. She gently set the cups down and turned to Chase. "I'm going to take a shower. You'll stick around?"

"I'm not going anywhere." He watched her slow but controlled walk into the bedroom, shoulders held back. She was incredible. She had to be a mess, but she continued, refusing to give in.

He didn't know what to make of the threat against him. He knew Dylan was a sick fuck. Dylan had made enough mistakes, but he still had an advantage, bigtime. Dylan knew their routines, where they lived.

They didn't know shit about him or his thugs. Over the past decade, he'd stayed off the radar. They were having way too much trouble tracking him. Couldn't fucking find him. Didn't have a clue what else he may be planning. Surely, he'd have a back-up plan.

Chase was more than a little freaked out right now, which was not a normal feeling for him. He felt broken year after year his father pulled away and chose liquor. Not knowing where if he'd have a home when he got out of school, or where his next meal was coming from. Despite all that, his heart had broken when Henry had died. That didn't hold a candle to the fear he felt now.

29

After a long, hot shower, Maddy towel-dried her hair. She stared at herself in the mirror, daring herself to show a sign of weakness. Dammit, he was not going to win. He thought he won last time, but she became so much stronger than she used to be.

Because of him, she'd fought harder for every little thing she wanted. His craziness and the attack weren't a good thing, but she fought and ended up all the better for it. Her eyes squinted together, lips forming a determined grin.

Maddy threw on some eye make-up, hair product to reduce the mass of frizz, and her favorite distressed jeans and strappy tank. Shallow, she knew. But the extra touches boosted her confidence. She grabbed her laptop and headed to the living room. She may not be able to work on this officially, but she could do some research on her own.

While she was in the shower, Chase had made her an omelet and fresh cup of coffee. He sat at the kitchen island, his own plate already empty. "Feel better?"

She sat next to him at the island and dug into her breakfast, suddenly ravenous. "Much better." She grinned at him.

He smiled but looked more concerned than he was before. "You're awfully perky considering how your morning has gone so far."

"I'm done with the pity party. For now, anyway. We're going to take this asshole down."

"Ok, I'm on board. I thought you weren't supposed to work on this?"

"Not in any official capacity. Right now, I'm a civilian at home with internet access and a telephone." She scooped a huge bite of omelet and practically shoved it into her mouth.

"I'm in. What's your plan?"

She swallowed the huge bite and washed it down with a gulp of coffee. So hot, she nearly burned her throat. "I spent a year and a half with that asshole. I know a lot about him, his interests. I'm going to see where that leads. You, my friend, get to start with the law firm and the cruise ship company."

Chase smiled back. "On it. I'll grab my laptop from the truck. I'd planned on getting some work done, but something tells me the boss wouldn't mind if I took a personal day."

"He'd better, or his daughter will call to beg." She bumped his knee with her own playfully. It felt good to have a plan.

Hours later, both with eyes red from hours researching on their laptops, Maddy slammed shut the device. She took a deep breath. "Ok. Need a break. Hungry?"

Chase looked to her, groggy and confused. "Yeah, starving. I think we missed lunch." He rolled the tension from his shoulders and stretched his neck. He looked around the house, gathering his bearings. "When did it get dark?"

Maddy stood and stretched her body like a sleepy cat. "No idea. Frozen pizza or delivery?"

"Delivery, for sure. Pepperoni sound ok?" Chase picked up his phone to put in the order. He walked to the front door and looked out the side window. He saw the patrol car waiting outside and held off on the call. He stepped outside and trotted over to their car. The window was down before he got close.

Ian sat inside. "Hey Ian. You on guard duty? I thought you were stuck with Maddy as her partner?"

Ian smiled. "I sure am, but she's off today, and I'm getting overtime for parking outside her house all night. I'm saving up for a truck prettier than yours."

"Nice, let me know if you want any tips; I researched the shit out of that thing. Best on the market," they nodded, enjoying the manly truck moment. "I'm glad you're here, really. I know it's your job, but I'm grateful. I want this asshole behind bars... or preferably castrated and eviscerated—in that order—so Maddy can have some peace." Chase was enjoying his particularly violent fantasy. Ian laughed, nodding in agreement. "I'm ordering pizza, you want any?"

Ian nearly drooled, clearly starving. Dorito and Slim Jim wrappers made a nice pile on the seat next to him. "I'm sure I should say no. But I've never been on a stakeout before—this may not technically be a stakeout but that's what I'm calling it. Or maybe stalking the stalker, that sounds good. I'm not sure I'm supposed to accept pizza from the people I'm guarding, but as she's my partner, I think we can make an exception. Where are you ordering from?"

No wonder Maddy didn't mind partnering up with Ian. Just a good guy. "Scarpelli's."

"Ah, my favorite. Mind ordering me the Carnivore and add jalapenos?"

Chase laughed. "Sure thing. 'Night."

Chase dashed back inside. He ordered the pizza, with special instructions to deliver Ian's pizza right to his patrol car.

Maddy shook her head and smiled. "Thanks for thinking of him. That'll make my next shift much more pleasant. That man loves food. I would hate to see what he would look like if he didn't hit the gym every day."

They sat side by side at the island again and chatted about nothing in particular, a pleasant distraction for the moment. She couldn't concentrate anyway with her stomach rumbling so loudly. At the doorbell, she felt stupid when she about leaped off of the stool when she'd been expecting the doorbell to ring. Chase paid for the pizza and gave a wave to Ian, who was already devouring a gigantic slice outside in the patrol car.

As they dug into their piping hot pizza, Maddy grabbed a notepad. "Ok, now I'm ready. What have you accomplished?"

"Can I eat first?" Chase garbled out through a huge bite.

"I suppose so." She smiled and wolfed down her own. Her stomach yelled at her for not having thought of this sooner. She hadn't realized how hungry she was. She leaned into Chase as she finally slowed down on the pizza. "Beer?"

"Nah, better not. Not only do I need a complete brain, I had some last night and the night before. I usually try to keep it at a maximum of every other day."

Of course he was careful. She knew a lot of others who didn't drink at all to compensate for their parents. Chase enjoyed an occasional drink, but she'd never seen him drink more than one. "Would I look like a total lush if I have one?"

Through a very full mouth, "It's fine." She was not a big drinker either, but decided to splurge tonight. She cracked open a stout and poured it into her favorite glass. She poured him a water and led them to the couch, laptop tucked under her arm. "I found a few things that may be helpful. Andrea's likely long gone for tonight, so I'll call her in the morning with updates."

"I found a little too. You first." Chase sat beside her on the couch, his socked feet on the coffee table. Maddy sat facing him, feet tucked under his leg.

She set her beer on the coffee table and cleared her voice to give her official report. "His current residence is listed as an apartment in Georgetown. I searched around the area. He works out of an office not far from there. There's not a lot about his business available online, but it looks like he owns a corporate realty company. I'll have to dig some more; something just feels off about it."

"What feels off?" Pulling her feet onto his lap, he pulled her closer and covered her legs with a blanket.

"I couldn't say for sure. Almost like their website had too flowery of a description about its ethical business practices, some raving client reviews, but actual useful information was pretty slim. Like the site is there just for show."

"Huh. Weird. Let's keep digging."

"Agreed. I searched another route as well. Dylan was always active in the best teams and clubs, captain of the sailing club in high school and active in the community organizations while we were in college. I sent some emails to see if anyone kept in contact with him. I didn't ever see him develop any close friendships though; more superficial relationships, so I don't think that's going to go anywhere. He has no presence in social media. Unfortunately, if Andrea and Mike can't find school records for him after he was arrested, I'm not sure many of his old friends will know much." Maddy shook her head, frustrated.

"Maybe if we could get in touch with his old cellmate from jail, that might get us further."

She nearly laughed, but realized that actually could be a better lead. "Hmm. I wonder if Andrea can get that information."

"I was kidding, but maybe that will help."

Maddy pondered. She nudged her foot closer to Chase's hands, grinning as she subtly requested a foot-rub. "Well, anyway. He played baseball in college; said he'd never be able to give up the sport. I've looked around to different amateur baseball leagues near his house. Luckily, I didn't have to expand my search too far out so far. He just finished up with a local rec league; they won the local championship this year. His photo is right there with them. I emailed the link to Andrea and Mike to let them do some digging there, see if they want to interview any of his teammates."

"Sounds like a good plan. Anything else?"

Maddy picked up her beer and took a few sips, thinking. "Actually, I didn't get to it yet, but should have. His only other interest was sailing. He loved to sail. Lived in stark white boat shoes, even in winter. I wonder if Andrea can see if he owns a boat."

Continuing her train of thought, Chase paused his foot-rub, distracted, "We're not too far from the marina. Is your dad still part of the yacht club?"

Sitting up, Maddy reached for her phone. "He sure is. We could go check it out, but I'll behave and text Andrea first. See if she wants to send out a unit to look for any sign of him." Her fingers flew across the screen as she texted her boss. A few seconds later, her phone buzzed.

"She's on it. She's sending out a unit to look around the marina, find out if anyone has seen him. I hope they find something."

Not ready to stop yet, she gulped the last of her beer and continued. "I also spent some time researching stalker behavior. Trying to predict his next moves. Trying to map out his patterns. I know he's a control freak, a total narcissist. He's fixated on showing a successful front."

"He's fixated on you. Maybe you are part of his perfect picture, but I think it all comes back to you. He wanted you all through school, finally got you and kept you close. He tore you down until you didn't question him anymore, abusive behavior toward you."

"He was only violent the one time. The last time I saw him before he was arrested."

"True, but physical abuse is not the only kind of abuse."

"I know. I talked a whole lot with my therapist about exactly what happened, and it was a whole lot more than I'm willing to think about anymore." She sighed, eyes looking down.

"He's got that creepy obsession with secretly taking photos of you and using them against you. You broke free from him, you left him, and he ended up with nothing but photographs. And, he's clearly been adding more photographs over the years."

Maddy agreed with that. "I'm sure he could find someone else to worship him. Someone who might even let him take creepy pictures. It took a lot of therapy to allow anyone to take normal pictures of me. I had a bit of a complex for a while though."

"I'll bet." She'd had to go through so much because of that asshole. "I gotta say again, I hate that you went through all that. That I left you alone," Maddy tried to interrupt, "I know. I had to get out. But I wish things had played out differently."

"Me too. But, I'm glad of where everything ended up." She curled into his side.

"Whatever his deal is, he's fixated on you. Maybe this town and his success, but I still think it's all about you. Revenge or obsession or who the hell knows." Chase shook his head in frustration. "I'm sorry. I just can't seem to get my head into a psychopath stalker's head."

"I just hope we figure this out before he does anything. Did you find anything in your research?" Maddy felt near to the point of actually pouting.

"A bit. There are a number of cruise lines that pass along our lovely little coast, but no stops around here. I suspect a new cruise company would love to move in, as many of those already in the state are pretty popular and have a good thing going. Our little town, with its growing tourism, would be a perfect spot. So, I don't doubt he has at least one big fish on the line."

Maddy agreed. "No doubt. Not that they're welcome here."

"I'll keep digging on that. It took a while to find the law firm. Not much online for them either. I know Andrea's working this angle, so I'd like to compare what she's been able to find, if she lets us."

"I'm wondering about looking into his parents. Sounds like he's starting a business pretty similar to his dad's. Maybe we can look into his dad's business, see if any of his ventures account for Dylan's activities over the last decade. I'll give Andrea a call in the morning. In the meantime, I'll email her what we have so she can find any connections on her end.

"For now... want to watch a movie and snuggle up in bed?" She looked up at him with a smile, changing the subject. It had been a long day. Some shallow tv time sounded perfect.

He smiled back, as ready to change the subject as she was. He pulled her up from the couch and they walked hand in hand to bed.

Dylan punched the steering wheel again and again until his knuckles bled through his bandages from the last time he lost control. Bitch. Things were getting out of hand.

She had a police car stationed outside of her house now. That asshole was inside with her, locked up behind her absurdly fancy alarm system. He had a call in to a tech, but finding someone to disable the system would be costly and was taking too damn long anyway.

The deal for the business was solid and would go through without a hitch. He had the cruise line owner eating from his hand with the deal he'd negotiated; he could easily transfer the deal to another town if needed. But, more than ever, he needed buy-in from his crew. They knew Madelyn was a crucial part of his plan. However, they'd been immediately attracted to the lucrative deal despite his dual motives.

Biggest damn deal he'd negotiated; would set them up for years. His father had built an empire buying and selling businesses, but he wouldn't have been nearly so successful if he'd had to pay full price. Dylan had learned well and taken it to the next level. He'd made good connections in jail and had quickly built his own kingdom.

His father was constantly under a microscope as his deals typically involved international trade. Dylan was smarter than his father. Smaller, local businesses didn't have the oversight. Nor the resources to investigate when things went awry.

Dylan gave a satisfied smile as he pulled past her house, returning to his motel room. He'd started small, modifying deliveries of alcohol to some of the local bars around Georgetown. He gradually expanded his operations. Some business owners gave in with some roughing up, others with small steps to de-value their properties, and others when competition moved in – or at least when they thought competition was moving in.

He couldn't understand why Chase wasn't falling in line. Most recently, he'd sent in a crew to adjust the temperatures on the coolers and called in the health department to perform an "unscheduled" inspection before the change was detected, but by the time they arrived all had been set aright. They had even tried to compromise some of the fishing gear and boat engines, but they'd made repairs before anyone was hurt.

He should have started laying the groundwork before arriving in town, but Frank was a damn hawk. Didn't miss a thing. Would have smelled something fishy right off the bat. He knew Chase suspected, but he didn't know the business well enough yet, nor did he have the support from the employees. No, it wasn't his timing that was off.

The orange glow of the motel sign came into view, and Dylan pulled the sedan into a vacant spot. As he stepped from the car, he knew what he had to do. He could use Madelyn to his advantage after all. Chase always seemed to be a step ahead of him in business, but if Madelyn were out of the picture, he wouldn't have a choice but to sell out in order to get her back.

Not that Chase would actually get her back. Dylan faced the facts. He began to realize that he wouldn't be able to stick around to finalize the deal. But, he could earn a nice bonus on the business transaction to add to the nice nest egg he'd built for he and Maddy.

The bed squeaked in protest as he laid down in his motel room. What a dump. In trying to keep a low profile, he'd made do with the only motel near Seaview that took cash and didn't ask for ID. Painful, when nicer digs were so close, but it was a necessary precaution. It wouldn't be long now; she was almost back in his life.

30

Morning came bright and early, the sun's rays filtering in through the curtain. Maddy rolled to her side to find the rest of the bed empty. Rumpled sheets, no Chase beside her. She sat up, clutching the sheet to her chest.

She wasn't going to panic. She was a strong, independent woman. It was ok to be alone. She's been alone for years. Intentionally. She preferred it that way. She heard a crash in the kitchen. Pushing the growing panic aside, she sat and listened.

"Dammit." She heard a shout from across the house. Chase. She felt like an idiot. She'd have to control the jumpiness.

A moment later, coffee delivery arrived in the form of a very sexy, tousled man with sleepy eyes in jeans hanging low over his hips, chest bare. "You're up. I hope it wasn't the crash that woke you. Sorry, but your favorite Captain Marvel coffee cup shattered. Never make coffee while sleepy. That's my new rule." Chase handed her a not-broken, not-favorite mug and sat on the corner of the bed with his own steaming cup of joe.

"No, I'd just woken. You owe me a new mug, that's my power mug I use when I'm feeling like I need the extra boost." She grinned at him across the cup.

He studied her frazzled appearance, a pallor that was slowly diminishing. "Hope you didn't worry, waking up alone."

"Of course not. I wake up alone all the time." She didn't mean to, but the snap just came out.

"Wow, ok. What's up?"

"Sorry. I don't know where that came from. I'm just bitter and angry. I worked my ass off to be a strong, fearless woman. I woke up, saw you were gone and panicked. I'm just mad at myself."

"Maddy, you are a strong, fearless woman. You have a crazy stalker. It's ok to be a bit jumpy, whatever the reason. Everyone's all worked up with this whole don't-go-anywhere-alone business. I hope you don't mind me staying over so much; I'm also a bit wary of sleeping in my own house with its deadbolt-only security system right now. Not that you let me sleep much last night anyway..." he winked at her with a wicked smile.

"Hey, you're the one that woke me at 2 a.m." She stared him down across the top of her coffee mug.

He grinned at her, accepting full responsibility. He got up and opened the curtains to let the daylight in. Standing at the window and sipping his coffee, he turned back to her, "Maddy, I know you didn't want to date again. Maybe not ever, and I get it. I know you are scared of where this may go. You asked me for one night, and yet I keep coming back..." Might as well put the cards on the table, "I don't want this to end. I want to spend a hell of a lot more nights with you. Maybe all of them," with a sheepish smile, he added, "Days too."

Maddy's throat went dry. Her heart was thundering under her ribs. She asked for one night. Then she wanted another. And another. She didn't want it to end either. She'd gone and fallen in love with him.

But then, she'd always been in love with him.

She was all in now. And that thought was more terrifying than having a stalker after her. Against her will, her eyes welled. Without a word, she hopped up from the bed and about ran to the bathroom to take a long, hot shower.

What was wrong with her? Why couldn't she just accept and move forward? She knew she was obsessive about being able to protect herself. Her life and her heart. Other women had undergone more years of worse abuse and managed to hold down relationships. Why couldn't she?

She let the hot water pour over her body, feeling ripped to pieces with indecision. She trusted Chase completely. He'd pushed her away and left before, but she'd pushed too, and run away nearly as far.

She was completely herself around him, which was actually pretty marvelous. Her body and her heart were safe with him. The past few weeks, he occupied most of her thoughts. When they were apart, her heart ached to get back to him.

She needed help. Maybe Payson could swing by for breakfast; she was brutally honest and wouldn't let her continue this wallow.

Stupid. He shouldn't have pushed, not with everything going on in their lives right now. He knew she was scared. He didn't blame her.

Her longest relationship was stalking her and expressing his intentions for her new boyfriend to be very dead. Not a good time, he got that.

He pulled on a McAllister Fisheries black t-shirt and padded across the bedroom carpet. He needed to think about something else before it drove him crazy. Thinking about the what-ifs. If she didn't feel the same way about him. If she wouldn't let him in.

Aiden would be in court today. Frank was in a distant time zone, and he wasn't ready to talk to Frank until he knew where he stood with Maddy. Oddly, he wasn't worried about Frank's reaction like he'd been about Aiden's. The guys were all out on the boats. He could head into work.

Chase hollered to Maddy, still in the shower. "Hey Maddy, I'm going to run some errands. I'll pick up a few groceries while I'm out. I'll check in with Ian, or whoever's on duty."

She hollered out in a broken voice, "Ok."

Shit, he hoped he hadn't blown it.

He slipped on his usual work boots, loosely but quickly tied so he didn't trip, and dashed outside so he didn't have to face her again, not just yet. Not until they both sorted out whatever had happened this morning. Ian had gone for the night and a cop he hadn't met yet was waiting outside. "Hey, I need to run a few errands, Maddy's still inside."

The cop, a forty-something guy, rather gaunt with a clean-cut beard, replied in a monotone voice, "Sure thing. I'll call for someone to cover Maddy. I'm assigned to you."

Chase nodded and hopped in his truck. He hung out in the driveway long enough for another unit to arrive and then took off north across downtown. They had a pretty good system; Andrea ran a tight ship. Apparently, when she'd been hired about eight years ago, she had applied for some impressive grants and managed to triple the number of officers and update their tired equipment.

He tried to keep his speed reasonable; when being tailed by a cop for his own safety, would they give him a ticket? His adrenaline was out of control; the roar of the engine echoing his own torment.

Zipping past work, he drove a few more bends until he reached Winter's. Not realizing until now it had been his destination all along. Good idea, though, he ought to touch base about the buy-out offers. The parking lot at Winter's was empty as he pulled in, aside from an old but pristine purple Honda Protégé. Perfect, the old man was in. He dashed up to the door. Finding it locked, he knocked.

Winter threw open the door, his thick gray hair wild, classical music playing softly in the background. "Chase, my good man. What can I help you with? Come on in."

Pleasantly surprised at the welcoming reception, Chase followed him in. "I know you're not open yet, but I wanted to talk a few things over with you."

Winter nodded and headed behind the bar, apparently this was a normal occurrence. "Sure thing." He poured a cup of coffee for each of them and leaned across the bar, ready to listen. "I'm glad you called about the ridiculous business proposition from that dumbass and his antics. I've installed a pretty basic security system, and the police have been good about increasing patrols. So far they've left me alone."

Chase nodded, appreciating the coffee. "I'm glad. I hope it stays that way. You going to their little presentation meeting Thursday?"

"Wouldn't miss it. I've made a little presentation of my own. Hoping to personally run them out of town," he nodded, gesturing to his gigantic laptop set up at a nearby table.

"Impressive," Chase nodded. "I've asked the crews to come out and add to our show of force."

"Excellent. You sure have everything set." Winter went about his business, dusting bottles, organizing glasses behind the bar. Fucking obvious. Bartenders. The longer he sat silent, the more Chase accepted that he hadn't come by just for business.

Winter finally opened the door to the change in subject, "You were looking awfully cozy with Maddy the other night. You hook up with my best girl?"

Chase smiled, impressed with the other man's intuition. "Are you a psychic or a bartender?"

Winter laughed. "They oughtta require psychology courses in bartending school."

"Yeah, I actually would like to talk about Maddy. I was hoping to be more discreet and tell you about a friend, but I might as well get to it. Although, she wouldn't be too thrilled if she knew I was here, talking about her."

"Maddy is stubborn, but a smart woman. She's been through a lot. More than her share. Think that's why she's always the first one to come to the rescue." Winter kept working, but his mouth was turned up in a smile, glint in his eye. "Like someone else I know."

Chase didn't even know how to start. He wasn't even sure how he'd ended up here. Maybe he was more like his dad than he knew, finding himself in the bar before noon. "I should go."

"Chase, stay," the older man put his wrinkled, yet warm hand on his before he could stand up from the stool. When Chase sat back down and relaxed, willing to stay a bit longer, Winter continued his daily preparations. "Did I ever tell you I knew your dad?"

Chase couldn't respond, but desperately needed to hear what Winter wanted to say.

"You're probably not surprised that your dad knew the local bartender well. Regardless, he was a good guy. Had a red nose and a belly like Santa, but we all knew it was not because he was so jolly," he chuckled at the memory. "He used to tell me the best stories about you. 'My boy, nothing keeps him down... that Chase can cook up one amazing meal... that Chase holds my world together, don't know what I'd do without him.' Shortly before he stopped coming in, just before the fire, he told me all about how proud he was of your accomplishments. Told me about your diving, about you helping him financially, even though you should hate him. Hated how he'd disappointed you, that he could never be enough for you.

"I didn't have to tell you all that, I know, but I just wanted you to know."

Chase didn't even try to hide the sudden sniffle he'd developed. "Thanks, Winter. He was a good guy, just blew it as a dad. I don't blame him like I used to. Just hate that he lost the battle with alcoholism."

Winter, of course, had an answer to that. "Which is why you're always strong enough. For everyone. Every time."

Chase shrugged, knowing he was right. Chase had spent years rebelling from his dad while keeping them both afloat. The balance hadn't been easy. Maybe that was why he'd taken so well to diving. The ridiculous danger had been the appeal, but the steadfastness required had kept him there so long.

"Which is why you and Maddy are a good fit. Obvious to all of us. You're both overly driven to compensate for the past. Never give yourselves a break." He paused, and looked Chase not uncomfortably deeply in the eyes, "does she trust you?"

"I think so." Chase shrugged, but he knew deep down that she did.

"Does she look to you for advice?"

"Yes."

"Does she lean on you when she's feeling down?"

"So far."

"Does she celebrate with you when she's happy?"

"Yeah, she does."

Winter grinned. "Then stop worrying; she'll come around. Make a gesture, so she knows you're here for good, something that tells her she can count on you–but not something to scare her away. She's skittish, and for good reason. Try getting off your ass and tell her you love her and see where you end up."

Chase looked down at his untouched coffee and grinned. He slid off the barstool. "Thanks, Winter."

"Anytime. Just send me an invite to the wedding."

Chase laughed as he headed out the door. Making a plan, he hopped in his truck and headed back to the dreaded retailers to do some important shopping.

Maddy jumped and practically ran to the door when Payson rang the bell. "About dang time! I'm having a crisis here," Maddy shrieked, hair wild, face bare of make-up. But, the inside-out shirt was probably the most telling.

Payson walked in the door, carrying fresh, warm croissants from the bakery. "You're not having a crisis. You just need to find peace and acceptance." She rolled her eyes as she parked herself at the kitchen island, patting the stool next to her for Maddy to sit. "You look terrible."

"I don't want to give him up." Maddy pouted. "But I'm scared." Her head crashed down against her hands on the countertop. Were those whimpers coming from her? She sounded like a sad puppy. Or maybe a wet cat.

"No shit. Of course you're scared. What can I do to help?" Payson tore into her own croissant, smiling down at her bedraggled friend.

"I don't know." Another pout.

"Do you love him?"

"Of course I do. Why do you think I'm so terrified?" Maddy shook her head, overwhelmed.

"Ok, let's back up. Do you trust him?"

"Yes. Without a doubt." She nodded emphatically after she pulled her head up from the table.

"Is the sex incredible?"

Maddy sighed, a stupid grin taking over her face. "Yes," she replied dreamily.

"Do you want to be with him so much it hurts?"

"Yes. And it's a very new, very weird sensation."

"Do you want to spend every day with him?" Payson eyed her friend, "Eat your croissant." Maddy obeyed without argument, taking a big bite of her croissant. As she chewed, Payson fired away, "Have you pictured him holding a tiny baby? Practiced saying Mrs. Anderson? Have you thought about how sexy he'll look with gray in his sideburns? Can you picture yourself with anyone else ever–"

Maddy tried to quickly chew so she could swallow and stop her friend from continuing, but had taken too big of a bite. Putting her hand over Payson's mouth, she chewed and chewed. Finally, she was able to swallow the large bite. "Slow down, woman. I get it."

Payson nodded, "So, again, why are you terrified?"

Maddy felt her eyebrows push together. Her brain hurt from thinking so hard. "I don't know. I just didn't like who I was this morning when I was afraid and felt alone."

"Haven't you ever felt afraid before?"

"Of course I have." Stupid logic.

"One thing I know about you, is that you are damn stubborn. And tough. When you're scared, you face it head on."

"So, you're saying I should...?" Maddy's eyebrows raised in question, awaiting a brilliant response.

"I think you'll figure it out. You're almost there." Payson pulled her friend into a half hug.

Maddy managed a small laugh, "You are crazy, but I love you Payson."

They finished their breakfasts and enjoyed some time to just *be*. Without worrying about crazy stalkers, relationships, the future.

31

M ADDY WAS GLAD TO be back on duty Thursday afternoon. It was going to be a late night, but she was suffering from a nasty case of cabin fever. She was also glad to get her mind off of Chase for a bit. She knew what she had to do. What she wanted. But needed to gear herself up for it.

Last night, he'd come back from work late. Apparently, they'd had some issues with the boats and even a few processers suddenly quit. Chase had no doubt that Dylan was responsible, but Andrea still hadn't been able to track him down. They were forced to remain incredibly diligent to keep things running smoothly and safely.

He must be so stressed out. But he didn't show it. As was classically Chase, he simply kept moving forward, doing what needed to be done. Her dad would be home tomorrow morning, hopefully giving Chase some relief. Not that he needed help or would even consider asking unless absolutely necessary, but he would appreciate it all the same.

She'd made him dinner last night, had greeted him with a warm meal. They'd hardly talked. Both tired and overwhelmed. He dragged her to bed shortly after and made love to her all night. He'd been so attentive, so passionate.

It hadn't been the desperate fire like it had been that night after the beach party. Rather, it was softer, more intimate. Dragged her more deeply in love with him.

Pleasantly drowning in her feelings for him. An oxymoron, but that's how it felt. She thought she'd be afraid, but the further she fell for him, the more... empowered she felt. Somehow, she wasn't afraid anymore. Must be that peace and acceptance Payson was talking about.

"Ahem," Ian's loud throat clearing brought her back to the moment. He sat at the corner of her desk, the corner of his mouth turned up in full-mock. "What's with you, space cadet?"

"Sorry, a lot on my mind." Maddy forced an innocent smile back.

"Let's get to work then; I'm sure picking up a few drunk and disorderlies will soothe your nerves beautifully." He hopped up and tipped his head towards the exit, motioning her to get moving.

"Aye, partner." She mocked him right back. She pushed back from the huge desk and adjusted her gear. "You wearing a vest?" She demanded.

At that moment, Andrea poked her head out her office door. "Ian, put on a damn vest." While Ian grabbed his bullet-proof vest, Andrea waved them into her office. "I wanted to update you on our progress. Ian, you too. Sit." Maddy and Ian obediently sat in the chairs facing Andrea's desk. She was uncharacteristically short tempered. "Everyone is armored and packing until further notice."

Ian hadn't known her long enough to know when to shut up. She may be a softy, but when she was serious, Andrea was a force to be reckoned with, and lost her infamous patience. "It's too hot for these damn things," he whined as he held the armor out, disgusted by it.

"Put the damn thing on Ian." She stared him down, demanding his compliance. He silently obeyed, but he didn't hide his scowl.

Taking pity on her partner, Maddy broke the tense silence, "What did you find?"

Andrea broke her stare from Ian, looking Maddy in the eye, "It's a bit worse than we feared. You were right, Dylan is no dummy. He didn't just sit around and pine for you all those years." Maddy tensed, knowing she wouldn't like where this was going. "As you learned, Dylan owns his own business. As you suspected, it's shady. Has a handful of employees. All with a record or history of suspicious activity. I spoke with a real detective in Georgetown who's been trying to pin down Mayberry for years, but they haven't been able to prove anything.

"He buys out businesses that were doing well but are suddenly on the brink of collapse. He gets a hell of a bargain, then breaks it down or merges it with another acquisition, then sells it for a hefty price. Briggs and Johnson represent him and his company; they don't appear to represent anyone decent. Nielsen is an attorney, but has a hell of a record himself, although he keeps his nose just clean enough to maintain his license. He negotiates most of Mayberry's deals."

Maddy knew the rest, but couldn't help but ask, "And what makes those businesses suddenly so affordable?"

Andrea's lips pressed together tightly, "The Georgetown detective hasn't been able to find proof. He knows most of Mayberry's 'associates' have long lists of convictions: breaking and entering, armed robbery, destruction of property; you can guess the rest. They're smart in business; nothing ever ties back to them."

Maddy's heart sank, even though she had expected this was where the investigation had been heading. "And what does this mean for us? Have our arrests been enough to nail them down once and for all?"

Andrea's face was grim. "It'll have to be enough. I'm hoping we can gather some last-minute evidence over the next few hours and make the arrest at the meeting tonight; all three of them. I've doubled protection for Chase. You two are to stay in public areas tonight while you work. I'd like you to stay in the Explorer for the most part."

Ian stood and paced the room, as angry at the situation as Maddy was. "Where is this asshole? Let's go after him."

Andrea glared again, but let him continue his frustrated pacing, "We're looking for him. No one has seen what he's driving or where he's staying. We have eyes and ears everywhere right now, but nothing. Not in any of the hotels or rental houses, not at his parent's beach house, not with any of his old friends. He had a sailboat docked just outside of Annapolis, but I just received confirmation this morning that he sold it six weeks ago."

Maddy interjected, remaining in her seat and keeping her voice steady, "What if he doesn't show up to the meeting?"

Andrea nodded, knowing Maddy was following her thoughts. "The meeting is in three hours. I'll be at the meeting with Mike, and we'll have another unit stationed discreetly outside, ready to grab him if he comes near. Since the photos, I've been running a constant search for him. We're taking him into custody as soon as we find him. I've requested assistance from the county, so we'll have some deputies on hand at the meeting, a few more searching the area, watching the roads in case he decides to run for it. You two are to stay far away. Patrolling. Handling unrelated activity."

Maddy nodded. "Understood. You'll let me know when you get him?"

"You'll be the first to know."

Maddy and Ian left the station shortly after, both armed and armored as instructed. Neither spoke as they headed for their Explorer. Maddy didn't even argue when Ian hopped in the driver's seat; normally she liked to drive, or she got restless. She sat in the passenger seat, arms calmly in her lap, eyes facing straight ahead.

"How are you so calm?" Ian asked. His left knee vibrating so fast he about shook the car.

"I just want this over. I thought it was over years ago when I watched him hauled away in handcuffs after he was sentenced. I'm ready for it to be over, for good this time." Maddy sighed, resigned.

Once Ian calmed his body enough to drive safely, he pulled onto Beachside Avenue and started a basic patrol. Some of their patrols like this were more to establish police presence in town. The occasional traffic violation wasn't what they were looking for.

Hours went by as they drove all over Seaview. Town was quiet, as she normally would have appreciated, but tonight the quiet was aggravating. Grating at her frayed nerves. Neither would admit it, but they were hoping for some sign of Dylan. The meeting would be starting any minute, so Maddy supposed he was already there anyway.

32

CHASE PULLED INTO THE grange hall, the parking lot full of other local business owners and fishermen. Aiden must already be inside, his car parked right in front. He checked his surroundings, not wanting to be caught unaware. He'd love for Dylan to come after him.

Chase had never been in a fight he couldn't win. Not that he was conceited, he was more... tenacious. He'd had a few fights almost not go his way, but his opponents had never shown the same relentlessness; Chase was prepared to fight until the last breath.

He checked his rearview to see his bodyguards coming to join him. Their eyes scanned as they walked, following him into the hall. Nielsen and the other goon were already standing up front, playing with a projector to format their presentation. Half of the town had turned out. Standing room only, with doors propped open so those standing outside could hear. He went to join Aiden, standing with arms crossed in the back of the room.

He stood at his friend's side and looked around. Odd. "Where's Dylan?"

Aiden's face was grim. "Not here yet. I asked Thing One and Thing Two, they said he's on his way. Said he is bringing the refreshments. That the order was messed up, hence the delay. Load of shit if you ask me."

Maddy and Ian were tense as 7 o'clock rolled around. Town was eerily quiet. Many of the locals would be at the meeting, either supporting Chase or looking for the promise of quick cash from Dylan and his associates. They distracted each other reminiscing about some of the crazier moments of their partnership. Not much was going to beat the recent back alley blow job.

Although, the bank robbery 3 months ago had been pretty interesting. Perp had tried to escape via bicycle. And wasn't much of a biker. Maddy had only needed to tackle him at the second intersection, and Ian had come around the side and had him in cuffs before the light had turned green.

The radio interrupted, Quinn's voice came through clearly, "Unit 3, we have a situation on Marsdale Road, are you able to respond?"

Maddy picked up the radio, "Sure thing, what's going on?"

"We have a report of a domestic dispute at 334 Marsdale." Quinn filled them in on the details as she knew them.

"On our way." Ian turned on the lights and headed southeast, lights flashing and siren blaring.

As they pulled in, the house was dark. "Hmm, looks quiet. I hope everyone's ok."

Maddy nodded, "I hope so. Isn't this where Mateo and Lucy Rivera live? I wouldn't have pegged them for a domestic dispute. Let's check it out."

They parked on the street outside the house. The house was pretty isolated. The next houses down were not visible through the trees with the sun setting. The house lights were all off. Maddy rolled down her window to listen for sounds of a dispute. A scream came from inside the house and the sound of a man's voice yelling followed. They leaped out of the car, moving into position.

Maddy was nearly to the front door, weapon drawn.

A few feet behind her, Ian hollered, grabbed his chest and was down.

As she turned, she was grabbed from behind, a foul odor on the rag smothering her face. The world went dark in seconds.

33

"THERE, THERE. LET IT out. Let it out my sweet."

Maddy gagged at the sound of the hated voice talking to her. Despite her confusion, not being able to see or hear, her head pounding, she lunged for the voice and spewed vomit towards his devious voice. She coughed and expelled the last of the foul mixture.

She managed to open her eyes and stare right into Dylan's eyes. Seemingly distant, she heard her own deranged laugh echo through the room.

Dylan leaped up and hollered, "Bitch. You'll learn your place." He shook the vomit off of his hand, disgusted. With his other hand, he smacked Maddy across the face.

Her cheek stung from the sharp slap. She tried to hit him back but found herself hog tied. She looked around, trying to identify her surroundings. She was on a mattress in a tiny room, angular and oddly shaped.

Once the nausea faded, she realized they were in a boat. She could hear the sound of waves crashing against the hull, the resonant roar of a sailboat engine.

"Madelyn, we have so much catching up to do. For now, you just rest. We're heading for a nice tropical vacation, just the two of us. Just like you always dreamed." He looked to her softly for a moment, then turned and shut her inside the room, alone.

She heard the scraping of a lock on the outside of the door. When had she ever dreamed of a tropical vacation with him?

She racked her brain, trying to retrace how she had gotten here. Ian. Shit. She'd seen him fall just before she fell asleep. He'd been wearing his vest; she could only hope he was ok. Hopefully calling for back-up.

Maybe if he'd seen where she was taken? Who had shot him? Had Dylan been alone? She hadn't seen anything.

Maddy pulled at her bindings, trying to find a weakness. He'd used zip ties. Dammit. The room was bare except for a sleeping bag on the bed and an analog clock ticking loudly on the teak wall. She searched for a way out.

Even if she could get out of the room... even if she could get out of the bindings, she was likely still heading out to sea and couldn't just dive in and hope to find shore in the dark, especially when she was still foggy from the drugs he'd used on her. She had to assume Dylan still had the gun.

She fought the overwhelming urge to cry. Later. She could cry later. When she was back home safe and sound.

Quinn answered the phone to hear Miss Hanson's frantic whisper before she could even say hello.

"They're here, there are bad men here. I'm watching them break into Chase Anderson's house as we speak. They're up to no good, I know it. He's not home. I think they're waiting to jump him."

Quinn calmly, but quickly, asked Miss Hanson to stay on the line and notify her of any updates. She kept the line open while she called Andrea immediately. "Andrea, please respond immediately."

Andrea, who had been at the meeting inside the grange, responded, "Go ahead Quinn." Andrea snuck outside the front door to take the call.

"Miss Hanson is calling. She says there are two men dressed all in black that just broke into Chase Anderson's house."

"On my way, please keep Miss Hanson on the line, I want to know every detail about what's going on." Andrea opened the grange hall door and motioned for back-up. Chase and Aiden caught the movement and raced out the door to follow.

"You two, hop in the backseat. You are not to leave the car for any reason, but I'm not leaving you alone." Without argument, they jumped in the backseat, fearing the worst. She filled them in on the way. As she drove, she radioed for Maddy and Ian. "I repeat, are you ok? Are you there?"

Nothing but radio silence. "Shit. Shit. Shit. Quinn, I'm not getting anything from Maddy and Ian, what was their last known position?" Andrea drove lights on, siren blasting across town.

"334 Marsdale, checking out a domestic dispute. I last heard from them thirty minutes ago. I'm sending out the closest unit. I have a county deputy about a mile out, he's on his way to their last known location."

Andrea radioed to the cars behind them, "I want 2 units at 334 Marsdale right now. Find Maddy and Ian. Be careful." Chase looked back to see there were several other units falling in line behind them, two of them veering off southward.

Panicked, Chase leaned to Andrea, "Come on, let's go find them. My house can wait."

Shaking her head, Andrea continued on her trajectory. "We're stopping at your place first. The chance Maddy is still there is slim. If we can catch the intruders at your house, we may be able to find out where he's taking her... we have to assume that he's taken her." Andrea got back on the radio, "Mike, it's time. Gather some back-up and make the arrest," she referred to the presenters. That would make a nice message for those who were planning on the quick sale and promise of a more lucrative venture.

They pulled onto the street to Chase's house. Quinn's voice came through, "Miss Hanson said the men just drove. Says they didn't go inside. They ran up to the front door, took a few moments, then ran back down the road. Says they're long gone and is blaming me for taking so long."

Andrea growled, "It's been 6 minutes since you called. We're pulling in now." At the house, Andrea barked orders for Aiden and Chase to remain where they were, or she'd arrest them herself. Chase had never been so scared in his life. Every second he didn't hear Maddy's voice, the risk increased that he'd never see her again.

Dylan hadn't been at the meeting for a reason. His attorneys had been presenting, saying Dylan would be there any minute with refreshments. They'd clearly been stalling.

Andrea sprinted out of the car, a few other officers following. She returned less than a minute later with a note. She passed the note, already bagged as evidence, to an impatient Chase and Aiden frantically waiting in the back seat. Lights still flashing, she whipped out of the driveway so fast, Chase was glad he was still buckled.

Chase could hardly read the note, his hands were shaking so violently. Aiden snapped, "You can't help her if you don't calm down." Aiden snatched the note from his tremulous grip.

Quickly reading the note, Aiden inferred, "Mayberry's got her. He's got Maddy. The note says he'll tell you where to find her after you sign over McAllister Fisheries."

Aiden scowled, "This doesn't make any sense. Even if you signed everything over to him, which wouldn't hold up in court, he wouldn't be able to do anything with the business. He'd be arrested on sight."

Andrea nodded. "I agree, it doesn't make sense." She took the note back and handed it to one of her other officers that had jumped into her passenger seat at Chase's house to aid in the pursuit. Picking up the radio, with exasperation she connected back to Quinn. "Anything on Ian and Maddy yet? When did you last hear from them?"

Quinn's voice echoed back, "Deputy is there; he found Ian. He's alive, but unconscious. No sign of Maddy"

The rig nearly caught air as Andrea flew down the street towards Marsdale. She radioed for back-up as they flew down the hill. Chase shook with rage. He needed to get control, or he wouldn't be any good to her. With a deep breath, he imagined himself deep underwater, letting his mind calm.

The radio chirped again. At the sound of Ian's voice, Chase's ears perked up and his heart stopped. Ian's breathless voice came through, "He's got her. He took her."

Andrea grabbed the radio, "Ian, are you ok?"

"Yeah, glad you made me wear the vest. Single shot, in the chest. Hurts like a son-of-a-bitch though, knocked me out for a bit there. I don't see any sign of other gunfire; no blood anywhere, no signs of a struggle," he added, knowing they'd be desperate to hear news of Maddy. "Hurry over. Area appears to be secure. Hoping there's a clue I've missed. One of the deputies is searching the area and one of ours is just pulling in."

Tires squealing on the pavement, they rounded the corner and pulled in front of the house on Marsdale. Ian stood out front of the dark house, surrounded by red and blue police lights.

Chase was out of the SUV so fast, Andrea hadn't even come to a complete stop. "Where is she? Which way did he take her?" He ran up to Ian, putting his hand on the other man's arm to steady him.

Still breathless and grabbing at his chest, Ian managed to point. "I was in and out, but I saw flashes. I knew I had to stay awake long enough to watch where he was taking her. She was unconscious. He carried her over his shoulder like a ragdoll towards those trees." He pointed to the trees in front of the beach, handing his radio to Aiden.

Chase didn't hesitate. He sprinted full speed down through the patch of trees Ian had pointed to, heading straight for the beach. Passing the officer already scanning the area. He didn't hesitate, knowing full well Dylan had taken her to sea.

He heard Aiden and Andrea right behind him. As he broke through the last of the trees, he scanned the beach, looking for any sign of them.

The deputy was running back towards them, "There's a sailboat in the distance, might be her."

Chase could see the track of a small craft that had been beached but was now long gone. He scanned the horizon and saw a mast and white sailboat in the distance. He fought the ridiculous instinct to swim after her, knowing the boat was travelling too fast for him to ever catch up.

Aiden's voice interrupted his thoughts. "Dad's boat is moored at the marina. Come on," he motioned. Both sprinted the 200 meters towards the marina without hesitation.

Andrea hollered after them, unable to keep up, "You keep in touch with me; I'm calling in the Coast Guard."

As they ran, he asked Aiden, "You got a key?"

"Did that ever stop us before?"

Chase shook his head, "No, I guess it didn't." They'd taken Frank's boat for a number of joyrides back in the day. Frank must have known, as there was always plenty of fuel and good snacks on board. Out boating, they were much less likely to get into trouble.

At the marina, they raced straight for the dock entrance. Without hesitating, Chase ripped his pocketknife out of his pocket and picked open the gate to the yacht club. Hardly missing a beat, they kept running down the dock. They nearly knocked over the woman coming the other direction, carrying a heavy ice chest.

"Sorry," Chase panted, then stopped to talk to her. "You haven't by any chance seen a lanky guy with white blond hair, or a sailboat setting out recently?"

The tiny woman looked back at him like he was crazy. "We just got in from a long trip, sorry." She dragged out the words as she shook her head.

Chase hollered back, as he hadn't stopped to hear her response, "Thanks anyway," as he followed Aiden to Frank's Hinckley. He leaped on board the 38-foot Hinckley. "Glad your dad hates to sail. We should make good time." They each untied a line before hopping in.

Aiden was already at the ignition, hotwiring the boat. Chase scanned the horizon as Aiden backed the boat out of its slip. He could see a hint of the boat in the distance and chanted over and over in his head, *Let that be her. Please let her be ok.*

The other boat was moving faster than he expected. Much longer and it would have been gone from sight.

Aiden radioed on Ian's handheld as he picked up speed. "Andrea, we're on the water. We're heading toward what we hope is Dylan." Chase couldn't hear much over the roar of the engine and the wind. Aiden continued, "I understand; get here as fast as you can... You know we're not waiting... I know, we'll be careful. Thanks." Aiden looked to Chase, "We're on our own. There's a Coast Guard cutter a few miles out. They are going to try to intercept."

Chase nodded. He belatedly pulled in the bumpers he could easily reach into the boat. He looked around for anything resembling a weapon.

34

Maddy strained her ears, listening for any sounds to tell her where they were, figure out what was going on. There were no voices. A roll of thunder echoed in the distance, the tiny porthole splattered with rain. It didn't sound like anyone other than Dylan, was on board.

With the weather, it would be hard to make out their position when she made it on deck. Her feet and hands were zip-tied behind her. They moved at a steady clip along the ocean, some of the waves bounced her on the bed, aggravating the nausea that lingered still. She pulled and strained against her bindings, but they weren't loosening, and her wrists were threatening to go numb. The odor of her own vomit from before was strong, so she scooted away from the stench.

She looked around for something, anything that would help. She rolled onto her back to look up at the ceiling. Dammit, no skylight. Under her hands, she felt the sleeping bag zipper.

She listened closely for sounds of Dylan. Nothing. She gripped the narrow metal zipper pull and tried to wedge it into the clasp of the zip tie that bound her hands. If she could just release the locking mechanism on the thick plastic of the zip tie, she could loosen it. Her wrists and shoulders strained under the pressure, her fingers aching from gripping the narrow zipper pull at the awkward angle.

A creak from the hatch opening echoed across the hull. She quickly rolled onto her side and dropped the zipper as she heard the lock rattling as Dylan unlocked the bedroom door.

"Madelyn, I'm so glad you're sitting quietly. You have no idea how much I've missed you," he gazed at her, patting her leg in what he supposed was a comforting manner. "You'll forget about your job, your family, and that asshole anyway. He'll get what's coming to him. I've already made the arrangements."

Maddy wanted to scream at him, to spit in his face and tell him to fuck off. But first, she needed him to leave so she could finish undoing her bindings. "Dylan, please. I'll do whatever you want, just leave him alone."

He tilted his head and smiled sympathetically. "Oh, my dear Madelyn, I wish it were that simple. You're coming with me, as far south as the wind will take us. Chase will be signing over your father's business as we speak to try to get you back. At least, that's what he and my associates think. And that's what your ransom note implies.

"But, I'm ready to retire someplace sunny, and I want you with me. Since our separation, I've been building us a nest egg. Once Chase signs over the business, my associates can move forward with the building plans. Well, that's what they think.

"I'm sure your colleagues are arresting them as we speak, taking care of that little mess for me. Meanwhile some of my... more specialized associates, will be taking care of Chase tonight. He's a stubborn one, and I can't have him trying to hunt us down."

Maddy allowed the tears to come, giving him a sense that she'd given up. That he'd won. That she was giving in. "You monster. You'll never get away with this." If he knew her as well as he thought he did, he'd have known it was for show. She hid the smile. With his narcissism, he couldn't see past his own success.

"I know you feel that way now. But you loved me once, and you'll love me again." His poorly placed confidence was revolting. He leaned as if he were going to kiss her, but pulled back, thinking better of it. Remembering what had happened last time he tried to get close. "Soon," he reassured her as he stood. He begrudgingly left the bedroom and locked the door behind him. She listened as he climbed back up the ladder.

She quickly rolled back over and grasped the sleeping bag's zipper. Grunting as she strained, she strained to push the zipper into the clasp until the zip tie released, freeing her hands.

As she worked to free her feet, she planned out her next steps. Break down the door, she could easily do that with a kick. Even with the cramps in her legs. Dylan would see her as soon as she opened the door if he'd left the hatch open, so she'd need to find a weapon quickly.

With any luck there would be a fire extinguisher or fishing knife or something outside the door. Maybe a kitchenette. She couldn't count on any of that. She knew some good moves, but it was risky to try to attack from a lower, enclosed position against an armed opponent. The way he'd taken out Ian and grabbed her, she realized she wasn't the only one who had been training for the day he came back for her.

She'd need to wait until the right opportunity arose.

Chase was suddenly grateful that Frank had a bit of a boat obsession. He'd upgraded since Chase had last been on one of his boats. The engine was powerful and a lot quieter, the ride smooth. They were catching up.

"We need a plan," he nudged Aiden. "He's going to see and hear us coming; might put Maddy at risk."

Aiden nodded, his eyes focused on the dark ocean, lit only by the glow of the moon and stars. Hard to see at night in the best of circumstances, but running dark was downright reckless. "I agree. We can't wait for him to dock, if he even decides to dock, which could be days, or even weeks from now. And, I don't want him to have enough time to hurt her. I don't think he has any intention of returning her, no matter what ransom we give up."

"Agreed. I think this is our best chance. If we can get close enough without him seeing, somehow slow him down, I can swim over and board the boat. You can distract him."

Aiden looked at Chase as if he had totally lost it. "Are you nuts? That water is way too cold for you to swim very far. And with the currents, waves; there's a hell of a wind and this rain is picking up – you'll drown yourself trying."

Chase shook his head, "Are you forgetting what I did for a living for the past decade? I've been in colder water with stronger currents and bigger waves."

Aiden laughed out loud and shook his head. "You're fucking nuts. If you say so."

In a lightbulb moment, Chase asked, "Does your dad keep a flare gun on board?"

"Of course. What's your plan?" Chase grabbed the wheel as Aiden ducked down beneath to grab the flare gun. He re-surfaced carrying a big case. "You ever shoot one of these?"

"I can handle it." Aiden took over the wheel while Chase checked and armed the flare gun. With every moment, they got closer to what they hoped was Dylan's boat. Fuck. If it wasn't Dylan, she was gone. He ignored the shred of uncertainty. No one else would be desperate enough to be out with the approaching storm.

As if on cue, a crack of lightning lit up the sky in the distance. Yep, summer storms were in full force. The raindrops against the windshield grew fatter and fell faster. The storm seemed to be moving closer, picking up more steam. The rain was just enough to reduce visibility, which might just work in their favor.

Chase pulled off his button up shirt he'd worn specially for the meeting in his attempt to look business-like. He pulled off his shoes and socks. His jeans followed. He kept on his briefs and undershirt; considering a totally nude rescue... he'd swim faster without the extra layers. The humorous visual brought him at least a brief respite from worry that engulfed him.

They were getting closer. If Dylan looked back, he would easily see them now. "Slow down a bit, I don't want him to hear our engine. I'm going to fire a flare at the engine. If I get lucky, I'll disable them enough to slow their trajectory."

Aiden couldn't hide the worry as he slowed the engine to a dull roar. "No way. We could blow up the fuel tank and risk Maddy. I'm willing to bet he's got lots of fuel on board; he's trying to get away far and fast."

"Fuck, you're right. Dammit." Chase shook his head, brainstorming a new plan. "Swing wide so we stay out of sight. When we're ahead of him, I'll jump and swim. As he passes, I'll board the sailboat. Then, you can come around from the other side as a distraction."

"Don't fuck up. I'm not losing my sister and my best friend on the same night."

"Trust me. This is not even close to the craziest thing I've ever done. Remember when I jumped off of Hopeless Bluff north of town, in the middle of October, just to see if I could? I made it to the water but didn't think about how I was going to get to shore. I must have swum in the frigid water for half an hour before I found a scrap of beach. Then I had to climb 50 feet of rocks to get back up."

Aiden shook his head and laughed desperately. "My sister is clearly drawn to crazy men."

Chase smiled. Thinking of Maddy bolstered his adrenaline. The plan sucked. He had little chance of success, but he couldn't come up with anything better and was out of time. If he failed, Aiden would be there with the flare gun and a faster boat.

He just hoped they weren't too late. He didn't think Dylan would go to all this trouble to kill her, but if he laid one hand on her... Dylan could be just crazy enough to take her out if to prevent Chase from getting her.

It took too damn long, but finally they were well ahead of the sailboat and it was nearly out of sight. Fuck, he hoped they weren't seen. If they were, he at least wouldn't be able to see Chase in the water in this storm. "I'm going in. Give me time to get to the boat. Swing wide around and make it look like you're approaching him from the right. That'll give me time to make a move, and you won't run over me. Hang back until the last minute but don't get too close; we know he's armed."

"I'm on it."

Catching one last sight of the sailboat in the far distance, Chase calculated his trajectory carefully, knowing he wouldn't see shit in the rough waves. Without hesitating, he dove in and was off, swimming all-out towards Maddy. He knew he was fast; could have competed if he'd cared enough, but he'd hated organized sports when he was younger. And the glory; he preferred to fly under the radar. The water was freezing, but he ignored the sharp prickling pain covering his body.

Exhausted, muscles on fire from the exertion and the frigid water, Chase saw the sailboat coming right at him. With everything he had, he threw his arm out to grasp the side of the sailboat as it whizzed past him. Like catching a freaking train leaving the station. The force nearly pulled his arm out of its socket, but he pulled with all his might to keep his grip, and his shoulder in place. Probably couldn't have done it without the rush of adrenaline pulsing through his veins.

Aiden had slowed to allow Chase time to reach the boat first, but now he fired up his engine and was nearing the sailboat. *Dammit, Aiden*, he was supposed to wait. Chase didn't want Aiden in the line of fire.

Dylan jerked as he heard Aiden approaching. He reached for the gun and took aim.

Chase took advantage of the distraction and hurled himself at Dylan, fists flying, knocking the gun out of Dylan's grip.

With a solid blow to the side of the head, he knocked Dylan to the ground. Dylan crashed against the wheel as he went down. With a pause, he feigned disorientation, coming up slowly grabbing at his head, his body rocking from the blow.

As he rose, he grabbed a nearby fire extinguisher and swung at Chase's head.

Seeing the move coming, Chase ducked and had to rotate away from the cylinder.

At the sound of the fight, Maddy came crashing out from below deck. Dylan went to grab Maddy as a hostage, but he underestimated her swiftness, and she slipped out from his grasp and bashed the heel of her hand straight into his nose.

As he grabbed for his bleeding nose, her knee came straight up and nailed him in the groin.

Expletives streamed from Dylan's mouth as he tried to recover. He stood up far enough to go for Maddy, but he didn't see Chase until it was too late.

Chase grabbed him and flung him to the back of the boat. Before he could stand, Chase was on him, pummeling him mercilessly.

Blood pouring out from his nose, Dylan went limp as he lost consciousness. Pulling himself away, Chase turned back to Maddy, ensuring she was ok.

35

BLINKING HIS EYES, CHASE shook off the rage and looked down at his bloodied knuckles. He glanced up at Maddy, his eyes still crazed, jaw twitching. "Chase, it's ok. I'm here."

She watched his eyes warming as he realized she was unharmed. He stood a few feet away, wearing nothing but a t-shirt and briefs, soaked to the skin, covered in goosebumps. The rain poured over him. He gradually released his tightly clenched fists, a slow smile of relief building as he looked at Maddy.

Maddy smiled as relief flooded her senses. He'd come. He outswam a sailboat in a storm to get to her. She pulled her handcuffs from her uniform and cuffed Dylan's wrists behind his back. She then rolled him onto his side and grabbed zip ties from his back pocket. She secured zip ties tightly around his feet for good measure.

Area secure, she flung herself into Chase's waiting arms. Looking up, she captured his gaze with her own, "Thanks for coming to get me."

"It was a nice night for a cruise." He smirked back at her, then leaned them together against the captain's chair to steady them against the rocking of the boat.

His lips were as freezing as the rest of him at first, but quickly warmed as he kissed her. He gently explored her mouth, pressing soft kisses along her lower lip, then held her close again, resting his forehead against hers. "Maddy, I love you so much. I don't ever want to be as scared again as I was tonight." Maddy shuddered in his arms, letting the tears come. "I'm so sorry." She allowed herself another minute to cry, clutched tightly against the man she loved.

Within a minute, she shook away the fear, the anger, and pulled back, remembering where she was. "I love you too. Let's get the hell out of here. I can't spend another minute on this boat." She looked up and saw Aiden waiting alongside, as close as he could without their boats colliding in the waves.

"Hey, sis. You ok?" His relief was evident as he saw she was safe and unharmed.

"All good. Thanks for coming; I wasn't fancying swimming back to shore in this storm At night," she joked, eyes puffy from her brief crying jag. She was done crying because of Dylan. Ready to live her life.

Aiden shook his head in relief. "Let's get the hell home," he glanced at the sailboat, debating what to do. "I'll contact Andrea and let her know you're ok. I'll have her meet us at the dock. Why don't you hop on over? Toss your prisoner in back here; we'll make good time. The coast guard is about three minutes out; they can take care of the sailboat."

"Absolutely. Get me off this boat. I hate sailing." Aiden got the boat as close as he could, and when the waves brought the boats steady alongside for a moment, Maddy leaped across into her father's boat.

Dylan's limp, but still living body landed on the floor near her with a thud after Chase had thrown him over. She tried not to enjoy that so much, but it was tough. Just a small revengeful moment.

Then, as the waves aligned just right again, Chase jumped the gap and landed next to her. "Let's go home." He leaned over, picking up his dry clothes.

Maddy sat under the cover across from Aiden, but kept the pistol she'd nabbed trained on Dylan, not risking him coming to anytime soon. Chase kicked open the cabin door, then ducked inside to get dressed, replacing the soaked underclothes.

Aiden laughed as his friend surfaced in his dry clothes. "You are totally nuts. How the hell did you swim like that in the middle of a storm?"

Chase smiled, "The North Sea. The coast of Maine in summer is downright balmy by comparison."

When they finally pulled into the marina, Aiden pulled the boat smoothly into the slip. Andrea and a few other officers were waiting at the dock. Maddy nodded at her boss as she tossed her the line.

Andrea smiled. "Nicely done Officer. You ok?"

Maddy smiled back, "Yeah, I'm good." Dylan stirred at her feet, for the first time since Chase had knocked him out. "You guys want to take care of this thing, so I don't have to look at it any longer?" Maddy happily watched as the nearby medics pulled Dylan out of the boat and wheeled him to the ambulance, with two police officers running alongside, while reading him his Miranda rights.

She smiled. "Be happy to." Andrea hollered over the Mike, "Mind making a few calls? Let the Coast Guard know it's no longer a rescue op, but an impound?" She looked back to Maddy, "While you were out for a sail, we kept digging. Found an empty slip, recently registered to a Darren Mayhew. Mayberry's parent's sailboat is currently missing, not in its registered slip."

Chase nodded, "Reported stolen?"

"Actually, no. Said they'd loaned it to an old friend but refuse to disclose more." Andrea nodded, mouth drawn tight. "So, they may know about this whole situation more than they're letting on."

Chase hopped out of the boat and leaned down to Maddy to lend a hand. Exhausted, wrists and ankles aching from her bindings, she gratefully accepted the hand. He pulled her toward him as she stepped up to the dock. Before she could crumble, his strong arms wrapped around her. She relinquished and let him support them both.

She nodded at her boss. "I'd like to be done with this whole thing. I know its late, but can we finish up tonight?"

Andrea nodded, "I need to get your statements, it can wait until morning..." she trailed off as Maddy shook her head, refusing to ruin her morning. Needing to be done with it.

"My parents will be back in the morning. I'd rather relax for a few days. Let's get it done tonight and be done with it." She knew there would be court dates and all that crap, but she'd have a reprieve after tonight at least if Andrea took her statement now.

"No problem. Hop in and I'll drive you home and get your statements at your place. Mike can take Aiden's statement and drive him back to the grange to pick up his car."

As they followed her to the parking lot, Andrea filled them in on what had happened while they were at sea. "We have Dylan's buddies from the meeting in for questioning regarding their part in tonight's events. They're doing some fancy footwork. But, give us time. We should have enough to lock them up for a while, share information with Georgetown to build a nice case against the whole business.

"The guys that left the ransom note at Chase's have been appre-hended; they were waiting a few houses down to nab Chase when he got home."

"How's Ian?" Maddy had to know, more than she cared to hear the rest.

"Ian's doing fine. We had the paramedics check him out; they took him to the ER for x-rays and a head CT. Nothing's broken, but I made him take off the next week as he's pretty sore. Hit his head on the pavement after his vest took the hit; has a hell of a headache. I've been keeping him updated; he's glad you're ok and says to tell you thanks for making him wear the vest."

"I'm so glad. I was so scared for him." A load lifted off her chest as she heard about Ian, knowing he was ok.

As promised, Andrea took each of their statements as the other showered, then together, curled up on the couch, in the comfort of Maddy's living room. Maddy feared she may have been mid-sentence when she couldn't hold open her heavy eyelids anymore and fell asleep. The rest of the night came in hazy glimpses.

Whatever drug Dylan had used was taking its sweet time to wear off. Or she was just plain exhausted. She vaguely remembered Andrea telling her to take a very overdue vacation for the next two weeks.

Chase carried her to bed, wincing but not complaining at the strain against his shoulder. Chase held her close as she sank into a deep sleep.

36

Early rays of dawn gently peeked through the gap in the bedroom curtain, teasing Maddy's eyes open. Feeling warm and cozy under the comforter, with Chase's muscled body spooned tightly against her, she couldn't resist the need to stay and snuggle. A nice way to start her vacation. Her first real vacation in years.

"Stop wiggling, I'm trying to sleep," Chase's cranky morning voice, more a groan, really, vibrated through the back of her head, his breath tickling at her hair. Feeling ornery, she wiggled her bottom against his already growing erection. Rolling her over, on top of her in under a second, Chase trailed kisses along her neck, "Fine. Work, work, work."

Her phone buzzed on the bedside table. Maddy glanced over at the clock, "Shit, it's already 10 in the morning. How late were we up?" She checked her text. "Aiden says they're half an hour out. He's having Payson deliver breakfast; says she wanted to check on me too, so Aiden conned her into bringing food. They're all coming over here."

Still lying atop her, Chase continued his trail of kisses along her neck, with a quick nip at her earlobe. "Plenty of time."

She slipped her knee out and rolled him over, swiftly switching their positions. "Nice try. I'd rather my parents not find out about us the way Aiden did."

Chase rubbed his tired eyes. "Yikes. Agreed. We'll move fast." He sat up and climbed out of bed, hauling her with him into the shower. Ignoring her fists hammering against his back, laughing out loud as she demanded to be put down. Which he responded to with a quick slap on her ass.

After a steamy romp against the shower wall, they were dressed and politely sipping coffee in the living room within 23 minutes. Setting their coffees on the table, Chase pulled Maddy snugly into his strong arms. He looked deeply into her ice blue eyes, "I love you, Maddy. I want you in my life. I know you're scared. Take as long as you need; I'll be here."

A slow smile crossed her face as she gazed back, enjoying the moment. Not wanting to wait a moment longer, she pressed her lips to his for a brief, soft kiss and pulled back, looking right back into his eyes. "Chase, I'm not scared anymore. I love you so much. Marry me?"

With a self-assured smirk, he smiled back at her. "Oh shit, I forgot something." With her standing there, waiting his response, he sprinted outside. Well, that certainly wasn't the answer she was expecting. He dashed back into the house in record timing, finding her still frozen where he'd left her on the couch.

Getting down on one knee in front of her, he pulled out a box with a blue sapphire set into an intricate band. "Maddy, I've loved you since the day we first met. Will you marry me?"

Eyes misty but smile huge, she laughed, "I thought I just asked you? Yes, of course I will." He sat up on the couch next to her and slipped the ring on her finger, pulling her in for a steamy kiss. Without breaking contact, she slid onto his lap and wrapped her legs around him.

With a shrill chime interrupting the moment, the doorbell rang. Chase groaned, shifting her off of his lap. "We've got to have a talk with your family about timing." Cock-blocks.

He hopped up to disable the alarm and held the door open for the troops. Preparing for the onslaught, he stayed back and played doorman. Not ready to tell anyone yet, she shoved the ring into her pocket.

Laura whizzed past him, barely more than a flash as she ran to her daughter. She threw her arms around her and started the barrage of questions. With a sigh, Maddy hugged her right back. "I'm ok mom, really." Maddy laughed, realizing she felt better than she had in... forever.

"Are you sure? Oh sweetie, I hate that we left you alone with that creep on the loose. That we weren't here for you." Her mother cried; Maddy couldn't tell who was reassuring who. Although, it was nice to have their roles reversed for once. Her mother rarely needed reassurance, and never sobbed.

She watched Chase over her mother's shoulder. He was so damn handsome, his beard passing scruffy again, hair still wet from their shower, but looking tousled already. Leaning against the wall next to the open front door with his arms crossed, he winked at her.

Frank came lumbering in next, carrying heavy bags of Italian booty. He shoved the heavy bags at Chase, who quickly grabbed them before they went crashing to the floor.

"Alright, alright. My turn." Frank walked up to his wife and daughter and wrapped his arms around them both in a big bear hug.

Once she'd calmed her tears, Laura slipped out of the group hug and walked over to Chase. Maddy leaned against her dad as he held her in one arm against his side. Laura threw her arms around Chase like she had Maddy, crying again. Chase set the bags on the floor before they went crashing to the ground under the force of Laura's exuberant hug.

"Thank goodness you're ok, Aiden told me about the whole ordeal. I can't believe you swam after a boat; you could have been killed," she sobbed, tears free-flowing again.

Aiden strolled in the door finally, helping Payson carry in bags of breakfast. Delicious smells flooded the house. Maddy felt her stomach rumble in anticipation. She hadn't eaten since lunch yesterday.

Never comfortable with tears, Aiden tore into the bags of breakfast burritos from the Mexican restaurant down the road. "We can fuss and fret while we eat. Come on, I'm starving. I've been up for hours. Somehow, everyone thought Maddy shouldn't have to wake up early after her ordeal to make the airport run, even though it was her turn," he ranted, "I was up late too you know." He grinned, totally kidding, but never missing a good opportunity to rile his younger sister.

Rolling his eyes, Frank spoke up. "Aiden, thanks for the ride, again. Thanks for bringing breakfast, Payson. And, Chase, thanks for all your good work keeping the business afloat. I couldn't imagine many who would have been able to keep things running with all that's been going on. All the damn repairs."

Maddy appreciated the subject change. She was ready to move on with her life. Ready to be her own person, stalker-free. They gathered around the rarely-used dining table with their steaming breakfast burritos and coffees, everyone speaking at once.

Laura was the loudest, "I brought back the best surprises. Maddy, I got you the cutest leather boots, and wait until you see the Murano glass I found for you. And, Payson, I hope you like it; they had the prettiest sundress at this open-air market that made me think of you.

We'll go through everything when we're done eating if that sounds ok? I'm ridiculously jet-lagged but buzzing on adrenaline and caffeine; couldn't sleep if my life depended on it. We had to buy an extra suitcase to pack all of this home in, and I can't wait for you all to see it."

Aiden nodded, "I know. It took you an extra hour to get through customs with all that crap," he teased.

Frank nodded his head in agreement, "At least you didn't have to carry it all across Rome." They laughed, but quickly shut up when Frank yelped in pain in response to a not-so-subtle abrupt kick in the shin from under the table. Laura had a fondness for pointy shoes for a reason.

Frank cleared his throat. "Chase, I..." Frank stopped mid-sentence, a look of suspicion darkening his face. "Chase... Your hair is awfully wet," he glanced down under the table, "And your feet are bare... like you just stepped out of the shower. Considering you must have just driven from your house this morning, I find that a bit odd. Your shower not working?"

Chase shifted uncomfortably in his seat. Across the table, Maddy looked the other way, suddenly finding the living room sofa incredibly interesting. Frank's glare was intense. Intimidating. Furious.

"So, Frank. I, uh..." Chase tripped over his words. "Can we, uh, talk in private?"

Aiden burst out laughing, anticipating the entertainment about to ensue.

Frank's face was stern, "I think right here is private enough." His normal jovial manner was gone. His tone threatening.

Searching for words, Chase finally spit out, "Sir, I'd like to ask for permission to marry your daughter."

Laura's happy screech shook the room, "Maddy, honey, I am so happy for you."

Frank broke out in a grin. He slapped Chase on the bad shoulder; Chase held back the wince. "I'm just messing with you. It's about damn time you two got your heads out of your asses and figured it out. We've known for a long, long time."

The End

Carrie Thorne is the author of kick-ass romance novels, specializing in white-hot chemistry, healthy relationships, and a mix of action and dreamily falling in love. Whether it's a sinuous flow down a lazy river or evil bad dudes hot on heels, Carrie's stories will draw you in and ruin your sleep. Happily ever afters are for everyone, and kindness is everything.

She's also an introvert who loves people, travel, fitness, video games, food, and is a true Pacific Northwesterner who lives for rain and outdoors and trees and mountains and ocean, and... she's a total dork. At home, she's lucky to have two creative and confident kids, a witty veteran husband she fell at-first-sight for, and a tiny pup snuggled at her side. In addition to writing romance, Carrie has been a nurse practitioner, a Martian and Earthling geologist, a banker, and she is usually elbow-deep in a DIY project in which she bit off more than she could chew.

Where is she now? Depends on the weather. Cozied up by the fire with a steaming mug of black coffee, or stretched out on the hammock with a frothy IPA in the shade of her forest. Either way, she's working on the next great love story to conquer your TBR list.

www.CarrieThorne.com